STRIKE POINT

A THRILLER

JOHN ETTERLEE

All rights reserved. No part of this book may be reproduced or used in any manner without written permission of the copyright owner except for the use of quotations in a book review. For more information, address: john@johnetterleebooks.com.

First edition, 2020

Edited by Griffin Smith

Book design by Damonza

ISBN: 9798620763849

Published by John Etterlee
www.johnetterleebooks.com

For my wonderful wife, Elizabeth, who put up with me disappearing into my office daily for hours while repeatedly messaging her excerpts.

"We seek the total elimination one day of nuclear weapons from the face of the Earth."

— RONALD REAGAN

PROLOGUE

MOSCOW'S WINTER CLUNG dark and dreary. Clouds loomed over the presidential executive office in the heart of the capital city. Russian winters were brutal, but this one was the most severe seen in years.

Harsh wind and snow swept through the center of the seemingly forsaken city, a city of millions who were mostly huddled around fireplaces, cooped up in their homes. It resembled a sign of troublesome times that had fallen on the Russian people. The economy had disintegrated around them.

Restaurants and shops once filled to the max now sat empty, their doors locked. People could no longer afford to be out and about. A decade of total disarray had begun. Many who were happy with the security they enjoyed under the communist regime resisted the idea of capitalism. And, the Russian military was all but broken down.

Behind the curtain of the almost desolate capital city, a secret meeting had been taking place in the Kremlin. The same conference room had held many communist gatherings for many years before. Reminders filled the building, from paintings of now-defunct Soviet State farms to busts of old Soviet leaders that lined the hallway that led to the newly appointed Russian President's office.

The fate and financial security of Russia, as well as freshly independent former Soviet republics, hung precariously with no guarantees. Poverty ran rampant. People who'd been used to being provided with the bare essentials could no longer depend on it. Many turned to criminal behavior just to feed their families. The former communist nation had utterly lost its direction.

A year earlier, the USSR had been bragging to the world about its nuclear capabilities. But, behind the scenes they were in crisis mode, attempting to salvage what was left of the Soviet Empire. However, Soviet power had been decaying for a while. The high price of a losing occupation in Afghanistan, as well as a faulty government system that could no longer sustain itself under the weight of its own corruption, left the country in near financial ruin.

A coup de état had been attempted by certain hardline supporters of the old communist regime who weren't thrilled with the changing liberal stance the new Russian President had expressed.

Boris Petrov, a former KGB officer, now a senior agent for the post-communist FSB (the government bureau referred to as the Federal Security Service) had been sitting in the corner with his boss as the meeting with Russian President Boris Yeltsin and leaders from the former Soviet republics of Ukraine, Belarus, and Kazakhstan commenced.

The day's issue was the destination of nuclear warheads that were left behind after the sudden downfall of the Soviet Union. They were the same nuclear weapons that had been employed to threaten the United States and the West for almost the entire duration of the Cold War.

However, with the communist system now broken, it appeared as though a nuclear Russia was no longer a viable option. But these weapons had been spread across the former Soviet states. Left behind, they'd risk them being ravaged by terrorist organizations or anyone who'd wished to sell them to the highest bidder, namely Russia's enemies. Something had to be done with them.

Petrov wasn't willing to accept what he was hearing. The United States had promised the Russian government millions of dollars in exchange for severely dismantling and reducing its nuclear imprint.

"We must comply with America and the international community," Yeltsin told them in his raspy Russian tongue. "This is the way of the new world order. We do not have a choice!"

"We always have a choice!" Minister of Defense, Sergei Lavrov, yelled as he pounded his fist on the table.

Petrov, sitting quietly in his chair, nodded his head in agreement with Lavrov. Though he wasn't a politician, Petrov had dreamt nightly of bringing back the glory days.

He craved it so badly he could taste it. To him, Soviet power had stood for something. It was the only thing he could ever really relate to. As a spy, he'd seen the effects nuclear warnings had on the West, America in particular. The mere threat of nuclear war sent Americans and their politicians into a state of turmoil. It rankled him as he sat in on the meeting that those days had long since passed.

President Yeltsin lit a cigar as he gazed back at Lavrov. He'd wished to keep the meeting calm. Yeltsin didn't see the purpose of making a stressful situation worse.

"Listen, old friend," he said to Lavrov. "I understand your concern. But this is what we have to do. We are not in a position to negotiate!"

With a deteriorating economy, Russia's leftover nuclear weapons had become a bartering tool—a means to regain some of the millions lost during the financial crisis that had plagued them just before the decline of the USSR.

In his corner, Petrov grit his teeth. His blood boiled at this degeneration of his country. He'd always seen Russia as a premiere world power. He and his boss, Mikhail Belsky, just glimpsed at one another without uttering a word. Petrov could tell by a single raised eyebrow they both were thinking the same thing.

But, he could no longer hold his tongue. The agent rose to his feet, scowling at the President from across the room.

"This is an outrage!" Petrov blurted out in anger.

Belsky clinched Petrov by the arm, trying to keep him from provoking the Russian leader.

"What the hell are you doing, Boris?" he asked under his breath. "Sit down now!"

The FSB agents weren't in the meeting to speak on the matter. Nor were they expected to. But, suddenly, all eyes in the room riveted on Petrov.

President Yeltsin looked back at Petrov in confusion.

"You have something to add?" Yeltsin asked with sarcasm. "If so, we would love to hear it."

Every person in the room stared at Petrov, waiting for him to speak up.

"Russia is my home," he said. "I have always done my job to the best of my ability, knowing that I was serving the greatest communist power the world has ever seen."

Their jaws almost dropped to the floor. Nobody in the room could believe the young agent would be so bold and brash in such high company. Now, everyone in the meeting was keen to hear Petrov finish; everyone except President Yeltsin. He wasn't the least bit impressed.

"But now we are bowing down to the international community?" he continued. "America, of all countries? Why must we reduce our nation's pride to please them? They have always been our sworn enemies. Now, we are making deals with them? This will not stand!"

President Yeltsin cleared his throat as he stared Petrov down.

"You finished now?" he asked with a bitter smirk. "Thank you for enlightening us all with your educated opinion, Agent Petrov. We are all so appreciative. Now, please sit down and allow us to finish this meeting!"

Petrov took his seat, his face twitching in frustration as Belsky looked over at him in disbelief for having the audacity to disrupt a Presidential meeting. However, he wasn't at all surprised. Petrov had a temper. And, he would never shy away from giving his blunt opinion to anyone, even those in power.

Many in the Russian government silently shared the same opinion as Petrov. But they were powerless to do anything about it and wise enough not to voice it. The attempted takeover of the Russian Government, although a failure, had set the tone for the fall of an empire. The only thing any of them could do was sit and watch in horror as it tumbled to the ground, hoping they could somehow gather up the ashes and build anew.

"This matter is now closed," Yeltsin said to his cabinet members. "All remaining nuclear stockpiles will be sent to our facility in Siberia to be broken down and made into nuclear fuel."

"But…" Lavrov interjected. "The young agent does make a point!"

"But nothing!" shouted Yeltsin. "This matter is no longer open for discussion! I have made my decision. This conference is now closed!"

As the intense hour-long meeting adjourned, ambivalence punctuated the air—an element of desperation in the minds of all who attended, especially Petrov, coupled with a powerlessness.

Petrov stepped out from the meeting room and headed straight down the long corridor to the door that led to the back of the old drab looking, Soviet-era building. His hood over his head and looking out at a blanket of white amassed on the ground, he lit a cigarette to calm his raging nerves.

Belsky moved in behind him, resting a hand on his shoulder as they both stood, silently staring out into the dreary winter day. Though not as outspoken and brash, he'd shared Petrov's disappointment. Both men were staunch supporters of the old communist regime.

However, it appeared as though those days had died, and neither could comprehend what would become of the motherland. Russia had once been a significant player in the world of nuclear nations. Now, they were reduced to accepting money in exchange for getting rid of the only thing that guaranteed them power.

"I cannot believe that the country I have served for so long has succumbed to this," Petrov said to Belsky as he balled his fists. "I am outraged, boss. Getting back at America was the only thing I ever cared about. Now, we are accepting donations from those God damned dogs? It's disgraceful!"

Belsky looked Petrov right in his eyes with all the weight of a life-long career in espionage.

"Listen, Boris," he said as he went in closer to him. "You are my number one. You have always served your country well, comrade. You will go places, I promise you that. Maybe you will become President one day, huh?

Then, you can fulfill the ideals of our former Soviet leaders, in all their glory!"

Exhaling a long string of cigarette smoke, Petrov clutched Belsky by his shirt collar.

"Long live mother, Russia!" he spouted.

"Long live, Russia!"

CHAPTER 1

BOZEMAN, MONTANA
TWENTY-EIGHT YEARS LATER

THAT RANCH WAS absolutely stunning, especially with the backdrop of the Montana Mountain scenery and rolling foothills rising high above its many acres of pastureland. The timber frame farmhouse and matching stables dotted the center of the massive property and its wooden perimeter fencing. Rooster's crowing and chickens balking echoed throughout the surrounding valley.

"O'Neil Ranch" marked the place on an old western-style wooden sign hung high above the entrance to the long, concrete driveway that led to a two-car garage. Horses grazed on the abundant, rich grasses as if they didn't have a care in the world. Ah, but that one horse; that one horse he loved.

Roger's fourteen-year-old son, Patrick, had named him Jack. He was a beautiful two-year-old Palomino Quarter Horse Gelding, standing at fourteen hands high. He'd picked him from a slew of other horses that could have easily been great companions to a young teenager. For Patrick, it was love at first sight.

He'd never ridden a horse before that day. But he swore to his dad that he would be a fast learner. Jack wasn't entirely broken yet, and Roger was a little hesitant to allow Patrick to ride him unsupervised. As the evening sun began to dip below the cloudless, spring sky, Roger had been watching Patrick sit atop him in the round pen, boots in the stirrup as Jack kicked up dust and dirt, bobbing him up and down while he squeezed his legs tightly against the side of the saddle.

"Come on, son. You can do it," Roger urged him. "Don't let him sense your fear."

"I'm trying, dad!" Patrick responded, pulling back slightly on the reins. "Jack just won't calm down."

"Rub his mane and talk to him." Added Roger. "You have to gain his trust. If you are confident and calm, he will be too."

But, before Patrick could react, Jack began to rear wildly, bucking Patrick in every direction.

"Dad, I can't hold on!" Patrick yelled.

"It's ok, son," Roger reassured him. "Just stay with it."

"I can't, dad!" Continued Patrick, as the strength of Jack's kick thrust him up from the saddle. "I'm losing my grip!"

Patrick tried to maintain his position, but he was no match for the remarkable power of that horse. He lost his glove, and his sweaty palm began to slip from the horn. Before he could say another word, Patrick was flung abruptly to the rear, tumbling down directly on his hip on the dusty ground with a loud thud.

"Damn!" Roger yelled, hurrying to Patrick's side and kneeling on the ground. "You ok, son?"

"Ugh, I think so," he sorely uttered, slowly pushing himself upward and spitting a glob of dirt from his mouth. "I'm pretty sure I'm going to have a fat bruise tomorrow, though. God, that hurt."

"Come on," Roger said, gripping his son by the arm and pulling him to his feet. "You're ok. Just shake it off and get back in the saddle."

"After that?" Patrick asked as he wiped the remaining dirt from his face.

"Especially after that," Roger replied. "You can't let Jack see your fear. If he can sense you're scared, it's going to make him scared, too. That's why he threw you. What you do teaches him what to do. Got it?"

"Fine," Patrick grudgingly agreed, brushing the dirt from his clothes, snatching his glove from the ground and stepping back toward his skittish horse. "Now what?"

"Now, pat him on his side," said Roger. "Let him see the trust in your eyes. Talk to him. You're just a boy with his horse, hanging out together."

As Patrick started rubbing Jack down and talking into his ear, the horse seemed to settle down a bit, as if he could see the change in the boys' demeanor. Patrick did exactly as he was instructed to. Jack's excitement seemed to wain as the jumpiness he had observed before turned to sheer composure. Or, so he'd hoped.

"Now, cowboy up!" Roger told him. "He's your horse. He's not going to ride himself!"

"Ok, Jack," Patrick said, placing his left boot into the stirrup and swinging his right leg over. "Here goes nothing."

The boy snagged the reins and prepared to take him for a spin. But Roger stopped him, grabbing the lead rope that was hanging from the fence and attaching it to the halter.

"Don't worry about trying to steer yet," he said. He needs to get used to you being up there, first. Just sit tight, and I'll lead him for you."

"Sure, Dad."

While Jack followed Roger in circles along the fence, Patrick was pleasantly surprised that he wasn't being thrown to the ground again.

"See, son?" Asked Roger. "He needs to get used to your weight before you try to teach him. Otherwise, it confuses him, and he'll get agitated."

"Where'd you learn all this from?" Patrick asked.

"Your great-grandfather taught me a long time ago," he answered. "I was much younger than you back then. He was a hell of a man, too. Rough as they come, but a straight shooter."

"I wish I could have met him," said Patrick.

"So do I," replied Roger, as he guided Jack back toward the metal farm gate.

"That's about enough for today," he continued. "Jack

needs to rest. We'll pick up where we left off tomorrow after we feed the animals."

"Ah, dad, you promise?" Patrick asked, hopping down from Jack's back.

"I promise," Roger told him as he opened the gate to direct the horse to the enclosure. "It's about dinner time, anyhow. Your mother and Emily are probably waiting for us. You head in, and I'll meet you in there once I get your horse settled."

"Yes, Sir," he answered.

Roger escorted Jack back toward the other horses, removing the saddle and the rest of his tack and prepared to carry them back to the barn. As he stood by next to him, Roger began talking to him and lightly brushing the side of his mane.

"It's ok, buddy," he said to Jack. "I know you didn't mean to throw him. You're going to have to learn to trust Patrick. He wouldn't do anything to hurt ya. I promise you that."

He looked the horse right in his eye. For a moment, as Jack neighed calmly, it was as if he knew precisely what Roger was telling him.

"If only horses could talk," Roger continued, patting Jack on his side as he pulled a horse treat from his pocket and held it out in his palm. "I wonder what you would say to me."

Roger took a square bale of hay and dropped it to the ground next to the water trough, left Jack to be with the other horses and headed straight for the tack room to put Patrick's stuff away. As he flipped the light off and slammed the barn doors shut, headlights beamed toward him from the end of the extended driveway.

"What the hell?" he thought, placing his gloves into the back pocket of his faded jeans. "We aren't expecting company."

As the strange vehicle moved in closer to the house, Roger walked into the driveway to greet the mystery person. The dark-colored Suburban SUV came grinding to a halt. Suddenly, the door swung open, and there stood a tall, bombshell of a brunette all decked out in a dark pants suit and matching shoes and looking like she'd just walked straight out of a James Bond movie.

"Can I help you?" Roger asked the woman as he continued closer to the vehicle.

The lady glimpsed over at the horses in the barnyard, then back at Roger, giving him the once over.

"Nice life you've made for you and your family out here, Mr. O'Neil," she said with a smile. "This place is beautiful."

"Thanks," Roger replied. "But I'm not buying whatever you're selling, lady. So, why don't you just turn your car around and leave?"

"That any way to greet a stranger?" She asked. "You haven't even heard my proposition yet."

As he impatiently waited for the woman to continue, Roger sidestepped and noticed the government license plate mounted to the front of the vehicle.

"Ok, enough with the games," he said. "Who are you, and how do you know my name?"

"I know enough about you, Mr. O'Neil," she answered. "Ex-Army Ranger, numerous combat tours, decorated. Now you're a family man, prominent lawyer, highly intelligent. Should I go on?"

"You still didn't answer my damn question," he said. "Who in the hell are you?"

"Name's Lacy Brown," the lady replied. "I'm Agent, Lacy Brown of Central Intelligence."

"Uh-huh, I see," Roger said sneeringly as he began marching back to the house, not desiring to have anything to do with the woman. "Well, Agent Brown, it seems they sent you all the way out here for nothing. I trust you can find your way out of here."

"Wait!" she shouted. "Just give me a few minutes of your time. It's all I ask. If you don't like what I have to say, then I'll leave."

Roger turned around hesitantly. He recalled that feeling well. Roger was sure that he didn't want to hear whatever it was that this young agent had to say. But, part of him was curious. Part of him had that fire burning deep in his gut. It was the same fire that he'd felt so many times before in combat. That patriotic button that seemed to turn itself on whenever it felt like it.

He knew there was only one reason that the CIA would ever come all that way to see anybody. Roger had a solid idea of where the conversation was going to go. Still, he wasn't convinced that he wanted to hear it. Once going down that road, would anything ever be the same? After all, he'd promised his family a simple country life.

"You've got five minutes," Roger said to her. "My family is waiting inside. As you can see around you, I'm a very busy guy."

"Thank you, Mr. O'Neil," she said. "Where shall we talk?"

"Let's go over here, by the fence."

Roger accompanied the agent toward the large horse enclosure next to the barn. As he leaned against the wooden fence, the post light gleaming down on them, Roger took a deep breath, letting out a sigh as Patrick's horse, Jack, came wandering near them.

"Know what's so interesting about horses, Agent Brown?" he asked her.

"I can't say I do, Mister O'Neil."

"You have to work to earn their trust," he said. "There is no middle ground. Either they trust you, or they don't."

"I see," she answered.

"Know what happens when they don't trust you?" Roger continued.

"Nope."

"You end up flat on your ass on the ground, looking up at the sky," he told her. "But, when they do trust you, they'd go anywhere and do anything for you."

"I don't see what…" Agent Brown got out of her mouth just before Roger interrupted her.

"I'm the same way," he said. "I would do just about anything for someone that I trust. But, cross me, or my family, and I'd bring hell raining down on that person."

"I see, Mr. O'Neil," the agent said. "I think."

"Call me, Roger," he told her.

"Ok, Roger," she added. "I'll get straight to the point, then. The United States Government is currently in a war of words with certain elements of the Russian Government. The US president has been pressuring the Kremlin to dismantle its nuclear weapons program and placed sanctions on their trade goods. In return, Russia has begun threatening to nuke the West Coast of the United States."

"Yeah," Roger stated. "I've seen the news stories. It's a sad thing, certainly. Nobody wants a nuclear war."

"Exactly," she said.

"What I am not understanding is what that has to do with me," he added.

"There are certain hard-liners within the Kremlin that we believe would fulfill this threat," she said. "They are a bunch of old, pro-communist fascists who'd love nothing more than to rebuild the Soviet Union to its former glory and destroy any nation that stands in their way."

"Again, what does this have to do with me, Agent Brown?"

"Well, simply put, Roger," she said. "We need someone like you on the inside. Someone we can trust to get in and disrupt their plans, permanently. If you know what I'm saying."

"Sounds a lot like you're trying to recruit me, lady."

"In essence, yes, that's exactly what I'm doing," she told him.

Roger began to stroke the side of Jack's head as he leaned over the railing, one boot resting on the bottom board, pausing for a moment to think about what she was saying to him, and everything he and his family had built around them. Not to mention all the crap that they'd been through over he years. He'd served his country honorably. Roger had nothing left to prove.

However, that burning desire to right wrongs was again smoldering within his soul. That feeling deep inside of Roger had always been there, and, probably always will be. It's what Special Operators are made of. She undoubtedly knew that. There was no other reason she'd come all the way to a ranch in the middle of nowhere, Montana.

"I've done my time," Roger said firmly. "I've given blood, sweat, and tears to this country. I've lost many friends in the process. I have nothing left to give."

"Oh, but I think you do, "she told him. "You aren't the type to back down from a challenge. Are, you, Roger?"

"You know nothing about me, lady!" Roger shouted, trying not to lose his temper. "You don't know what we have given to this nation, only to be shit on!"

"I've read your file, Mister O'Neil," she replied. "I know more about you than you realize. You may get upset thinking about it. But, inside, you're a true-blooded American Operator. Killing the bad guys is in your DNA. You'll only be disappointed at yourself if you don't come full-circle."

"Meaning what?"

"Do not dismiss who and what you are," the agent added. "Your country needs you, Mr. O'Neil."

"Well, I don't need this shit!" He shouted, kicking the side of the fence post with his cowboy boot.

Roger lifted his ball cap to wipe the sweat from his brow. As he stood there, hunched over the wooden fence, he glanced back at the agent with a pondering expression on his face.

"Who's your friend, honey?" Kate asked as she stepped out onto the front porch, their young teenage daughter Emily close behind her and brushing her long brown hair.

Two years younger than Patrick, Emily helped her mom around the house while the boys worked outside.

"Nobody!" he replied. "She was just leaving."

"Well, come inside before your dinner gets cold!" Kate added.

"Be inside in a minute, honey!"

Emily tugged on Kate's long dress as they withdrew back into the house.

Slipping the hat back onto his head, Roger wasn't quite sure how to respond to Agent Brown. The thought of leaving his family was daunting to him. He swore to them that he would never put them through that ever again. Still, if anything happened, if the US went to war and millions of people died, could he live with the fact that maybe he could have done something about it? Could he fathom a nuclear attack on American soil?

"I know you have some reservations," Agent Brown said. "It's ok. I didn't expect an immediate answer."

He didn't say a single word. He just glared at the agent in frustration. Will Roger ever know peace? Will he ever live the life he's longed to for so long? Would his family forgive him if he left?

"I'll give you forty-eight hours to think it over, Mr. O'Neil," the agent said as she withdrew back to her Chevy Suburban.

"Don't count on it," he said.

"I know where you live," she told him, swinging the vehicle door open. "I'll be in touch."

As the engine cranked up and Agent Brown sped out of view, Roger knew he had much to think about now. It seemed his life was about to change. He shook his head in disbelief as he watched the taillights disappear into the bright, full moon night.

"Why me?" he thought to himself. "Damn it. I really don't fucking need this."

Walking onto the front porch, his head felt like it was going to explode. Roger had no idea what he was going to do. Whatever it was, he needed to decide fast. War with Russia and so many innocent lives that would inevitably be lost wasn't something Roger wanted to imagine. The clock was now counting down. Tick-tock.

CHAPTER 2

THE WHITE HOUSE
WASHINGTON D.C.

THE NEWLY ELECTED American President, Republican Larry Cash, sat in his oval office desk chair, biting his nails nervously and doubting in his mind how he was going to answer to the overwhelming Public fear of an imminent war with Russia. He had to remain steadfast. Showing instability would only fuel the enemy and hinder public trust in him. If that happened, his presidential term would certainly go downhill fast.

Cash came from a long line of Republican Politicians from Texas. His uncle, Theodore, had been the Mayor of Arlington. His cousin, Brian, was the Governor of Arkansas. Cash's late father, Larry senior, had been the Secretary of the Treasury back in the early eighties under then, President Ronald Regan. It could have been said that politics ran in his blood.

He never envisioned that he'd ever be met with such a

national crisis, one that could very well define the fate of America for years to come.

"Mr. President!" National Security Advisor, Joe Rice, said as he hurried through the office door. "They are waiting for you, sir!"

Joe Rice was the President's most trusted advisor and friend. Cash knew that he'd never steer him wrong. He'd been a Colonel in the United States Army, serving in three different wars, including Operation Iraqi and Enduring Freedom, before retiring in 2010. Rice knew his stuff. To president Cash, anything that Joe said to him was gold.

The President didn't instantly answer. Instead, he peeped down at the mounds of paper on his desk, taking in a large breath as he prepared himself mentally for what was about to occur.

"Mr. President?" Rice continued.

"Yes, Joe," the President answered as his head shot up. "Yes, I heard you."

"The people are waiting, sir."

President Cash didn't say anything, only nodding his head. The truth is, he wasn't entirely sure of himself at that moment. He knew the nation was waiting for some kind of response amid growing concerns of war with Russia. He'd never been so uncertain of himself in his entire life. And, he didn't want anyone, especially his critics, to know it.

"Joe?" the President called out in a muffled tone.

"Mr. President?" he replied.

"Jesus," the President returned. "Come on, Joe. We've known each other for what, twenty years?"

"Something like that, sir."

"Call me Larry then, would you? You're making me feel old."

"Whatever you say, sir. I mean, Larry."

President Cash scratched his head and listened for a time to the relentless chatter coming from people and White House Staff just outside of the Oval Office.

"Answer one question for me," he said to Joe.

"Anything."

"What would you do?" the President asked. "If all these people were looking for an answer that you didn't have?"

"What would I do?"

"Come on, Joe," Cash continued. "We've been friends for too long. Don't patronize me."

"Ok," Joe replied. "What would I do?"

President Cash leaned back in his chair, waiting for an answer. The much-needed advice from a friend and National Security Advisor was all that mattered to him in that case. He'd gone over that speech dozens of times in his head. Before he walked out into the limelight, however, he needed one last reassurance from an old friend that he wasn't going to look like a fool.

"Quite honestly," Joe added. "I would go out there with the same unapologetic prose that you know how to do so well. Don't worry about the doubters. They are going to say what they are going to say. But, the American public needs you. They need to know they have a President who isn't going to back down from Russia, or anyone else.

They're just flexing their muscles. The Kremlin knows that nuclear war with the U.S. would be self-destruction."

The President rose steadily out of his chair, glimpsing at his trusted friend. Adjusting his light blue tie and the American Flag lapel attached to his Navy-Blue coat, he patted Joe on his shoulder and prepared to address the nation.

"Thanks, Joe," he said with a smirk. "I thought you'd see it my way."

"No problem, sir," replied Joe. "So, you ready to go?"

"Yep," he told him. "I'm right behind you."

As the Oval Office door opened, the gaggle of people who were awaiting the American President gradually parted away from the center of the hallway, allowing him and his advisor to proceed through. They made their way down the long hall and toward the waiting cameras, and he and Joe parted ways.

"I hope we've got this right, for all of our sakes," the President mumbled to Joe as he smiled at the crowd, allowing Joe to move off to his side.

"Trust me, sir," Joe replied into his ear just before slipping past him.

As the camera turned on, President Cash stood at the podium, forging a grin at the millions of people surely watching at home on their televisions. Of course, he didn't have much to smile about. However, he was bent on hiding behind that facade for as long as he possibly could.

"My fellow Americans," he began. "I stand here before you this evening, confident enough to say that the Russian people do not want a nuclear war with America. President Petrov and his administration are merely unwilling to demonstrate to their people that they don't want to face the United States in any kind of war. But, especially, a nuclear war. In other words, they don't want to look weak. But, rest assured, the United States is armed and more than capable of countering them, should they feel the need to test this theory. I want you to sleep soundly, knowing that Russia understands that attacking us would be suicide. Currently, my administration is in the early stages of peace talks with the Russian President. We expect to resolve the situation civilly, and, within a matter of weeks. Thank you."

As president Cash withdrew from the camera, Joe and the rest of the administration began following him straight down to the situation room in the West Wing of the White House, where they had an emergency meeting set up with the rest of his administration and top generals, along with CIA director John Cabot. They needed to get right to the bottom of the Russian President's threats.

"Think they bought it?" Joe asked, quickly trailing Cash down the long hallway.

"I hope so," answered the President. "I can't afford for this to come back and bite me in the ass. We don't need a nationwide panic on our hands right now."

"Right, sir," Joe replied.

"But I'll tell you something," the President added. "If they decide to get jumpy, we'll send a nuke straight into the heart of Moscow and worry about consequences later."

"That wouldn't be wise, sir," said Joe.

"I know it wouldn't," Cash replied. "Jesus, I'm not an idiot, you know?"

"Of course not, sir."

"But, America, and I have had enough of these pro-communist fanatics trying to assert their power over the rest of the world," the President continued. "If we don't find a resolution, and fast, this could very well end up far worse than the cold war ever was."

The American President was reasonably uncertain of the Russian president's motives, given his unpredictable and erratic past. Petrov was known to be outspoken against the West. But would he be willing to go to war over those beliefs? Nobody knew for sure. But it would be a travesty not to take his threats seriously.

Petrov was old school former KGB and the poster boy for communism. He was a small stature of a man, at five foot six, but as ruthless as they come. His father and grandfather both had held top positions in the old Soviet Government, both under Leonid Brezhnev and Joseph Stalin. Perhaps he was trying to live up to his family name.

CIA analysts had been studying him for some time since he rose to power five years earlier, following the death of his predecessor, who reportedly died of a sudden heart attack. Whether his cause of death was accurate was some cause for speculation. Some believe that Petrov had him killed. But, nobody knew for sure.

Petrov didn't want to appear soft to his people. Weakness, to him, was the ultimate disease. He came up at a time during the Cold War when the United States was always at odds with the Soviet Union. Many in the U.S. Administration and intelligence circles believed that he wanted to bring the empire back at any cost, even to his people. At present, that didn't seem like such a farfetched theory.

The door to the situation room swung open, and all in attendance quickly rose to their feet. Joe held the door open, and the President entered, eyeballing everyone in the room with a piercing gaze.

"Have a seat!" He thundered. "Please. We've got some work to do."

As the President lowered into his chair, he tapped CIA Director Cabot on the shoulder.

"You have an update for me, John?" he asked.

"Yes, sir, I do," he said, sliding a large photograph and some notes across the table.

Director Cabot had been a four-star general in the United States Army and rose to be a member of the Joint Chiefs of Staff before retiring from service in 2016. He was also the top officer in charge of American Forces during the initial stages of the war in Afghanistan back in 2001, as well as serving during the first Gulf War, Somalia, Grenada, and the end stages of the Vietnam War. Having devoted his entire life to serving his country, President Cash saw no other man more fit for the job.

"What's this?" the President asked him.

"That, sir, is President Petrov at a pro-communist rally in the Red Square in Moscow, two days ago."

"What the hell?" the President said. "How'd you get this?"

"We have sources inside Moscow, sir," said Cabot.

"That's good to know," the President continued. "But, still, I wouldn't put it past Petrov to become the new Stalin."

"Exactly, sir," Cabot replied. "Whether he has his citizens' support or not, a totalitarian regime doesn't need public support. They'll just force them into submission just like every other. It'll be the Soviet Union 2.0."

"Agreed," the President added. "Now, what about these nukes? Do you think he'll use them? Or, is he just blowing smoke?"

"Mr. President," Secretary of Defense Ronald Baker chimed in.

"Yes, Ron?"

"It is my firm belief, sir, that Petrov is just using this whole nuclear threat as a ploy to get us to stay out of Russian affairs."

President Cash thought about his answer for a bit. He'd wanted to believe that. But, it was hard to decipher what was real and what was being fabricated by the Russian government. He knew they could be far from trusted. However, would they risk attacking the most powerful nation on earth?

"You really believe that?" the President asked.

"I do, sir," the Secretary answered. "He has to know it would be self-destruction."

"Come on, Ronald," Joe interrupted. "This guy is talking about bringing back the old Soviet era. Just take a look at his family history. You think he's capable of thinking like a rational human being?"

"We have to take these threats seriously!" Vice President Mark Harris added. "It is this unpredictability which makes the man dangerous."

Harris, a tall Caucasian man from Saint Paul, Minnesota, had been a congressman representing Minnesota's second district in the nineties. Afterward, he'd risen to the positions of Secretary of State and National Security Advisor immediately following. By all accounts, Harris was a career politician, having served in the Republican Party for almost two decades. Knowing the man's stellar track record, President Cash graciously chose him as his running mate during the last election.

"So, what do you want to do, Joe?" Ron asked. "Destroy Moscow? Send in the troops? He's just testing us for God's sake!"

"Enough!" the President interjected. "This is entirely too much speculation and not enough fact! We cannot act until this threat is confirmed; Not until then. You all know that!"

President Cash tilted back in his leather chair, taking in a deep breath as he glanced at all in attendance. Looking over at the man sitting next to him, he knew exactly what was on his mind.

"What do you think, Joe?" the President asked his National Security Advisor.

"You know what I think, sir," Joe remarked. "We have to validate the threat. We aren't a nation that acts on impulse. The bottom line is, we will never garner congressional or United Nations support over a war of mere words, even if it is a credible threat. We don't know that yet."

"You're right," the President replied, dropping his head into his folded hands.

A brief silence came over the entire room as everyone paused and waited for the President to proceed.

"I can't believe my entire presidency has come down to this," he continued. "I could be focusing more on my campaign promises to create more jobs, lower taxes, support the middle class. But, No! I'm stuck worrying about some crazed Russian lunatic wanting to vaporize us all!"

Nobody said a word in response. Instead, they all sat, not wanting to rock the boat. President Cash could be a handful when he lost his temper. Everybody in that room knew it. Nobody in his administration wished to be on the receiving end of one of his rants, especially during such a stressful situation.

"I need more," the President said as he glared at CIA Director Cabot. "Get me more!"

"Yes, sir," Cabot replied. "I'll get my people on it immediately."

"You do that," the President added.

As everyone rose from their seats, preparing to depart from the meeting, President Cash knew that he did not want to act on empty threats until they could get more intelligence on specifically what President Petrov was planning.

The CIA had something going on behind the scenes, as they usually did. What that was remained to be seen by the Cash Administration. Black Ops was their specialty. What that required would be revealed in due time.

CHAPTER 3

THE BLACK, ARMORED Range Rover came barreling around the curve at 100 KPH, swerving to the side and barely missing a pedestrian in the crosswalk. The loud, piercing screech of brakes locking could be heard for blocks as the vehicle came to a skidding stop in front of the enormous building. The driver jumped out immediately and held the door as four occupants, exiting the backseat, swiftly made their way down the long footpath.

"Those damned dogs!" President Boris Petrov shouted in his heavy Russian accent as he and his security, Bizon submachine guns strapped to their bodies, headed up the steps to the Presidential Executive Office at Moscow's Staraya Square. "I'll show them how serious I am. The pigs!"

"They're just testing you, sir," one of his men said to him.

"When I want your God damned opinion," the President returned, punching the man square in his shoulder. "I'll fucking ask for it!"

"Yes, sir."

Petrov had seen the footage of the American President on television earlier that morning. He was outraged that the US didn't seem to be taking him seriously. Or, so he thought. Russian power was essential to him, as it was for most past Russian presidents. But, the fall of the Soviet Union had seemingly brought with it a new age of democracy.

For a long time, there was thought to be a new world opening up to citizens of the former communist nation. Yet, something else had been brewing behind the scenes. Petrov vowed to his closest associates that he would bring back the past in all its glory. What the Russian people thought, or were too ignorant or absent-minded to know was irrelevant to him. In his mind, Russian supremacy was the top priority.

"Leave me," Petrov said to his security detail as he entered the office and settled low into his desk chair, lighting up a Cuban cigar and taking in a long drag. "I need to be alone."

Blowing white cigar smoke high into the air, Petrov glared up at his men with a fierce gaze.

"Now!" He yelled to them. "Get the fuck out of here and close the door behind you!"

"Yes, sir," one of the men said in Russian as they scampered away through the office door.

Petrov kicked his feet up onto his desk, the whole place

reeking of cigar smoke and the open Vodka bottle he had sitting on the side table. Vodka was always a staple in the Russian diet, especially during those long, horrid winters when it's all they could do to keep warm. President Petrov never went anywhere without his favorite drink. Some might have said he was an alcoholic, but, not by Russian standards. Vodka wasn't just a drink to him. It represented something more—the strength and resilience of Mother Russia and her people, his people. He just knew they would persist through any storm, and rise from the ashes to be born again.

The President poured a little Vodka into the sparkling crystal shot glass sitting in front of him and raised it high into the air.

"K Materi Rossii," he toasted to himself in Russian.

As he leaned his head back with a long gulp, Petrov slammed the cup down hard on his office desk. Checking the time displayed on the Rolex watch on his left wrist, he seized the secure telephone from the table beside him and began dialing.

"Yes, Mr. President?" the old, scratchy voice, on the other end, answered in Russian.

"Hello, Adrian," Petrov replied. "Give me the good news. Is our plan still working?"

Adrian Ivanov, fifty-nine, was the head of the Russian nuclear weapons program. He'd been appointed to that position by Petrov immediately upon taking office. Ivanov had served alongside the Russian President since his days as an officer in the Russian military, and, also during

Petrov's time as a spy in the KGB during the late eighties and early nineties.

Ivanov was amongst the president's inner circle of true believers in the old communist regime. Additionally, he knew not to get on Petrov's bad side. He'd seen firsthand what happened when people crossed him.

"Yes, sir!" Adrian roared over the sounds of heavy machinery operating. "We just need a week or two to get everything in order!"

"You don't have a week or two!" The President yelled into the telephone. "You understand me, Adrian? You have four days! That's it! If it's not done by then, you will suffer the consequences!"

"Very well, sir," Adrian anxiously replied. "We'll get it done."

"That's what I wanted to hear," said Petrov "Now, stop wasting time talking to me and get back to work! We'll all have a celebratory drink when this is done!"

President Petrov slammed the phone back down onto the receiver and grabbed the remote that was sitting on his desk, switching on the flat-screen television hanging from the office wall in front of him. He'd been keeping a watchful eye on the American news media for some time. If the American public was sent into a panic, well, that suited him just fine.

"Reporting to you live from Manhattan, I'm Pamela Gray," the news reporter said over the loud noise from the massive crowd of people chanting close by. "As

you can see behind me, the protest is in full swing now. People are chanting for President Cash to put more pressure on the Russian President to disarm these weapons of mass destruction. They are absolutely in fear, for good reason, of a nuclear war with Russia! It feels like the Cold War all over again. Some of these protestors are even calling for the President to be impeached. This is not only happening here in NYC, either. Massive rallies are going on right now in LA, Seattle, Atlanta, Chicago, and the list goes on. As I look out over the sea of people who are here in the streets, it seems that President Cash has some harsh critics here in New York. The question on everyone's mind, now, is what he will do. I fear this crowd will only continue to grow and gain momentum as time goes on. I'm Pamela Gray, reporting from New York. Back to you, Tom."

"Perfect," Petrov said to himself as he downed another shot of Vodka and tossed the TV remote onto the luxury leather sofa in the corner.

It was exactly what he had expected. Petrov knew that the confusion of possibly going to war would send the American people into turmoil. He envisioned it. The fact that this American President wasn't that popular, to begin with, was just feeding right into his hands. With the Republicans and Democrats fighting over what action to take, and American citizens caught in the middle, it was the perfect opportunity to create hysteria.

Suddenly, Petrov heard a loud knock at the door.

"What?" he thundered.

"It's me, sir!" A deep voice sounded through the door.

"Come in, Ivan," Petrov replied.

Ivan Chernov, the Russian Presidents' Chief of Staff, entered the executive office and stood directly in front of Petrov's desk. Chernov was a tower of a man, with tree-trunk sized legs, and short, dark brown hair on top of a buzz cut. Charnov had obviously worked out regularly, with his bulging chest and enormous forearms. He was also among the few people that the Russian President truly trusted with his most intimate secrets.

"They are ready for you, sir," said Chernov.

"Very well," the President responded, nodding his head and clutching the leather-bound briefcase from the floor underneath his desk. "Come on. Let's go."

The two made their way outside to where the President's henchmen were waiting next to his armored car.

"Go!" Petrov shouted to the driver as they entered the back of the vehicle.

The FSB had sent the President's office a secret cable early that morning announcing that they had captured a suspected intelligence officer, an American. This was fabulous news to Petrov because he knew he could now use the American as a bargaining chip against the US. That is if the President cared enough about the fate of one man to come to the negotiating table.

The Range Rover sped rapidly across the city. As they neared the front gate to the prison, the two gate guards,

Kalashnikov rifles in hand, had noticed the presidential seal fixed to the front of the vehicle and promptly opened the gate to allow them to enter.

LEFORTOVO PRISON, MOSCOW

Within the old building, the overwhelming funk of urine, feces, and sweat could be smelled throughout the prison walls. The cell blocks reverberated with the thunderous sounds of prisoners cursing and screaming and tapping hard on the bars of their cells with whatever they could find. That place was most clearly not a den for the civilized human being.

Down in the cold, damp, and dusty basement, there was another kind of prisoner. Strung up by pipes connected to the high basement ceiling, cables wrapped around his arms, that man had seen better days. Blood ran from his head down to his beaten torso before forming a bright, red puddle on the dirty prison floor. Sweat beaded down his forehead as he coughed up blood, splattering all over his bare arms and legs. The filthy white rag wrapped around his face made sure that he wouldn't see the beating coming.

"You bastards!" the man painfully squealed, struggling to position himself, his legs barely touching the ground.

But it was no use. Nobody was listening to him. He was on foreign soil, now. Nobody there gave a damn about him or his reasons for being in Russia. The prison system in Russia was notoriously brutal for anyone, but, particularly for foreigners. However, if you were under suspicion of being a spy, they'd lock you up and throw away the key; if you were still alive after they battered and tortured you to exhaustion.

The slamming of the large metal prison door sounded down the dark basement corridor. Footsteps getting ever so closer to the captive tapped on the floor, warning the American that they were about to begin again. He'd expected it. Every time someone entered that area, the beatings started all over. The inmate felt a tenseness come over his entire body as the footsteps got closer.

Two of Petrov's security agents stood by the door as he entered the holding cell, stopping close enough to the American for him to smell the Vodka on his breath. The Russian President eyeballed the prisoner from head to toe, noticing the dried-up blood caked on his face and limbs.

"Who are you?" Petrov asked him in English. "What are you doing in Moscow?"

"I'm a tourist!" the man answered in distress, spitting blood onto the floor. "I just came here to see Red Square!"

"Bullshit!" Petrov yelled into his ear. "You're a fucking spy!"

"I'm not," the American replied in horror. "I swear to you!"

"I don't believe you!" the Russian President shouted, balling up his fist and striking the prisoner hard in his gut and causing him to double over.

As the American hung from the ceiling, cringing in pain, one of the prison guards approached Petrov from behind.

"Sir," the guard said, delivering Petrov the man's wallet. "This is what they found on him."

The President emptied the contents of the wallet onto the wet floor, picking up the driver's license and the passport that had landed by his feet.

"John Regan, from Bethesda, Maryland?" he asked, studying the document. "I am assuming that is not your real name."

"Yes, it is. I swear!"

"Really?" Petrov continued. "You know, somehow, I still don't believe a word of it!"

"Who are you?" the American asked.

Just before answering his question, however, the Russian President glanced backward at his men, grinning from ear to ear.

"Who am I?" Petrov added, kicking the man in the stomach as hard as he could and watching him cry out in agony. "I'm the one asking the God damned questions here, not you! I am the President of the country you are standing, well, hanging in. You better start answering me, or things are going to end very badly for you! Ponyat?"

"What does the Russian Government want with me?" Asked the prisoner, a tear rolling down his cheek. "I've done nothing wrong! Why is the Russian President here?"

"I said I am asking the fucking questions!" Petrov shouted, slapping the man hard across the face with an open hand. "I wanted to see your face, myself."

"Please stop!" the American begged, his head cocked

sideways from the blow. "I told you already! I am a student on holiday. I swear to you I am not a spy!"

"Shut the fuck up!" Petrov added, sliding the cloth slightly above his eyes.

"Look at me!" The President continued, gripping the American by his chin and raising him higher above the floor. "Look at my face! I am sick of you Americans thinking you can do whatever you want, wherever you want, and whenever you want. I am the man who is going to be responsible for destroying your pathetic nation, and leaving you in here to rot with the rest of the animals! Remember me for as long as you remain alive!"

President Petrov hit the man in the face one last time, the power of his punch causing the American to swing backward before turning to walk away and leaving him to bleed all over the cold prison floor.

"Open the gate!" He ordered the prison guard. "Leave him there to fucking bleed!"

"Yes, Sir."

"And, make sure you get some information out of him!" The President added. "Don't let him die until then!"

Petrov was enraged over what he considered to be an act of war against Russia. It didn't really matter that the American was innocent. In the current climate, Petrov was going to use him for all he was worth to the US. The man's rage was only misplaced by his aggression toward the United States. Aggression that would, without wavering, only grow as time progressed.

CHAPTER 4

BIG SKY, MONTANA

THE FORD F-250 Super Cab's diesel engine rumbled as they made their way down the long, twisting roadway to the expansive, fifty-acre Ranch on the outskirts of the tiny, mountain town.

As the morning sunlight peeked over the horizon, flashing a glimmer of light directly into the front windshield, the flatbed trailer tires rotated noisily beneath the weight of the large, round, hay bale that was held down in the back by long ratchet straps. Father and son were on their way home from the farm supply store, preparing to feed the animals and take in another hard-working day of farm chores and training Patrick's horse, Jack.

They'd left the girls at home on purpose. Roger wanted to spend some quality time with the boy, who was looking and behaving more and more like his father every single day.

"What do you think, Pat?" Roger asked. "You up for testing Jack's patience, today?"

"Hell yeah!" Patrick answered, almost forgetting that his father told him not to curse. "I mean, yes, sir!"

Roger loved the fact that Patrick was becoming a hard-working and respectful young man, not like when he was younger. However, He didn't exactly want the boy to end up just like him. He'd wanted him to be better like most fathers do. But Patrick looked up to his dad.

He wanted to emulate everything that Roger did. There was that one trait of Patrick's old man that Roger never wanted him to pick up—the rough around the edges, battle-hardened veteran that flinched from every loud sound or had nightmares of people dying in front of him. If Patrick could stay far away from that life, well, that would be ideal for him.

The massive pickup truck turned into the entrance to the Sprawling Ranch, pulling the trailer along the side of the barn and coming to a standstill next to the big, metal drive-through gate.

"Come on," Roger said as he leaped out of the truck. "Let's get this thing unloaded, shall we?"

"Can I do it, dad?" Patrick asked. "Please?"

"If you think you are up to it, sure," Roger replied. "The keys are hanging up just inside the barn door over there."

While Patrick ran inside of the barn to snatch the keys, Roger untied the straps that were holding the big hay bale to the trailer. As he tossed them into the toolbox in the bed of the vehicle, the loud roar of a tractor engine starting sounded from inside of the large, wooden barn.

Patrick guided the orange Kubota Tractor through

the double doors and around to the edge of the flatbed trailer, positioning the spear directly into the center of the round bale.

"Nice job, son!" Roger told him. "Now, lift it up slowly while tilting it back. We don't want it to fall over."

"How's that, dad?" Patrick asked, tilting the spear somewhat and watching the bale slide back.

"You are good to go," Roger replied. "Just don't hit my truck."

Patrick backed the tractor up a little and carried the hay bale straight through the metal gate to be dropped into the large hay feeder close to the middle of the horse paddock. Exiting the Kubota Tractor and tugging his gloves onto his hands, Patrick jumped off. They pushed the large bale until it slid off of the end of the hay spear, landing upright in the center of the feeder.

"Here they come," Roger said as they watched all eight horses head straight for the fresh hay bale. "It's mealtime, boys and girls!"

Father and son, both leaning against the metal feeder, watched in awe as their horses went about their daily business. It was something they did every single day. But, it never got old to them. Taking care of those horses tended to bring out the simplicity of life. It instilled a calmness within Roger that he'd been searching for in the past. Just watching them reminded him every single day of what life could be. Their beauty and tranquility were the only thing, other than Roger's family, that grounded him. Compared to his past, those horses were the ultimate symbol of peace.

"They sure are majestic, aren't they?"

"What, dad?" Patrick replied.

"These guys," he said. "I could stay out here and watch them all day. They are the most beautiful thing I have ever seen, aside from your mom, of course."

"Of course, dad," Patrick said, chuckling. "Can I ride Jack Now?"

As much as Patrick had grown up over the past year or two, he was still the impatient teenager, which his father felt he would grow out of working on the Ranch.

"We have to let these guys finish eating, son," Roger told him. "Besides, we still have other chores to do first. We'll bring Jack out this afternoon."

"Ok, Dad," Patrick answered.

Suddenly, as if to warn of an intruder, the racket of one of their roosters crowing rang out from its perch atop a nearby fence post. It was nothing new for life on a ranch. But, upon focusing his eyes on the bird, Roger's gaze met with a recently familiar and uninvited sight in the distance.

"Shit," he mumbled under his breath.

"What, dad?" Patrick asked. "What's wrong?"

"Nothing for you to worry about, son," Roger assured him. "Just get back to your chores, and I'll be around to help you in a bit."

Patrick went to the barn to grab a pail to feed the chickens while his father headed straight for the driveway to greet the visitor. The Suburban pulled up alongside him as the occupant slowly rolled the driver's side window down.

"Hello again, Mister O'Neil," she said to him. "Lovely morning for a horseback ride, isn't it?"

"What are you doing here?" he asked. "I told you. I have family and obligations out here to think about. I cannot leave them here by themselves."

"Yeah, I know," she responded, opening the door to exit the vehicle. "Let's talk about that."

"Talk about what?" Roger questioned as he leaned one arm onto the hood. "There's nothing to talk about, lady."

"I prefer Agent Brown or Lacy," she replied.

"Ok, Agent Brown. I have nothing else to say to you. Would you kindly leave so I can finish my work? I need to go help my son."

Agent Brown rested her back on the side of the vehicle, glancing out at the expansive ranch in all its beauty.

"You know, this life you've made out here, you and your family, Mister O'Neil?" She asked.

"What about it?"

"Well, somewhere in this country, other folks have made comfortable lives too," she added. "They are trying to live and raise their children in peace, just like you. But, unlike you, they don't know the true danger or costs of war, especially on our own soil. And, those lives will be in grave danger should we end up in a nuclear conflict with Russia. Get my drift?"

"Agent Brown, I see what you are trying to do here," he told her. "It's not going to work. With all due respect, I've given my heart and soul to this country, already, many times over. I have nothing left in me."

"They have an American, Mister O'Neil," she added.

"What!?"

"Yeah," the agent added. "An American student who was on holiday in Moscow. By all accounts, an innocent man. But, they suspect him of being a spy. That's what they are saying, at least. We believe they are beating and torturing him as we speak."

"Jesus! What are you doing about it?" Asked Roger. "You can't just leave him there."

"Nothing the agency can do about it right now," she answered. "Unfortunately, our hands are tied politically unless we can find a diplomatic solution. Due to the state of the current Russian administration, it's highly unlikely. We are certain they are just using him to get our attention. But, there's no telling what they'll do to him. President Petrov is a complete maniac."

"Why do you people have to come and fuck up my life?" Roger asked, standing next to her with folded arms and looking out into the distance with a blank stare. "I don't understand why it has to be me. There are plenty of operators out there who are still active. I just don't get it."

"The agency doesn't normally go out recruiting people, Mister O'Neil," she said. "You were recommended."

"By who?" he asked.

"Does it really matter?"

"I guess not."

"This is an off the books kind of operation," she replied. "You understand what I am saying?"

"Meaning?"

"Meaning, nobody will know who you are," she said. "Only the highest levels of government will have a clue. We must maintain complete deniability. You won't officially be a member of the agency. Instead, we will contract you."

"So, in other words, I'll have no support?" asked Roger.

"Not officially, no," she answered. "You'll be what we call a non-official cover operative, or NOC. However, you will have a case officer stateside, and a contact in Moscow who know your true identity and will provide guidance and support. They will be the only other people besides me, who know who you are."

Roger stood there for a brief time, thinking of his life up until that point. He thought about his family and how he swore to never leave them. He thought about the friends they lost in Afghanistan, and the remnants of war that never seemed to go away, no matter how much time had passed.

He thought about September 11, 2001, and where he was at that moment when the first plane hit the tower. That morning was when Roger had decided he needed to do something. Terrorists attacking American soil brought the fighter out of him. It was a trait that perhaps had always been there but was dormant up until that point.

After that, he'd dedicated his life to serving. But this was something different. This time around, It wasn't Roger and his Ranger team. This was new territory for him. It didn't seem to matter that the government that he'd served under liked to shit on him and other Veterans from time to time. It was about the people, the peace-loving people of the United States who had no clue of war, or what could happen to their way of life, a life that could very well go away at the push of a button.

"Dad?" Patrick called out to him from a few yards away. "Are you really leaving?"

Abruptly, Roger's focus switched back to reality. As he looked over at his son walking toward them, he knew of only one thing to say.

"Give me a few?" he asked Agent Brown.

"Sure," she said. "Take your time."

Roger gripped Patrick by the arm, escorting him closer to the barn. Obviously, he'd overheard the two talking. This was his son, and he had every right to be worried. But it was Roger's job to comfort his children. They wouldn't understand, fully. However, he would do what he had to do to ease their confusion.

"Dad?" Patrick said as Roger stooped down in front of him, arms resting on his shoulder. "Are you really going away?"

"Don't you worry about that right now, Pat," Roger told him, looking straight into his eyes. "Just run inside, and I'll be there in a minute to talk to you, your mother, and sister, ok?"

"Is everything going to be ok, dad?"

"Yes, son," Roger replied. "Everything is going to be fine. I promise. Just run along, and I'll be there in a few."

"Yes, sir."

Roger knew he'd have a lot to answer for now. He also knew that eventually, his family would understand. This was much bigger than Roger, bigger than anyone. It wasn't some local thugs threatening people. Nor was it al-Qaeda flying planes into buildings any longer.

This was a nuclear-powered nation threatening to make California cease to exist. Maybe it was the call to serve that he'd desired more than anything. He missed it. He craved it. In deep thought, he returned to the lone agent.

"Fine, I'll do it," Roger said as he leaned back against the Chevy Suburban. "On one condition."

"Name it," the agent replied.

"I get to do this my way," he said. "No micro-managing, if you or anybody else doesn't like the way I do things, I walk. It's that simple."

"Mister O'Neil," she said, sliding her black, Oakley sunglasses onto her forehead. "I wouldn't have it any other way. I'll be here until tomorrow evening before I fly back to Washington. Meet me at the Holiday Inn parking lot in Bozeman tomorrow morning at 10, we'll go over everything, and I'll introduce you to your case officer, the man who will be your handler throughout the operation."

Roger still wasn't entirely sure why he was doing this. Those damned government agents appeared to know precisely what buttons to press, though. He just couldn't manage to turn it off. After all this time, that patriotic fire was still burning inside of him. Maybe Roger was made for war. Perhaps war was in his blood. Either way, he was getting prepared to step into a new unknown. This time, he wouldn't have his fellow Rangers to back him up. These were unchartered and treacherous waters he was getting set to sail into.

As he stood in the drive, watching the agent's vehicle fade away into the morning fog, Roger wondered if he was doing the right thing. It all seemed surreal. However, as in everything else, only time would tell what the future held.

CHAPTER 5

BOZEMAN, MONTANA

ROGER TURNED THE pickup truck into the hotel parking lot, ten minutes early for his scheduled meeting time with the agent and her unknown associate. He was always early for everything, the gift of so many years of waking before the sun came up. He'd gone over in his head how everything was going to go the night prior, in between small periods of pleading with his wife, Kate.

His family wasn't pleased. They didn't want him to leave. Though, Kate knew who she'd married a long time ago. Roger was a patriot. She'd disliked what he was doing; however, she wasn't at all surprised. But, she didn't believe it was his fight.

Roger didn't see it that way. An American life was at stake. And Russia had been threatening nuclear war for some time Who else would step up to the plate to test?

As Roger came around the corner of the hotel, on the edge of the lot, all by itself stood the black Chevrolet

Suburban with its tinted windows and the outline of two occupants waiting in the front seat.

"I can't believe I'm doing this," Roger said to himself just before rolling up next to the waiting vehicle. "What was I fucking thinking?"

Roger shoved the gear shifter into park, and Agent Brown quickly hopped out of the front side, holding the backdoor open for him. But, before he could get in, a figure appeared behind him, pulling his arms out to the side and frisking him up and down.

"What is this?" he asked, the man pulling his pockets inside out. "What the hell, man?"

"It's just a precaution," the agent told him. "Nothing against you. We need to make sure no recording or listening devices are present. Leave your cell phone in your truck, too, please."

"Get in, Mister O'Neil," Brown continued, as he tossed his phone into the front seat of his pickup. "Please. We have a lot to discuss."

As Roger made himself comfortable in the back of the Suburban, he glimpsed at the stranger sitting beside Agent Brown, holding a manila folder with unknown contents. He could just about guess what was inside. The man was a mysterious looking gentleman, an older white guy, decked out in all black clothing and a round, black Panama hat and dark shades.

"Mister O'Neil, this is Richard Weber," said Agent Brown," Your handler. Weber, meet Roger O'Neil."

"Heard a lot about you," Weber said as he stretched his hand out to shake Roger's.

"I can't say the same about you," Roger returned. "But, nice to meet you."

Richard Weber was a thirty-year veteran of the Central Intelligence Agency and former Moscow Station Chief. He knew that part of the world well. Now, in his early sixties, Weber had taken up more of an administrative role pending his retirement in a few years. Because of Weber's extensive knowledge of the inner workings of the Russian Government, and, this Russian President in particular, he'd been handpicked for this role.

"So," Weber continued, plucking the documents from the folder and spreading them out on the center console. "Now that we got all the formalities out of the way, let's get down to business, shall we?"

"Sure."

"This is your passport," Weber said, Handing Roger the small document for him to study. "You'll notice, Mister O'Neil, that there is a different name under your picture. From now on, you will be known as Chris Hughes, a Canadian graduate student on holiday in Moscow. Make sure you know your identity inside and out before you land. Study it, know it, be it."

"Got it," Roger replied.

"Also," Weber added. "Your callsign for contact purposes will be Raven. You only use this should you need to contact me directly over a non-secure line. This is extremely important, so do not forget it."

"Roger that," answered Roger.

"Now," continued Weber. "I must reiterate to you if you are caught or captured, you will most likely be tortured or worse. If this happens, you are never to give up that you are American, or what you are doing there. If you do, we will deny all knowledge of your existence."

"But," Agent Brown interrupted. "If you do the job the way we suppose you will, you shouldn't need to worry about that."

"Right," Weber said in agreement. "Now, you'll be working out of a safe house in Moscow, close to the red square."

"Who's my contact in Moscow?" Roger inquired.

"A guy by the name of Demetri Gusev," replied Weber, slipping a photograph from the manila folder and placing it out in front of him. "He's former Spetsnaz and a veteran of the Russian war in Afghanistan, callsign, Spinnaker."

"What the hell?" Roger asked. "How is a former Spetsnaz soldier involved with us?"

"Don't worry," Agent Brown said. "He was pro-Soviet way back then. But, the Russian Government tried to have him assassinated for switching sides and fighting with the Ukrainians against Russia after the collapse of the Soviet Union. He was injured pretty badly. Now, he has a vendetta against them."

Roger took a quick glimpse of the picture, noticing the long scar running from one side of the man's face to the other.

"Can we trust him, though?"

"Yes, mister O'Neil," Weber stated. "Spinnaker has

been one of our contacts in Russia for many years now. We've never had a problem with him. He's given us some valuable intel over the years."

"That's good to know," said Roger. "But, what about the American student who was arrested?"

"We think he's locked up in Lefortovo prison," said Brown. "Rescue him if you can, but he is not a national priority for this mission."

Roger really didn't like the way that sounded. The thought of leaving an innocent American in the custody of the Russians, just to use for their own propaganda, spread chills throughout his body. He could've only imagined what the poor guy must have been going through.

"You can't just fucking expect me to leave him in there," Roger told her.

"I don't, mister O'Neil," she said. "But, if it comes down to him or the mission, the mission must come first."

"Whatever you say," replied Roger.

"Now," Weber interrupted, unveiling the remaining three photos from the stack. "These are satellite images of the only known locations of Russia's nuclear weapons facilities. We do believe there are more. In fact, we are pretty certain of it. Still, they have yet to be found. Our assets on the ground haven't been able to locate them, and the Russian's have done a good job of hiding them from aerial reconnaissance. If they really do plan to launch, it will most likely be from a mobile launcher, probably somewhere within the immense Siberian wilderness, which, as I'm sure you know, is a much larger landmass than the United States, itself. It's like finding a needle in a million haystacks."

"You have your work cut out for you, mister O'Neil," Agent Brown added. "But, a capable guy such as yourself should be able to work with it. Demetri will help you find your way around. Just trust in your instincts, and you should be fine."

"You two sure know how to make a guy feel confident," replied Roger. "But, I'm always up for a challenge."

"We thought you'd be," Weber told him. "Now, get your things in order, Mister O'Neil. Your flight leaves tomorrow morning at 0800 hours. Our contact will give you all of the supplies you need once you land in Moscow. From here on out, only your false name may be used. Understand?"

"I got it," Roger told him as he examined the passport held in his hands.

"Ok, then, Chris Hughes," Weber said with a grin. "Have a nice flight."

✧

A day later, as the late evening sun beamed through the aircraft window, warming the left side of Roger's face, he struggled to keep his eyes opened. It had been a long flight. He hadn't slept much the night before, and he didn't anticipate he was going to sleep much that night, either.

Roger was concerned about the mission, but he was more concerned about his family back home. He'd arranged for his uncle Franklin to watch over them while he's gone, so he wasn't worried about their safety as much as he worried that they didn't understand why he needed to leave.. He was troubled because he knew they didn't understand. Leaving them was far from easy for him. And, it's something he said he would never do again. Someday, perhaps, they would forgive him.

Roger's body began to sway as turbulence shook the airplane from side to side, upsetting his already jittery stomach. It felt to him like the first time he'd ever experienced combat, walking into battle as green as grass. But, in the end, he'd proven himself on multiple instants. He was an experienced combat soldier.

This was a different kind of war. A shadow game that Roger had yet to play. He felt once again like a rookie about to step up to the plate. That type of cunning can't be taught. There was a reason they'd selected him in the first place.

"Can I get you something?" the flight attendant asked as she pushed the drink cart up next to him.

"What?" Roger asked, snapping out of his daydream.

"Can I get you something to drink, sir?"

"Vodka on the rocks, please. Thanks."

Vodka seemed to be fitting for where Roger was headed. The flight attendant poured him a glass and proceeded down the aisle. As he took a sip from the cup, Roger glanced around the cabin, wondering to himself, as they go about their daily lives, how many of those people had absolutely no clue that two powerful nations were on the verge of a disastrous war.

Sure, it had been all over the media. But, these types of threats, on the surface, have happened over and over throughout history. Nobody, especially the American public, ever expected them to come true. People, as a whole, are feeble-minded and dangerous. They need, without ever even knowing it, people like Roger behind the scenes doing America's dirty work.

"Ladies and gentlemen," the pilot called out over the intercom. "Please fasten your seatbelts. We'll be entering the Russian capital in a few minutes and will begin our descent momentarily. As always, thanks for choosing United and enjoy your stay in Russia. Thank you."

As Roger buckled his seatbelt, he peeped out through the window, watching the tiny Russian cars, as small as ants, move gradually down the highway. The airplane was lowering beneath the clouds, and he could barely make out the city of Moscow skyline approaching from far off in the distance.

Roger could feel the power of the aircraft increasing as they began to make their descent. Reaching into the gray, carry-on bag laying across his lap and hiding it from view, he slowly uncovered the photograph of Demetri one last time. Roger wanted to ensure he would recognize Demetri wherever he might be waiting. He was positive there would be eyes on him as soon as he made his way into the airport. He was confident he wouldn't miss the long, deep scar across the man's face.

Roger removed the fake Canadian passport from the bag and slid it into the front pants pocket of his Khaki trousers.

"Here goes nothing," he thought to himself, feeling the sudden jolt from the aircraft underneath him as the wheels touched down on the long runway of the Moscow Airport.

Roger was in rival territory now. He was no longer, Roger O'Neil, a family man from Montana. But, now Chris Hughes, Canadian student from British Columbia. Roger was in town to see the sites, and perhaps try a few of the country's popular dishes—maybe take in the glamorous Russian architecture. At least, that was the story. He'd gone over it many times in his head during the lengthy flight. As Roger stepped off the plane, he knew that he'd need to bury his identity and his past deep down inside of him and not let it back out until this mission was a success. The time for games had long since passed. The fate of his country and its people depended on it, and him.

CHAPTER 6

THE IMMIGRATION OFFICER carefully examined Roger's face while glancing down at his passport photo numerous times over a couple of minutes. As she read through the information displayed under his name, he firmly kept his poker face, quickly grinning at her every time she looked back up at him.

She appeared similar to what he'd imagined the average Russian lady to be; very light, blonde hair, and pale white skin. She was very young, young enough that Roger thought a little flirting may go a long way.

"What is the nature of your visit to Moscow, Mr. Hughes?" She asked in a thick Russian accent.

"Just sightseeing, darling," he told her. "I'm on holiday from University. Plus, I'd like to try some of that world-famous Solyanka I keep hearing about."

The lady gave Roger a flirtatious smile in return.

"Yes, it is delicious," she answered, nodding her head. "Where are you from, Mr. Hughes?"

Remembering what Richard Weber had told him a day earlier in the car, Roger answered back without delay.

"Vancouver, British Columbia," he replied.

"And where do you attend university?"

"The University of British Columbia," he said. "I'm two semesters away from my master's degree."

"Very good," the lady said, stamping his passport and delivering it back to him. "Welcome to Moscow, Mr. Hughes. You can go down that way to retrieve your checked baggage."

"Spasibo," he said in Russian, winking at her before spinning around to leave.

As Roger made his way down the passageway, his eyes scanned the horde of people walking back and forth. He was looking for a man whom he'd never met but knew all about. He couldn't really forget a face like that, one that certainly would stand out in a crowd of people.

Roger was almost to the baggage claim when a stranger quietly cornered him from behind, tapping him hard on his shoulder.

"Mr. Hughes?" he heard the stranger say in a thick and raspy voice. "Chris Hughes?"

Roger twirled his body around. There the man stood; awful scar stretched all the way across his face from his neck to his ear. He was a tall man, taller than Roger at six foot five, thin gray hair and much older than Roger had expected.

"Yes?" Roger blurted out. "That's me."

"Welcome to Russia, Mr. Hughes," he replied. "I am Demetri. Please, come. We have no time to waste."

"After you, then," said Roger.

Roger promptly snagged his duffel bag from the carousel, putting it onto his back and followed the man out through the masses to the parking lot where he had a car waiting for them. It was an old 80's Mercedes with tinted windows and faded black paint. They both entered the vehicle, and Demetri hit the gas, whirling tires out of the airport parking lot.

The entire car stank of stale cigarettes, cheap cologne, and gun oil. Roger glanced down toward the seats and noticed the multiple cigarette burns all over it's partly ripped and worn, faded leather seats.

"Mr. Hughes?" Demetri said as he lit up a cigarette.

"Yes?" Roger asked.

"See that lockbox lying between your feet on the floor?"

"What about it?"

"Open it," said Demetri.

Roger clutched the box from between his legs, placing it into his lap. As he raised the lid, he was pleasantly surprised at what was revealed inside; a black, stainless steel combat knife, some surveillance equipment, and an MP-443 Russian pistol, small in size and the ideal gun to conceal under his clothing.

"Excellent," he said. "So, what should I call you, Demetri?"

"Call me Raptor," Demetri answered with a smirk. "And yourself?"

"Charlie."

"Well, Charlie," added Demetri. "Dig in."

Roger removed the gun from its case, clearing it and checking the magazine before placing it into the back of his Khaki's, hidden under his white, button-up shirt.

"You made sure you weren't followed, correct?"

"Yes, of course, Mr. Hughes," replied Demetri. "I'm no rookie, I assure you."

The safe house was roughly a thirty-kilometer drive away, near the city center of Moscow. Roger wasn't very keen on the idea of being so close to the Russian government buildings that were located there. But, it was just a feeling. If he did the job right, they'd never know he was even there. After all, he was a Canadian graduate student in town to see old Soviet artwork and to awe over the infamous Russian architecture.

"Any word on the American?" Roger asked.

"Not in a few days, Mr. Hughes," Demetri answered as he sped down the highway, wind whipping his thin, gray hair. "But you'd better believe they are working him over good."

Roger knew that any attempt to rescue the American prematurely would more than likely result in blowing his cover. If that happened, the mission would be flushed down the toilet along with any chance that they may have had to stop Russia from launching a nuclear weapon against

America. Not to mention the possibility of landing him in a Russian prison and never again seeing the light of day.

So far, President Petrov was doing an excellent job of aiming his rhetoric at the president of the United States. It would be a tragedy not to take him seriously. Even many of Petrov's former colleagues were now saying he was mad.

While Roger sat silently in his seat, following the white lines passing by them in a blur, he'd noticed that Demetri had pulled off of the highway going in the opposite direction of where he knew the safe house to be located.

"Where in the hell are you going, Demetri?" Roger asked. "Isn't the safe house the other way?"

"Yes, Mr. Hughes," he replied. "I just need to handle a little business first."

Roger started to wonder what in the hell he was talking about. He hadn't even been in the country for an hour yet, and already they were veering off mission. But, it's not like he had a choice. Demetri was Russian. He knew the area; he knew the people. Roger only hoped that he knew what in the hell he was doing.

Demetri steered the black Mercedes off the road a bit, turning the lights off and edging slowly next to the tiny houses that ran along the two-lane, dead-end street. The car made a faint screeching sound as he pressed the brake as softly as he could.

Demetri glanced to his right, noticing one light shining out of a neighborhood that was as dark as night. Grabbing his pistol out of the center console, he opened the driver's side door, leaving the engine running, and stuffed the gun into the back of his pants.

"Where the fuck are you going, Demetri?" Asked Roger.

But Demetri didn't say a word, only grinning back at him before running up the sidewalk.

"What the fuck is going on here?" Roger thought to himself. "He'd better not do anything stupid, or I'll shoot him myself."

Roger watched as Demetri crept through the bushes toward the back of the house, stepping onto the wobbly back porch steps until he walked out of view. Roger sat calmly in his seat for a few, listening to the sounds of dogs barking and faint traffic noise in the background.

Suddenly, from out of nowhere, there was a thumping sound coming from the house, then the light went out.

"What the fuck?" he thought, just in time to see Demetri appear around the corner with his arm around the throat of some other stranger.

Demetri forcefully carried the unknown man toward the back of the car and signaled for Roger to join them.

"What the hell, Raptor?" Roger asked, dashing toward the back of the vehicle. "Who in the hell is this?"

"This would be the guy who handed the American to them," Demetri replied. "I've been tracking this piece of shit for weeks now."

"It would have been nice for you to fucking tell me beforehand," Roger said.

Roger thought about what to do for a moment. He was utterly taken by surprise and wasn't happy about his new

Russian friend's complete lack of discretion. Snatching people up in the middle of a neighborhood for all to see wasn't part of the plan, no matter what the guy had done.

"Fine," Roger added. "Put him in the fucking trunk, then. You'd just better hope nobody saw you!"

Demetri lifted his hand from the man's mouth for a moment to tie his arms behind his back with a piece of rope he had in the trunk.

"What are you doing?" the man blurted out in Russian. "I've done nothing!"

"Shut the fuck up!" Roger said to him, punching him right in the jaw.

Roger snatched a dirty rag he'd found in the trunk, and pulled it into his mouth, tying it tightly behind his head.

"Come on before somebody sees us!" Roger said, clutching the man by his arms.

Demetri lifted him by the legs, and they tossed the man into the trunk before slamming it shut and running back to the front of the car.

They jumped in quickly, and Demetri hit the gas, burning tires as he whipped the car around in the other direction.

"What the fuck was that, Demetri?" Roger asked as they hurried for the highway. "Don't ever do some shit like that again without telling me first!"

"Sorry, comrade," he replied. "He's a bad man. An evil man."

Demetri pointed the Mercedes in the direction of the safe house. The cars on the roadway went by with a flash of light as they hurried toward their destination roughly ten kilometers away. Roger wondered what they would do with their new friend once they arrived. Whatever it was, he had to remain quiet and out of sight.

Roger just hoped Demetri hadn't fucked the whole thing up. If it came down to it, he would gladly shoot him in the head if it meant protecting his own ass. Roger wasn't entirely sure yet if Demetri could be trusted and would remain on his guard until he knew without a doubt that he wouldn't give up Roger's true identity. He was going to make it back home, no matter what.

They pulled into the driveway of the tiny, two-bedroom house. It looked like what he'd imagined the typical Russian lower-class home to be. The place was drab and plain-looking with absolutely no color other than the faded, worn out gray paint peeling from the siding The torn screen porch, barely hanging from its hinges, seemed like it would break off at any moment. Crumbled front steps led up to the top of the small, square porch.

The long street ended where an old apartment block began. The apartment building was suggestive of the old Soviet-style structure, dark, bleak and cookie-cutter in appearance; a little run down and looked like nobody had lived there in years.

No other houses around and the apartments being a kilometer down the road meant no neighbors to worry about. That suited Roger just fine. He trusted nobody. Except, Roger had to trust Demetri. At least until he knew he couldn't. But he'd hoped it wouldn't come to that. The Russian's just seemed to have a different way of doing things than he was used to. But, from now on, it would be his way or no way. Roger was going to make that perfectly clear to his new associate.

"Grab his legs," Roger said as they popped the trunk open. "Hurry. We need to get him inside."

"I got 'em," Demetri said as they quickly marched up the drive to the concrete steps.

Demetri grabbed the keys from his pocket with his right hand, holding onto the stranger with his left.

"Hurry up!" Roger told him.

Demetri turned the doorknob, and the cracked, wooden door creaked open slowly. He put the keys back into his pocket, nudging it the rest of the way free with his foot.

"Come on, Chris," said Demetri. "Let's get this asshole tied up."

Demetri repositioned his hands to get a better grasp on his legs, and they brought the man down the hall to the other side of the old house, the old wooden floors creaking beneath their feet.

"Come," Demetri said, pointing to a room at the end of the hallway. "Let's put him in here."

They took the man into the bedroom, dropping him down onto an old, stained mattress, and tied his arms and legs to the wooden bedposts, leaving the rag stuffed in his mouth so he couldn't squeal.

The man muffled, hardly understandable under the cloth wrapped around his head.

"Shut the fuck up!" Roger shouted, booting him in his side.

As they got prepared to leave him in there, for the time being, Roger snatched Demetri by his shirt collar, shoving him up against the wall.

"No more surprises!" Roger yelled. "From now on, I am calling the shots! You are not going to get me killed! You get it?"

Demetri didn't immediately answer, so Roger pinned his arms tightly against his throat.

"Do you understand?"

"Y-E-S!" Demetri struggled to say under the weight of Roger's arm.

Roger loosened the grip on his neck a little.

"I'm in charge," he said. "Got it?"

"Yes, ok!" Demetri replied. "I understand. Will you let me go now, please, comrade?"

"Stop calling me comrade!"

"Yes, yes, ok," Demetri replied. "Just let me go, please."

Roger released him from the wall as Demetri struggled for air, his face flushed bright red from the blood rushing to his head.

"Now," Roger said. "He's your hostage. You fucking watch him! I'm going to catch up on some rest."

Roger was in no mood for playing games when he was suffering from jet lag. He went to the other bedroom and tossed his duffel bag to the floor. Snatching the gun from his waistband, Roger set it under one of the pillows, laying his head back onto the bed. Roger's eyes began to fog up as he slowly drifted off to sleep. Tomorrow, his mission begins.

CHAPTER 7

CIA HEADQUARTERS
LANGLEY, VIRGINIA

CIA ANALYST, JENNY Montgomery flashed her ID badge to the gate guard as she pulled into the checkpoint at the agency's Langley, Virginia Headquarters. With her strawberry blonde hair put up in a bun and her black glasses and matching pants suit, she had the look of a true professional woman.

Jenny had been working for the agency for just under two years. She'd already gained a reputation for being a no-nonsense woman. She'd been recruited into the agency straight out of Harvard, where she rose to be in the top ten percent of her class in International Relations. Before her college career, Jenny had graduated from her Pensacola, Florida High School, at the young age of seventeen.

Currently, she was a part of a group of analysts who were tracking every movement of the pro-communist segments of the Russian Government. Jenny had been working on it for almost the entirety of her short career. She knew that Petrov and his closest associates needed to be monitored closely if they were going to prevent the rebirth of the Soviet Union and an attack on American soil. So far, the Russian President had been talking a big game. But, many in the CIA considered him to be just the type of hardliner that would risk his country's fate.

The gate guard waved her through, and she drove her red, Jeep Wrangler, top-down, to the vast parking lot just outside of the entrance to the massive structure. Swinging the vehicle into the parking space, Jenny hurried out and made her way up the long cement walk to the glass double doors at the front of the building.

Central Intelligence Agency, United States of America displayed under her feet across the shiny white floor as she strolled through the lobby to the elevators on the other side.

"There you are!" Jenny heard her colleague, Antione, yell out to her from behind as she swiped her keycard at the elevator entry. "I've been looking all over for you!"

"What? I'm not late," she replied.

"Of course, you're not," he said. "I just couldn't wait to tell you!"

"Tell me what?" She asked as he followed her into the elevator. "What's going on? You seem flustered."

"I think I got something," he told her.

"You serious?"

"I'm dead serious."

Antione Gonzalez was one of the other analysts who worked in the same office as Jenny, keeping a close watch on President Petrov and every move he made with his military and known nuclear launch sites and (ICBM) Intercontinental Ballistic Missile capabilities. Antione was a second-generation Mexican American. His mother had immigrated to the United States decades earlier. It was always his dream to serve the nation as a thank you for giving him and his mother a new life.

Antione had been at the agency for almost a year. And, he was one of a handful of analysts who were trying their damnedest to find intelligence on the Russians. Long before Petrov began spouting his mouth to the West, the CIA had obtained a leak, a former Russian spy who'd defected to Europe, Codename: Hound.

They'd never met him. And, nobody knew what he looked like. But, every piece of intelligence they had received from him had proven to be accurate, so far. But this was the big one. Though Russia was the largest country in the world, they were far behind America in terms of military power, and most of their equipment was now outdated, except for one.

Russia's newest nuclear power capability, which begun development in the latter part of the Cold War, but was scrapped until President Petrov came to power, was thought to be around fifty times more potent than the bomb dropped on Hiroshima during World War Two. Coupled with mobile missile launchers, it was definitely a cause for the American Government's concern.

"So, what is it?" Jenny asked as the elevator dinged, and the doors sprung open.

"You won't believe this, but I think I've got a third launcher!"

"Really?" She asked.

"Yeah!" He said. "Out in the middle of nowhere in the Siberian forest. Come here, I'll show you."

Jenny followed Antione to his cubicle, and she sat beside him in a folding chair next to his. She watched impatiently as he pulled up and zoomed in on the satellite imagery.

"See, there it is!" He said, pointing to a spot on the image. "Looks like a mobile launcher to me."

"Yeah, it sure does," Jenny replied. "You can barely see it. But it looks like they're trying to hide it in the woods. How the hell did you find it?"

"I don't know," he answered. "I just had a hunch. My eyes are about to glaze over from staring at the freaking computer screen. But it is fairly close to where the Soviets tested ICBMs in the '80s."

"Ok, good job," she said. "We need to get this to Cooper, right away."

"Get what to me?" Sylvia Cooper asked as she approached them from behind.

Sylvia was their supervisor. She'd been working for the agency for going on twenty years and knew her stuff. Luckily for her, Sylvia also had a top-rated team of analysts in her department. She trusted them, And, why wouldn't she? They were an exceptional group of people, regularly early and always staying late. Sylvia, forty-five and unmarried with no children, was more or less married to the job. With a sparsely furnished Alexandria, Virginia apartment, she was rarely at home and didn't have much of a social life to speak of.

"Oh, hey, boss," said Jenny. "Didn't see you there. Antione has something he needs to show you."

Sylvia moved in near to his seat and squinted at the screen. Her vision was beginning to fade a little from years of staring at computers.

"Shit," she said, putting her glasses onto her face and glancing a little closer. "Is that what I think it is?"

"Hell, yeah it is, boss," said Antione.

"Ok, damn it," she replied. "Are we certain? We need to be sure."

"Yes, mam," Antione said. "About as positive as we're going to get."

"Ok," Sylvia continued. "Keep monitoring for activity. I'll send it up."

"Copy that, boss."

Sylvia snatched the secure telephone from the receiver on her desk, getting prepared to make a critical phone call. She'd been instructed to notify her higher-ups immediately, should they find anything more in the realm of high-value intelligence to alert those operating in the field. In this case, that meant Roger. The intel would need to be confirmed on the ground before it could be acted upon.

"Deputy Director?" Sylvia said into the phone. "Yes, sir, this is Cooper. I'm sorry to bother you, sir. But we have an update."

She'd paused for a brief moment, waiting for the deputy director to respond.

Deputy Director Anderson Riley had come up with Director Cabot, appointed at the same time by President Cash. However, he hadn't been a career politician or a military officer. Riley was a thirty-five-year veteran of the CIA, first as an agent, then rising up the ranks through various supervisory positions to become the CIA's representative to PACOM (Indo-Pacific Command).

Afterward, he rose to be the Vice Chairman of the National Security Council. Having seen action on three continents during his impeccable career, and knowing the job inside and out, Cabot had come to depend on him for professional advice and guidance.

"What is it?" the deputy director asked Sylvia.

"Yes, sir," she continued. "We believe we found another launcher."

"Ok, Coop," he replied. "I'll send someone over as soon as I am out of this meeting. In the meantime, keep your people digging. We need to find them all!"

"Yes, sir, will do," she answered just before hanging the phone up.

Miles away in Washington, Deputy Director Riley and Director John Cabot were on their way to the White House to meet with President Cash and his National Security Advisor. They'd been roaming through the halls of The White House, discussing the action President Cash should take in response to the public outcry that had been gaining momentum across the country. He was also receiving immense backlash from the people, as well as critics, to pressure the Russian President into giving up the American prisoner.

The media had done an excellent job up to that point of making Cash look like a pushover who feared Russian hostility. That was far from the truth. But it didn't seem to matter to them. Outside of the boundary of the White House grounds, protestors were going through, carrying signs and yelling obscenities at the uniformed Secret Service officers guarding the gate as they marched up and down Pennsylvania Avenue.

"What do these people have against me?" Cash asked his advisor, taking a deep sigh as he glimpsed through the window at the crowd in the distance. "All I ever wanted to do was to keep America safe."

"Sir," said Joe. "Don't worry about them. The people are just scared and looking for someone to blame. They don't want war any more than we do. The highest office in the nation is the easiest target. In the end, they'll see. Don't let it cloud your judgment."

"I know," the President said. "You're right, Joe. But I fear war is exactly where we're headed. I just don't know what to do anymore."

"Let our people do their jobs, sir. That's all you can do. We have the best and brightest this country has to offer. But, until Petrov makes good on his idle threats, there is no need to worry."

"Tell that to the American people," Cash replied.

Public distrust in the American President was getting worse by the day. Cash knew that he couldn't just bury his head in the sand. His words had seemed to have the habit of being widely misinterpreted, lately. It was a thin line he'd been walking. If he came across as aggressive, he risked provoking the unstable Russian President into a war. But, if he said nothing, the public made him out to be a coward.

"Sorry we're late, sir," John Cabot said as he and the deputy director came around the corner to greet the President and his advisor. "It seems there's a little debacle going on outside."

"That's an understatement if I've ever heard one, John," said Cash. "These people hate me, it seems. Being the highest office in the land, one expects criticism. But this has reached an entirely different level."

"They don't hate you, sir. They just don't understand what's happening."

"That's one way to look at it, I guess," the president replied. "So, what do you have for me? Please, tell me you have something."

"Not a hell of a lot, sir," the director replied. "We've found a few of their mobile launchers. But, there's not much activity, otherwise."

"What assets do we have on the ground?"

"We have people working on it as we speak, sir," said Cabot. "If there is anything to be found, they will find it."

President Cash wasn't entirely convinced. Despite the many threats that had come out of the Kremlin in recent weeks, the CIA had yet to find one single shred of concrete evidence to back up President Petrov's claims. All that had been found were some mobile missile launchers, which may or may not be used as tools in Petrov's intimidation game.

However, agency analysts knew that the Russian President wasn't a stable man. Nor was he known for being level-headed. Any warnings made by him had to be taken seriously. The last thing Cash wanted was to be put in a situation where the two nations had their thumbs rested firmly on a nuclear launch button.

"And the prisoner?" President Cash asked.

"They are working on that as well, sir," replied Cabot. "It's a sensitive situation. But we have our people on it."

"Well, tell them to work harder!" He shouted. "I don't need this poor guy turning into a pawn for the Russian's to use in a twisted game of nuclear chess!"

"Yes, sir," Cabot answered. "We are on it."

They all knew the President was right. The American people would all but crucify Cash if he didn't manage to get him out of there. They knew that the Russian president was using him as a pawn. It had been all over the news. It was a blight on his presidency, as well as America in general. But, politics aside, that man didn't deserve to be locked up. The President could only imagine what he must've been going through. However, dealing with the Russians was never going to be that simple. There were some very long days ahead, indeed.

CHAPTER 8

RED SQUARE
MOSCOW, RUSSIA

THE SERVER SET the hot, steaming cup of coffee onto the plain, white bistro table at the Bosco Cafe at the side of Moscow's Red Square. Pigeons littered the walkway, picking for any crumbs being dropped by patron's eating their lunch at each of the various cafes bordering the square opposite of the Lenin Mausoleum.

As the waitress, a beautiful, blonde thirty-something Russian woman placed a napkin under his cup, Roger smiled at her, adjusting his red and white Canada hat.

"Thank you," he said to her in her native tongue.

"You're most welcome, sir," she replied in Russian.

Roger was in awe, ogling at some of the most perfect architecture he'd ever seen in his life. Saint Basil's Cathedral, just at the end of the dark brick square, was a pretty bright red color, showcasing the Russian dome-like roofs that the country was well known for.

Nikolskaya Tower, with its bright red star fixed atop it, appeared to be watching over the central administrative building located near to Senate Square. Everything in sight was in immaculate condition, with not a piece of trash to be found anywhere around. The Russians seemed to be a proud people, at least, in the capital city. But, Roger wasn't there to sightsee; Not officially, anyhow.

He'd gotten a tip-off from he and Demetri's gracious captive, Igor, that a man named Andrei Smirnov was going to be there shortly. Smirnov had supposedly been the head of the nuclear weapons program with Russia's civilian nuclear agency, Rosatom. Apparently, he had a top-level government clearance. Andrei was a high-ranking official until he was fired for disobedience and expressing western views, ideas that went against the fabric of a pro-communist regime.

Roger sat in silence, momentarily glancing up and surveilling his surroundings.

"This man better be fucking right," he uttered to himself. "For his own sake."

Peeping below the table at the photo he removed from his pocket, Roger studied the face for a time. Andrei looked to be a middle-aged man, maybe forty-five, with a bald head and a big, pointed noise. He was bleach white and thin, with freckles down both sides of his face. If he were out there as suspected, Roger would have to assume that he was wearing some type of disguise.

Surveilling his surroundings, Roger watched as the

many locals and visitors alike, who dotted the middle of the large square, went about their daily lives, not recognizing that an operation was being carried out right under their unsuspecting noses. Roger blended in thoroughly, his red and white Canadian shirt, matching his cap screamed out tourist to all passers-by.

Swiftly, dark clouds began to form above the center of Moscow, and the wind blustered through the square, warning of an oncoming storm. Folks started taking cover beneath overhangs that rose above the shops filling the single stretch of walkway. As Roger turned his head toward the long wall that separated Senate Square from the public, he caught a glimpse of an isolated individual ambling along, headed past Nikolskaya Tower, directly toward Mokhovaya Street.

The man looked very conspicuous for the time of year, wearing a heavy, black coat with a hood that partially covered his head. Roger could barely make out his face. To the untrained eye, he was just another wanderer. But, to him, he stuck out like a sore thumb.

"Game on," Roger thought to himself, rising from his chair to follow the loner straight to wherever the hell he was going.

But, as soon as he'd stood up, he spotted another suspicious-looking individual trailing carefully behind him. There was no doubt in Roger's mind that because of the supposed knowledge that Andrei had of the inner workings of Russian's nuclear weapons program, and knowing that the Russian Government guarded it's secrets carefully, that there would be people after him. Roger fell behind them at a distance, tracking both men from the other side of the State Museum to keep from being spotted.

"Ok, asshole," Roger mumbled to himself. "Where the fuck are you going?"

As Roger peeked out from the sidewall of the museum, he noticed the fellow he believed to be Andrei picking up the pace and aiming for a white Land Cruiser parked on the edge of the busy street. Behind, the pursuer increased his movement to a brisk walk, almost a slow jog.

Andrei took a quick glance behind him, quickly darting for the Cruiser and taking off in haste, spinning tires, running the red light, and coming dangerously close to ramming into two vehicles in the intersection. Roger watched as the Land Cruiser disappeared around the corner and out of sight. Suddenly, the mystery man ran for a parked Kawasaki Ninja Motorbike, and Roger hurried in chase toward the road.

"Follow that motorcycle!" He said to the Taxi driver who witnessed the action, smoking a cigarette and resting against the door of his car.

"Right away, sir," the driver said in broken English, flicking his cigarette out into the street.

Roger jumped into the backseat, and the cabbie hit the gas, the motorcycle quickly gaining distance from them.

"Step on it!" Roger told him. "That guy owes me money!"

"Yes, sir," the driver replied. "YA nenavizhu dolzhnikov!"

Of course, Roger was lying. But, he had to tell the man

something. There was no way he was going to give away his true intentions. The Taxi sped across town, tracking the bike all the way out to the highway just outside of the city. Up ahead, the bike driver made an abrupt right turn toward the town of Korolyov, an industrial suburb of Moscow.

As the cab followed suit and edged up gently, Roger noticed the motorbike, kickstand down, sitting on the sidewalk next to a large, gray three-story apartment complex. The driver put the car into park and waited for Roger to exit.

"Thanks for the ride, mister," Roger said to the driver, tossing a wad of Russian Ruble bills onto the center console. "Keep the change."

"Good luck to you!" The cabbie replied in Russian as he counted out the money that Roger had overpaid.

Roger crouched, making his way between cars in the parking lot until he located the bike driver walking up the flight of stairs at the corner of the building. He snatched the pistol that was stuffed in the back of his pants, hidden under his shirt, and screwed the suppressor onto it tightly.

"Ok, whoever you are," he said to himself. "Let's see what you really want."

Hiding the gun under his arm, Roger ripped across the parking lot toward the staircase. Midway up the steps, he began to hear a struggle coming from the next floor up. As Roger hastened quietly around the corner and up the last bit of stairs, he saw Andrei's pursuer holding him by the neck in a headlock in an attempt to strangle him.

Roger slowly lurked up behind the man, his gun aimed directly for his head.

"Don't fucking move," he said, the tip of the suppressor pressed firmly against the man's brain stem.

The attacker suddenly relaxed his grip, and Andrei scuttled backward on the ground, holding his hands up and leaning back onto the front of his apartment door, trying to regain his composure.

"What the hell?" the man said in Russian. "Who the fuck are you?"

"I'm the man who is about to kill you," Roger told him. "But not before you tell me why you are after this, man."

"Who's asking?"

"I'm asking, asshole," Roger replied.

"Who the fuck are you?" the man continued. "I was hired for a job. You have no idea who you are messing with."

"Oh, I think I do," Roger added, taking the man by his shirt and forcing him into the apartment and onto the floor.

As Andrei followed behind them, he watched in horror as Roger began kicking the man in his ribs, not quite comprehending what was happening, or who either of them were.

"The fucking Russian government!" The man screeched in agony. "That's who you are fucking with! You kill me, and they will chase you to the ends of the earth!"

"Well, in that case," said Roger, closing the front door and locking it. "I'll send you some company in hell."

Roger held the barrel of his handgun against the man's forehead and squeezed the trigger, blood spurting from the quarter-sized hole all over Andrei's floor, the intensity of the blast blowing his head back against the sofa.

"What the hell?" Andrei said in fear as he wiped his head with his sleeve. "What is happening right now? I don't understand what is going on!"

Roger cleared the gun and put it on safe, sliding the weapon back into the small of his back.

"You are Andrei, correct?"

"Yes," he replied in his Russian accent. Why?

"Andrei Smirnov, scientist and former head of Russia's nuclear weapons program at Rosatom?"

"Yes, mister," he answered. "Why? What is going on? Will you answer me?"

"That man was sent to kill you, genius," Roger said. "You're lucky I got here when I did."

"Who in the hell are you?" the man asked. "What do you want from me?"

Roger didn't immediately answer him. Instead, just shrugging his shoulders.

"Who I am is not important to you," Roger said. "What I need? Well, that's a different matter."

"What are you talking about, mister?"

"I am talking about your previous occupation, Mister Smirnov. I need everything you know about President Petrov's plans against the West, including all of their launchers, as well the locations of the nuclear reactors where they make their plutonium."

"I can't tell you that," said Andrei. "They'll kill me for sure!"

"I'll kill you if you don't!" Roger said in a raised voice, holding him by the collar. "Now, speak!"

Andrei had a look of pure terror on his face. He knew what it meant to go against Petrov's regime. What Andrei just experienced would only be the beginning.

"Shit!" Andrei yelled. "They will kill me for sure now! You think this is the last man? They will just send someone else to finish the job!"

"That may be so," replied Roger. "But we can protect you, so long as you cooperate with us.."

"You can't protect me from this people!" He continued. "They will find me no matter where I go!"

"Just take a breath, would you?" Asked Roger. "It will be ok as long as you talk to me. Or we can just do this the hard way!"

Andrei's life had already been flushed down the toilet. He had never agreed with Petrov's plans or his hatred toward America. But he'd had a career. It was never his place to agree or disagree, only to do the job that he'd loved. But, all of that changed once he truly realized what a psychopath Petrov was. He cared nothing for his own people, only his twisted bitterness toward the United States, as well as the rest of the West. He'd gladly sacrifice his own over his bloodlust toward them.

Andrei quit and never looked back. Only, he had a reason to look over his shoulder. Deep down, he always knew they would retaliate. Now, it seemed, things were beginning to take a much darker turn for him.

"Fine!" Andrei said. "Fine, I'll talk. But you have to promise me protection. I won't last a day out here alone after this. I need protection!"

"You got it," Roger replied. "We'll protect you. But, if you lie to me, or cross me in any other way, I will kill you and dump you so far out in Siberia that nobody, but the wolves will ever find your body! You understand?"

"Yes, mister," Andrei answered. "Whatever your name is. I understand."

"The name is Chris Hughes."

"Well, Mister Hughes," continued Andrei. "Please sit and make yourself at home. This will take a while."

Roger flopped down on the sofa next to the dead man and took a drink from a bottle of Beluga Vodka sitting on the end table.

"My God, you Russians love your Vodka," he said. "You don't mind, do you? I did just save your pathetic life."

"No, of course not, sir," replied Andrei. "But what about the body? You can't just leave him here. He'll stink up the place."

"Don't worry about that," Roger told him. "I'll dispose of him far away from here. Nobody will ever find him. But you're cleaning up the mess."

They both settled in for a long discussion about Russia's nuclear plans. Andrei had much to say, and Roger, as well as the CIA and the American President's administration, had yet to understand the true scope and magnitude of President Petrov's hostility, or what lengths he would go to achieve them.

CHAPTER 9

MISSILE TESTING SITE
THE WHITE SEA

THE RUSSIAN PRESIDENT'S motorcade approached the Nyonoksa Missile Testing Site, thirty-one kilometers from the town of Severodvinsk in northwestern Russia. Established in 1954, the site had been the premiere missile testing facility for the Russian Navy since the height of the Soviet Union.

Knowing better than to disappoint President Petrov, they'd been preparing for days ahead of his arrival. The Presidential Seal fixed to the hood of the four-wheel-drive Range Rover glimmered in the sunlight as guards promptly raised the gate to enable them to pass through.

Russia had toyed around with nuclear weapons since before the Cold War. But, this was unlike anything the West had ever seen. For some time, and out of the watchful eye of America and the rest of the international community, they'd been working on a nuclear super weapon, a prototype that could avoid current American missile defense systems in Alaska and California.

President Petrov didn't care to cave to international pressure to dismantle his nuclear weapons, quite the opposite. He was looking forward to seeing their latest creation come to life right before his eyes.

The three-vehicle convoy came to a stop in a set of reserved parking spaces adjacent to the base headquarters building. The President's driver held the door open as Petrov exited the Rover, his security team from the other two vehicles lingering close behind him.

"Admiral!" Petrov shouted in Russian as they made their way toward the two-story office building at the center of the base.

"Yes, Mister President?" Admiral Lebedev answered, hustling across the parking lot.

"Give me a status update, Admiral. Is she ready?"

Admiral Maxim Lebedev was a career officer in the Russian Navy and the Admiral in charge of the Navy missile testing site. A forty-year military man and closing in on retirement after a very long and distinguished career, Lebedev had also served under communist rule. It wasn't his job to agree, only to obey orders. Anything otherwise was a dereliction of his duty. He knew better.

The Admiral had attended the Kuznetsov Naval Academy under the Soviet Union in the late seventies and had seen combat in Afghanistan, Chechnya, Georgia, and numerous other conflicts. He was, by all accounts, a professional Naval Officer of the Russian Federation. He would have rather died than to let his country down.

Lebedev had been running around, barking orders to his men and anxiously waiting for the Russian President to appear as scheduled.

"Yes, sir," Lebedev replied, snapping to attention and rendering a swift salute. "My men are just awaiting your orders, Mister President."

"Excellent, Maxim," Petrov said, returning the salute. "That's what I wanted to hear."

"If you would follow me, Mister President," Lebedev continued. "I'll have my driver take us out to the site."

The Admiral escorted the President, along with his security, across the lot to a parked, Soviet-era military jeep sitting at the end of the headquarters offices.

"Kozlov!" The Admiral called out loudly to his driver. "Get your ass over here!"

The young, Navy Seaman put his cigarette out, tossed it into the ashtray, and scrambled toward the vehicle.

"Sir?" he said, snapping to attention and giving them both a salute.

"Get in," Lebedev ordered him. "You are to drive the President and me out to the testing area. Hurry up. We have no time to waste!"

"Yes, sir," Kozlov replied. "Right away, sir."

Kozlov, fumbling through his motions and almost tripping over himself, opened the door for him and nimbly jumped into the jeep. His shaky hands switched the vehicle into gear as he hit the gas, speeding across the parking lot and onto a two-lane road that ran down the center of the base through a sparsely wooded area before reaching Dvina Bay on the other side.

As the jeep rolled up alongside the observation point overlooking the water, the waves from the White Sea pounded the shoreline as if they were angry at something. The Admiral stepped away from the jeep and led President Petrov and his entourage up the metal steps to the observation deck, where they would have the best view of their latest weapon. Smelling the aroma of sea water on the slight breeze, birds chirping overhead, it appeared as though a peace lingered in the air. But that image was a deceiving one.

The brand-new Russian Prince Vladimir nuclear-powered submarine lay ready in the water as if she was awaiting her sole purpose; to launch the latest Russian ICBM, the Buluva Missile, from anywhere on the planet. A scary proposition, surely. However, the weapon was still in the development stage and had yet to be tested.

"She's a beauty, isn't she, Admiral?" Petrov asked as he glanced through high powered binoculars toward the submarine dock five hundred meters to the front of them. "Nobody will be able to stop her."

"That's the idea, Mister President," Lebedev replied. "My men have been working long and hard to make this a reality. Now, we get to see the fruit of our labor."

"Then what are you waiting for, Admiral? Get on with it!"

President Petrov was more than a little hopeful, having

waited months for developments to be complete. He bounced his leg rapidly, waiting for the countdown to start. But he wasn't a patient man

"Fucking get on with it!" Petrov shouted. "You told me things were ready, Admiral. I don't have all day!"

"Yes, Mister President," the Admiral said, fumbling across the platform for the radio box.

Admiral Lebedev snatched the radio mounted to the side of the sitting area.

"Captain!" He said into the handset. "We're ready for the show. You and your crew better be ready! We cannot afford any mistakes!"

"Yes, sir!" The voice, on the other end, shouted. "Just waiting for orders, sir!"

"You have your orders, Captain! Now, get your asses in gear!"

"Yes, sir! Very well, sir!"

The Admiral hung the radio up just in time to see the submarine begin to take off toward open water. As the bright sunlight began to reflect off of the dark hull, President Petrov and the rest of the men anxiously waited for the launch to commence.

The sub reached the center of the large bay and started to dive. On the surface, it seemed as though everything was in order. Neither Petrov nor Admiral Lebedev anticipated there being any issues with the launch. The Admiral, as well as the scientists who'd developed the new technology, assured the President that everything would operate as expected. There was no way they'd wished to disappoint the Russian leader.

As the group sat, waiting, Headquarters Command had initiated the launch over the radio, broadcasting aloud throughout the base over the extensive PA system.

"Get ready to fire, men!" The submarine captain yelled out from the helm as two senior sergeants settled into their seats, fingers resting firmly next to two missile launch buttons.

"Countdown initiated," said the voice over the PA, the decreasing numbers displayed on a board next to the observation deck.

The President remained restlessly glued to his seat as he waited for the minute-long countdown to expire.

"Ten seconds," the voice continued, pausing for a brief time. "T-minus 5, 4, 3, 2, 1. Go time!"

Petrov and his group watched as water from the sea surface kicked up forcefully from the power of the missile thrust. Smoke began to bounce from the ocean surface as the ICBM was ejected from the submarine, spitting flames and rising faster and higher into Russian airspace, headed for Kura Missile Test Range in Russia's far east.

However, just as the missile was almost out of sight, a cumbersome explosion rocked the sky high above them. Admiral Lebedev could only watch in horror as it exploded in mid-air, sending fragments of what remained of it crashing back down to earth.

Suddenly, the Russian President saw red.

"What the fuck is this?" he asked. "You told me it was ready, Admiral! You fucking told me!"

"Mister President," the Admiral answered apprehensively. "I don't know what happened, sir. I don't know. We took all of the necessary precautions!"

"Really? You did, did you? Then, why is my missile nothing more than a huge piece of fucking scrap metal in the middle of the sea right now, Admiral?"

"I don't know, sir. I don't know!"

"Tell me what you do fucking know, then!"

The Admiral stopped for a moment, frozen in silence. And, certainly not wanting to irritate the President any further. But, to his dismay, it was a little too late for that. President Petrov raised his sidearm from its holster and pointed it directly at Lebedev's head.

"Now, what else do you have to say to me? You dishonorable piece of shit!"

The Admiral was utterly terrified, holding his hands high above his head. Not only was his Naval career now in jeopardy, but the volatile Russian President had a gun pointed directly at him. There was little doubt from anyone that he would actually use it. Without wavering, Petrov stared Lebedev right in the eyes, the barrel of his weapon aimed at the center of his forehead.

"I should just fucking kill you right here and now!" Petrov sounded.

Instead, the President removed the gun barrel from the Admiral's head and aimed for the driver. The young, navy enlistee began to tremble. He was scared out of his mind as he watched the uproar from the stairs.

Petrov moved in closer to the driver as his trigger finger began to squeeze. Seaman Kozlov closed his eyes, his body going numb from head to toe. President Petrov inched the gun down from his head toward his chest, not wanting to get any blood splatter on his expensive Armani suit.

Without further delay, Petrov pulled the trigger in anger. The Seaman's body fell limp on the hard deck floor while his head smashed into the side of the metal railing with a loud clink.

"Good fucking riddance," he said as he brought the pistol back down to his side.

The Russian President gave the weapon to one of his security personnel to wipe the blood off as he moved in closer to Lebedev.

"Now," Petrov said to him. "Let that be a warning to you, Admiral. If you ever fail me again, it'll be your body lying on the fucking ground. Your family will only have your grave to talk to for the rest of their lives. I will not tolerate incompetence in my ranks! Do we have an understanding?"

Admiral Lebedev stood silent for a moment, glancing down at the body of his driver and the mass amount of blood spilled onto the metal stairs, dripping onto the ground below. He was frightened of this man. And, for a good reason. Petrov was a man who'd come undone at the drop of a hat. Nobody, especially Lebedev, wanted to be on the business end of his gun.

"Admiral?" the President continued. "Do we understand each other now?"

"Yes, Mister President," Lebedev replied. "Understood, sir."

"Good," Petrov added. "Get your people together and fix this mess! The next time I come back here, I'd better be impressed, or I'll bring havoc down on all of you, I promise you that. Now, get the fuck out of my face!"

The Russian President and his security withdrew back to where the Presidential motorcade was parked. On the way back to the Presidential vehicle, as he rode in the back of the jeep, Petrov received an alarming call on his cell phone. The President reached into his coat pocket, brought the phone up to his ear, and pushed the button.

"Mister President," the caller said.

"What is it, Ivan?" he asked. "This better be important. I am a little busy right now."

"I apologize for disturbing you, sir. But we have a problem. We have a big problem."

"So, you waiting for an invite? Spit it out, Ivan!"

"The man we sent after the scientist?"

"Yes? What about him?"

"Well, sir. He's missing."

"What in the hell do you mean he's missing?" Petrov asked.

"I don't know, sir," replied Ivan. "He never reported back in. And, now, the scientist is also missing. I sent someone to his house. But he wasn't there. I don't know what happened. He could be anywhere by now!"

"Fuck!" The President shouted into the phone. "Don't do anything else until I get there, Ivan. I'll be back shortly, and we'll get to the bottom of this! Meet me in my office."

"Very well, Mister President. I'll be here."

Petrov furiously threw his phone down onto the seat beside him.

"Damn it!" He yelled.

The Russian leader was worried that Andrei would end up defecting, and possibly give away Russian nuclear secrets. Now, he had a reason to be troubled. The hit hadn't gone according to plan. They had no idea where he had gone, or even if he was still in Russia.

However, Petrov was determined to find out at any cost. He couldn't afford for the United States to figure out his plan before he could bring it to life. Andrei was the one man who knew all of their secrets and was a real danger to the homeland. President Petrov had no idea that his worst fear had already begun to take shape.

CHAPTER 10

THREE CIA PARAMILITARY officers dressed in civilian clothing escorted Andrei to a waiting Silver BMW with tinted windows parked at the end of the dark, quiet street. Roger stood at the end of the walkway, watching as they shoved the former Russian Nuclear Scientist, hood over his head, into the backseat of the inconspicuous vehicle.

They were headed to a remote location, a safe house located somewhere in a neighboring country. But, he wasn't being held captive. Andrei, whom the agency had given the Codename: Fox, had now become an intelligence asset, an ally that the CIA needed to protect, no matter the cost.

Knowing that they'd be after him, their orders were to extract the man, and get him out of the country before the Kremlin figured out why their assassination attempt had failed. They were to debrief Andrei and learn as much as possible about President Petrov's dirty little secrets regarding his revamped nuclear weapons program.

"Don't worry, Andrei," Roger said as he cracked the back door open. "These men will take care of you. Just do what they say, and you'll be fine."

Andrei remained speechless as Roger slammed the door shut. He was trembling, scared. Andrei had never been in that position before. He certainly never thought he would ever defect from his country or his job. But, there he was, headed into the unknown, hoping that, at the very least, his actions might prove to do some worldly good in the long run.

Roger watched as the vehicle sped away, quickly gaining distance into the foggy night before vanishing around the bend and out of his sight.

"God speed," he said to himself.

Earlier that night, Roger had gotten information from HQ about the missile explosion over the White Sea. He breathed a sigh of relief, knowing that the launch wasn't successful. But, he knew it would only be a matter of time before they got it right. There was no time to waste.

"The Fox is secure," Roger said into his small, pocket-sized radio. "I repeat, the Fox is secure."

"Roger that, Alpha-1," said the voice on the other side. "Operation Stingray is a go."

Roger ran back into the safe house to grab his gear and fill up on ammo. His next stop—somewhere out in the middle of nowhere.

✦

Later that night, screwing a suppressor to the tip of the long barrel, Roger positioned himself behind the scope of the high-powered .338 Lapua Remington 700 Sniper Rifle. Lying at the top of a Church bell tower overlooking the small town, he and Demetri had the best view of the warehouse six-hundred meters away from their position.

Roger had learned about the place from Andrei. He'd claimed that the Russian Military had occasionally used the warehouse to store nuclear materials and munitions away from prying eyes. The structure wasn't even labeled. For all anyone knew, it could've contained stored fruit. According to Andrei, the locals had no idea what was in there or the danger it posed to residents. Though, they'd seen soldiers at the site from time to time. But, fearing the Russian Military, they weren't going to ask any questions.

Roger glanced through the night vision scope, the perimeter around the warehouse illuminated in a light green tint. He began to scan the surrounding area. But the only thing in his view was a pack of barking, stray dogs crossing the deserted street.

"You see anything?" Demetri asked.

"Nope, all quiet so far," Roger replied. "Except for those damned dogs. I don't like it one bit."

"I agree," Demetri added. "I hope we aren't wasting our fucking time. Are you sure this information is accurate?"

"That's what he told us," Roger answered. "I guess we'll see, won't we?"

"I guess so."

Demetri took a glimpse through the spotting scope, noticing the bright glare of headlights moving in their direction from far off down the roadway.

"Wait, I got something," he told Roger. "Hold one."

Roger peered the glass left toward the approaching transport.

"I got 'em," he said. "Let's see where they go."

The vehicle, an old Soviet military-type cargo truck, pulled up to the front of the warehouse, coming to a rest just shy of the big, drive-thru bay door at the front of the building.

"Well, who do we have here?" Roger uttered as they viewed five men in Russian Army uniforms and boots hopping from the covered truck bed.

"Shit," said Demetri. "These are Spetsnaz soldiers."

"You sure?"

"I am positive," he continued. "I can tell by their uniforms. See the camouflage pattern?"

"Yeah," Roger replied.

"They aren't typical Army."

The pair kept a close eye on the men while one of them, who appeared to be their leader, began snapping orders at the other soldiers.

"What the fuck are Russian Special Forces doing here?" Roger asked.

"That's a good question."

Demetri couldn't help but stare at the man as he ordered the others to begin unloading the back of the truck.

"Fuck," he mumbled, hanging his head low.

"What?" Asked Roger. "What is it?"

"I know that, man," Demetri replied. "That is Colonel Orlov, Commander of the Spetsgruppa A, Or, Alpha Group in English. They are the counter-terrorism wing of the Spetsnaz, formed under the umbrella of the KGB."

"How do you know all of this?"

"Because," Demetri answered. "I used to be one of them. That is until I deserted. They're nothing but a bunch of untamed killers. I had a disagreement with my commander and punched him in his face. Now they want to kill me. I'm better off now. I no longer need to worry about following their stupid rules. I make my own."

"I see," said Roger.

He wasn't quite sure what Demetri meant. But it sounded to him as if he didn't like following orders. If that was the case, they could have trouble along the way. For now, Roger chose to put it out of his mind.

Roger and Demetri kept surveilling the group of men as they went back and forth, toting large metal barrels from the bed of the truck into the inside of the warehouse.

"What do you think is in the containers?" Asked Demetri.

I'm not sure," Roger replied, glancing back through his sniper scope, his left eye closed. "It can't be good, whatever it is. Here, in the middle of the night, this far from a military base. It has suspicious written all over it. They're trying to hide something.

"You can say that again, my friend."

Roger positioned his earpiece firmly around his ear lobe and pressed the button on the radio.

"On target," He whispered into the mic. "I've got eyes on five tangos, Spetsnaz soldiers unloading an unknown substance into the warehouse, out copy, over."

"That's a good copy, Charlie 1-3," the voice said into the radio. "Continue the op, but proceed with caution. You don't know what you're walking into, over."

"Roger that, Charlie 1. Charlie 1-3, out."

Roger peeked through his sniper scope once more.

"What's the plan, Chris?" Asked Demetri.

"Well," replied Roger. "We need to get over there and see what the hell we're dealing with. But, first, we need to wait these guys out. We can't get into a shootout in a residential area. The police would be all over it."

"So, what's your plan, then?"

"We wait." Roger replied.

"Yes, ok."

Demetri grabbed his binoculars and continued watching the group of men Roger moved his scope higher until he saw the group of soldiers roaming along the parking lot in front of the depot. Colonel Orlov began to wander around to the other side of the truck, out of sight of the other four men. Standing there, isolated, Roger noticed a tiny spark as the Colonel lit a cigar. He was obviously waiting for his men to finish unloading the cargo.

Suddenly, Demetri began running down the stairwell and across the grassy field toward the group of soldiers.

"Raptor, what the hell are you doing?" he asked into the radio. "I told you to stay put!"

At that moment Roger began to understand why Demetri had been kicked out of the military.

Roger peeped into his scope again, right in time to see the Spetsnaz Colonel catch a glimpse of Demetri.

"Fuck!" Roger yelled, training his scope onto the Colonel's forehead.

"Goodnight," Roger said to himself, before squeezing the trigger and watching the Colonels' uniform top dyed bright red, his body collapsing like a sack of concrete to the hard surface below.

Demetri moved in closer to the men, his suppressed handgun pointed at them as Roger viewed the group through his scope. One man overheard the Colonel's body hit the ground and began marching to the other side of the transport to investigate.

"Oh, no, you don't," Roger uttered, squeezing the trigger and dropping him right where he stood.

One of the men saw the body and alerted the others.

"We have intruders!" He shouted to the men as they snatched AK-47's from their backs.

Demetri began firing his handgun into the gaggle of soldiers and dropped two of them before they had a chance to fire. Roger had the third in his sights and sent a .338 caliber bullet flying into the man's head and splattering blood all over the side of the building.

"Tangos down," he said into the radio. "Regroup on location. We need to get those bodies hidden before anyone sees them."

Roger collapsed his tactical rifle and placed it inside his bag, strapping the pack onto his back.

"Tangos down," he said into the radio. "I repeat, tangos are down."

He quickly darted down the stairs and across the field to where Demetri was waiting. Roger grabbed him by his shirt and shoved him against the Russian cargo truck.

"What the fuck is your problem?" he asked. "You want me to shoot you myself? I told you to wait you fucking prick! You pull any shit like that again, I'll kill you! You get it? You will not jeopardize this mission or get me killed!"

Roger stared right through Demetri with his cold eyes. Squeezing him tighter, he rammed his fist into Demetri's neck.

"I said, do you get it? This is the last time, asshole. Do not test me again!"

"Yes, yes," Demetri said under the weight of Roger's arm. "I get it. I promise! The Colonel wasn't supposed to be here!"

"What the hell did you just say?" Roger asked.

Suddenly, it sounded as if Demetri knew more than he'd been leading on. Roger moved in closer to Demetri's face.

"What do you mean he wasn't supposed to be here?" he continued. "If you know something I don't, you better talk, or I will end you right here!"

"I meant I didn't think anyone was going to be here!" Demetri screamed.

"One more fuck up," continued Roger. "Or if you plan to double-cross me, you're a fucking corpse!"

"Ok, ok," Demetri replied. "Will you please let go of me now?"

Roger released Demetri's shirt and shoved him hard to the side. In his best judgement, he was going to keep a close eye on his Russian associate. Something about the man wasn't adding up.

"Now, come on," Roger said. "Give me a hand, damn it. We need to hurry!"

One by one, they grabbed the feet of every dead Spetsnaz soldier and dragged them inside the warehouse, laying their bodies in a pile hidden in a dark corner.

"On me," Roger added. "We need to get these barrels open!"

Roger glanced around for a second, spotting a pile of gas masks on a table on the other side of the room.

"Grab a couple of those," he said. "We have no idea what's in here. I don't want to take any chances."

The men each donned protective masks and stepped toward the large blue containers that were stacked up on pallets in the center of the room.

"Shit. The lids are sealed," Roger said, looking around for a tool they could use to open it. "Check that toolbox over there!"

Demetri searched inside the large box, pulling out a metal hammer and a pry bar.

"That should do it," said Roger.

Demetri handed the tools to Roger, and he inserted the metal bar under the barrel lid and began hammering it as hard as he could.

"Ahhh, come on," he said, bending the bar with all of his strength. "Come on, damn it!"

Demetri helped Roger push the bar downward, and slowly, the lid began to pop open.

"Got it!" Roger said as he flipped the cover over onto another barrel. "Now, let's see what we got here."

Hovering over the open container, he had a puzzled look on his face.

"Oh my God," he said to Demetri.

"What?"

"It's much worse than I thought," Roger added.

"What is it? Let me see."

"It's fucking yellow cake!"

"Yellowcake? The stuff they use to make nuclear weapons?"

"Well, it certainly isn't what your mom bakes for your birthday, jackass!" Roger said. "Shit! This isn't good."

Roger snagged the high-resolution camera from his pocket and started to snap photos of the substance, as well as the dead Spetsnaz soldiers, to send up to HQ.

"Come," Roger said. "We need to search this room. This stuff came from somewhere."

The pair began to look around the space for any clues they could find that pointed to the possible origin of the Yellowcake. However, Roger knew that finding something like that just lying around was highly unlikely. But then he got an idea.

"Check the Colonel!" He said to Demetri.

Demetri hurried over to the Colonel's body and pulled his uniform pockets inside out.

"Some loose change, a wallet," said Demetri. "let me see. Wait a second. I got a phone! Here, catch."

He tossed an old flip phone across the room to Roger, and he opened it, scouring through the Colonel's most recent text messages.

"I think I got something here!" He said. "It's in Russian. Here, translate this for me!"

Demetri began to translate the text into English.

Protect this shipment with your life, Colonel, the text read in Russian.

You can thank our friends in Niger. And they said there is more where that came from too! Too our success! Nikolai

"Holy shit!" Roger said. "It's from Niger? I can't believe it's right there in black and white. But, who the hell is Nikolai?"

"Nikolai?" Demetri asked. "Is there a last name?"

"Nope, It just says Nikolai."

"The only man I know by that name is former KGB, now an agent with the FSB. Not the kind of guy you want to mess with, either. He's one of Petrov's right-hand men. A guy he calls to handle his dirty work."

"Well," Roger answered coolly. "I'm sure he's going to be pretty pissed when they find the bodies."

"Oh, he will be," said Demetri. "There's no doubt about that. And, if he finds out who you are, he will come after you!"

Roger didn't breathe a word back. He just grinned and nodded his head.

"So, what do we do now, then?" Demetri asked.

"I send this info to my boss, and we get the fuck out of here. I don't want to be around this shit any longer than I have to be."

CHAPTER 11

TWIN GAZELLE AH1 Helicopters from the 658 Squadron of the British Army Air Corps were carrying a team of SAS (Special Air Service) soldiers just above the sand dunes of the vast desert landscape in northwest Africa.

MI6 had received some valuable intelligence, documents that were seized from a nighttime raid in the heart of London in which six Islamist terrorists from Niger and surrounding countries in Africa were killed. The intel suggested that to raise funds for their terrorist activities, the group, known as IMN (Islamic Movement of Nigeria), had set up shop in Niger and partnered with and were selling stolen nuclear materials to the Russians. The intel pointed straight to a compound in the remote desert of the small country.

They were looking for a man named Aqib Amir, the leader of the organization. Aqib, a Saudi born Muslim cleric, had moved to Africa in 2005. Shortly after that, he started the Islamic movement in Nigeria that would later be named IMN. Supposedly, IMN had recently established an alliance with the Russians and were planning attacks in various locales in the West, including the UK. An odd couple, for sure. But, IMN and Russia had two things in common: their hatred for the West and their willingness to go to great lengths to turn that hatred into violence. The SAS needed Aqib alive, as he might be a useful intelligence asset, after they broke him, that is.

Captain William Price, the SAS team leader, tapped the bottom of the magazine in his M6A2 assault rifle and swung the door of the helicopter open.

"Five minutes!" The pilot shouted over the radio.

"Five minutes!" Price resounded to his men in his strong British accent.

The Captain secured his rifle sling to the carabiner that was hanging from the front of his tactical vest. He positioned himself next to the open door, preparing to fast-rope from the chopper.

Price, decked out in his camouflage uniform, black helmet, and a goatee, was a fifteen-year veteran of the regiment. As a young bloke from Cambridge, England, all he ever wanted to do was serve in her majesties armed forces. During selection, he'd injured himself on many occasions but regularly refused to give up.

As an operator, he'd seen combat in Afghanistan, Iraq, Africa, as well as terrorist attacks across the United Kingdom. He was a seasoned soldier. Price's men would've followed him to hell and back, and they have. The Captain hadn't lost a single soldier in eight years. He wanted to keep it that way.

"Ok lads," Price said to his men, securing his NVG's (Night Vision Goggles) to his Kevlar Helmet. "Get ready. It's time to earn your paycheck."

The helicopters began hovering over a tiny, flattened area as Captain Price kicked the thick ropes down to the earth.

"Go, go, go!" He yelled over the sound of rotor blades whipping.

The Captain stood by as each of his men slid down the ropes to the ground below. Price followed quickly behind them as they knelt, holding rifles pointed forward outward. The helicopters regained altitude as they left the area.

"Good luck out there, 3-1," one of the pilots said over the radio. "See you on the other side."

"Roger that, Eagle-1." Price replied, flipping his NVG's (Night Vision Goggles) over his face. "Thanks for the lift, Major."

The men took up positions behind the Captain as they got ready to move.

"Ok, men," Price said. "Form up on me."

The team, rifles at the ready, began to quietly advance over the sands in front of them, disappearing one by one over the red hills. The desert was covered with sandy hills that made it virtually impossible to move in a direct line.

The men, assault packs on their backs, hiked over four kilometers in just under an hour before they noticed anything that resembled being man-made. Crossing over a large rock formation, Captain Price overheard voices up ahead of them. He held a fist up, halting the formation to get a better look at what they were dealing with.

The Captain dropped himself to the ground, holding a finger over his mouth. The team froze still. Price crawled his way forward, dragging his weapon along the ground underneath his chin. As Price made his way to the edge of the compound wall, he spotted two stragglers out in the open, chit-chatting and smoking cigarettes. The team leader caught a glimpse of weapons, AK-47's slung over the front of their bodies.

Captain Price motioned for Sergeant Maxwell to join him. Maxwell was a five-year member of the SAS team and had proven himself to his leader. Price trusted him. He knew that Maxwell would never let him down and always obeyed orders.

"What you got, Captain?" Maxwell whispered as he crept up next to his team leader.

"See those two men over there?"

"Roger, sir. I see 'em."

"I'll take the left one. You get right," Price told him.

Price and Maxwell both retrieved the suppressed Sig Sauer P229 handguns from their holsters and flicked the safeties off.

'On my mark," the Captain said in a hushed tone.

Captain Price pointed his weapon at the head of the insurgent closest to him. Both men squeezed the trigger in unison, blood spilling from the back of the head of each man as they fell to the ground.

"Good kill," said Price.

They each clutched an insurgent by the feet, dragging them back over the hill.

"Come on, men," Price continued. "Let's get this done, shall we?"

The team quietly made their way around to the front gate of the dark compound, the only noise coming from the blackened desert behind them.

"3-1 Actual, Alpha 3-1," the Captain said into his radio mic. "Preparing to breach."

"Roger that, Alpha 3-1. You are clear to engage hostiles."

"It's a little late for that, isn't it?" Price said, grinning back at his team.

Sergeant Kyle Hall, a three-year member of the team, stepped to the front of the file and began placing the breaching charges right over the gate lock.

"Good to go, Captain," he said, fixing the explosive device to the metal gate.

"Fire in the hole!" Captain Price said as they took cover behind the tall concrete wall.

The charges blew, and the small explosion tore a hole in the gate, causing it to fly back and allowing them to enter.

"Ok, listen up, chaps," Price said to his men. "Aqib is here, somewhere. We split into two teams. Bravo team, take the back entry and deal with any runners. Alpha team, you're with me. We need to clear this building. Check your shots. There may be civilians present."

The men split up, with Bravo making their way around to the rear of the structure. Advancing through the gate as a single unit, Price's team silently making their way forward through the dark, the only glow coming from the inside of the two-story house.

Captain Price halted the formation and brought his rifle up to his cheek. With a single shot from the suppressed weapon, he turned the porch light off, broken glass falling to the surface below. He motioned for the men to push forward, and they continued up the steps, stacking on the front door to the building. Price raised his NVG's above his head, and the rest of the team followed suit.

The Captain reached out and quietly turned the knob, nudging the door open little by little. Peeking his head around the corner, the team leader progressed slowly into the long hallway, coming to a stop beside a door that led to one of the bedrooms.

"I hear voices, Captain," Maxwell whispered.

"Yeah, I got 'em. Get ready."

Captain Price held his fingers up one at a time. 1...2...3, and kicked the door in as three tangos with submachine guns began rushing toward them from the other side of the room. All three hostiles dropped in a hail of bullets as the team opened up on them before they had the chance to shoot back.

"Clear," Captain Price said as he inspected the bloody bodies. "Let's keep moving, Aqib is not here."

Alpha team made their way further down the hall, creeping along a little at a time.

"Watch your corners," continued Price.

But, as they turned the corner that led to the living area, machine-gun fire erupted from a hole in the wall of the second bedroom.

"Take cover!" Price shouted as his men dove behind the wall.

"Shit, Captain!" Maxwell yelled out. "That was fucking close!"

"You're telling me!"

Captain Price removed a smoke grenade from his vest and prepared to throw it.

"Max, you're with me," he said. "Once I toss this, you know what to do."

"Roger that, Captain."

Price pulled the pin from the grenade, tossing it right in front of the machine gun position. Pausing for the smoke to build up, the Captain signaled for Sergeant Maxwell to follow as he dashed for the door to the room. Hugging the outside wall of the room, Maxwell snatched a frag grenade and tossed it into the hole and jumped out of the way. The explosion jolted the entire floor and threw the insurgent, flipping him over in mid-air.

"Machine gun down," Price said as the rest of the team joined them, moving through the dust toward the stairs that led to the top floor.

Before they could advance up the steps, however, a

hostile with an AK-47 begin firing at them through the stair railing.

"Man down!" Sergeant Kyle Warwick shouted as Captain Price continue firing into the top story, cutting down the insurgent in a burst of gunfire. "Jones is hit!"

"How bad is it?" Maxwell asked.

Price knelt down beside his injured team member and grabbed his gloved hand, assessing the damage while Sergeant Maxwell kept his weapon aimed at the upper floor. Jones had a gunshot wound to his lower stomach, but, would most likely be ok if they could evacuate him soon.

"Get him out of here now," Price told them. "Prepare him for evac! We'll clear the rest of this shit hole."

Warwick carried Jones through the building and back to the edge of the field just outside of the compound.

"Come on, Max," Price said. "Let's get this bloody bastard."

"Right behind you, sir."

Price and Maxwell began ascending the steps to the next floor, each man pointing his rifle in opposite directions and anticipating gunfire from anywhere.

"It's too quiet up here, Sergeant," said Price, his eyes focused on the doors to the front of them. "I don't like it one bit."

"Got that right, Captain."

The pair gradually moved ahead to the remaining rooms on the second floor.

"Hold up a second," Captain Price added. "Do you smell petrol, Sergeant?"

"Now that you mention it, yes. I do."

"Get back, Max," Price continued. "Something isn't right."

As Captain Price and Sergeant Maxwell backed up gently toward the top of the stairs, one of the bedroom doors cracked open. The unknown figure tossed a lit match into the middle of the floor, instantly igniting the petrol and sending flames expanding across the surface and onto the walls as Price and Maxwell darted for the bottom of the stairwell.

"Shit!" The Captain shouted. "This place is going to go up!"

The man ran through the upstairs hallway into the outdoor balcony, where he vaulted onto the ground fifteen feet below. As Price and Maxwell escaped through the front door to meet up with the rest of the team, they heard shots coming from the rear of the building.

The two hurried for the back of the property and saw him lying in the sand, a bullet wound to his thigh.

"Aqib Amir, I presume?" Captain Price asked, kicking the high-value target in his side. "Nice to meet you, Aqib. You're coming with us!"

"Fuck you, you British piece of trash!" Aqib screamed.

"Well, that's not very polite, is it?" Price added, pulling the man up from the dirt and placing cuffs tight around his wrists. "You like killing innocent people? Selling nuclear shit to the Russians? I'm going to ensure that you hate life from now on!"

"Alpha 3-1, in possession of high-value target, ready for evac, over," he said into the radio.

"Roger, Alpha 3-1," the pilot replied. "We'll be at your location in five mikes (minutes)."

Captain Price shoved Aqib forward as the team followed after them.

"You are going to die for this," Aqib said. "My people will not let you take me!"

"Shut your trap!" Price shouted, smacking Aqib in the side of his head. "I'm the reaper. And, if we don't get answers from you, you will surely die a slow death!"

"I welcome death!" Aqib answered. "Anything for the cause!"

"Well," the Captain returned, "Your seventy-two virgins might be just around the corner. Now, move!"

As the choppers began to land, Price pushed Aqib toward the helicopter door.

"Get him in there, and don't let him move!" Price told Maxwell. "How is Jones?"

"He's stable, sir. But we need to get him out of here."

"Wheels up in two mikes."

Supervisory Agent, Jennifer Holloway of MI6 hopped from the first chopper and addressed the Captain.

"Good catch, Will," she said in her Scottish accent. "My agents have been tracking this asshole for months. They'll interrogate him. I'm glad it was your team that finally caught up to this maniac."

Jennifer was a twenty-year agent with MI6 and had also spent ten years in the British Army doing military intelligence. She knew her job inside out. She'd served in multiple capacities across Europe and in conflict zones such as Iraq and Afghanistan. There was no better agent to be working with the SAS.

"Nice to see you too, Holloway." He replied. "Always a pleasure."

"Is it now?" She asked, leading him further from the helicopter noise. "Then you're going to like what I'm about to tell you."

"I'm listening."

"We have traced the destination of the stolen goods to a secluded area in central Russia. But there's no way you and your team can go in there tactically if you know what I mean."

"So it's an off the books operation?"

"Exactly," she replied. "We have been in contact with American intelligence. The CIA has been working on it, also. They have a non-official cover operative in-country posing as a Canadian tourist. You are to link up with him and provide support as needed."

"This a joint op, now?"

"Yes, it is, Captain. I'll be in your ear throughout the mission. But, bear in mind, if you are caught or killed, we will deny any knowledge of who you are. I know you understand."

"My kind of work," Price answered.

"Good," Holloway said. "Get your team together and get some rest, Captain. Move out tomorrow at 1700."

"Roger that," he continued, smiling back at her. "Let's get the hell out of here, shall we?"

Captain Price headed for the chopper, taking a seat beside Maxwell. The helicopters lifted high into the sky, the Captain watching as the flames down below engulfed the entire building. He wondered where this mission was going to lead them. If this was a one-way ticket, and he could help save lives in the process, he'd gladly do it. But, first, he wanted to make them feel pain.

CHAPTER 12

MI6 SECRET DETENTION FACILITY
SOMEWHERE IN ENGLAND

IT WAS A concrete, dome-like structure located in the middle of the woods, somewhere in Britain. The site housed the most hardened of terrorists, anyone who was considered a threat to national security and the Western way of life. Mainly, it was the UK's Guantanamo.

Those who ended up there rarely ever made their way back out, or even saw sunshine again. Working German Shepherds barking from their enclosures ensured detainees never got a good night's rest. Most of them, having come from the middle east and Africa, were frightened to death of dogs.

The helicopter arrived just off of the entry to the building. The latest arrival was ushered through the locked entrance and to the basement, down a long passage and past a giant metal door with biometric security.

"Get your ass in there!" Agent Bradford said in his

English accent as he pushed Aqib through the metal prison door, causing him to fall onto the cold, damp, concrete floor.

Mark Bradford was a junior agent with MI6, also known as the SIS (Secret Intelligence Service). However, he wasn't new to the intelligence field, having served as an intelligence officer in the British Army. He'd gathered top-secret human intel from Afghanistan to Iraq and across the globe.

After ten years in the military, Bradford wanted to continue service to her majesties forces and quickly garnered the attention of his superiors through his methods and dedication to defending the West from the evils of terrorism.

The sharp sound of detainees shouting repeated down the corridor as Bradford slammed the prison door shut with a deafening crash.

"You won't get away with this!" Aqib shouted to Bradford. "You all will die!"

"I believe we already have, Mister Amir," Bradford said as he retreated to the dimmed control room on the other side. "Now, shut your bloody mouth! You'll get your chance to speak, trust me!"

As Bradford secured the door behind him and glared at Aqib through the one-way bulletproof mirror, Holloway approached him from behind.

"So, what are you thinking, Bradford?" She asked. "You think he'll break?"

"Oh, he'll fucking break," he replied. "It's just a matter of time. They always break."

Their methods were simple, starve Aqib of food and sleep until he was too weak to resist.

"We'll see how he likes this," he continued, pushing the button on the PA system radio and listening as it echoed throughout the cell portion of the secret prison.

Bradford left the radio blasting into the cell all night long as he kicked his feet up on the cot in the back of the building, far from earshot of the piercing noise. The bright light above shined fiercely into the cell, not allowing the detainee even a moment's rest. But Bradford would surely sleep well that night.

The next morning, bright and early, the racket stopped. The team was preparing to question Aqib. This wasn't going to be a friendly interview. Aqib was to be treated for what he was, a terrorist who'd been selling nuclear materials to the Russians. The evidence was right there in black and white. The main question was, why?

As Agent Bradford got the interrogation room ready, another figure entered the building. Richard Law, a veteran of the SIS (MI6) and a proud Scot, was an experienced interrogator. He'd been in the same room as countless senior lieutenants of the Taliban, al-Qaeda, and several others. He knew how to obtain information from a person and wouldn't stop until he got what he needed.

"You ready, mate?" Law asked Bradford.

Bradford nodded his head.

"Get him in there, then."

Agent Bradford jerked Aqib from the floor of the cell, his hands cuffed behind his back, and placed shackles around his feet.

"Move, you bloody bastard!" He said, pushing the man forward as he stumbled toward the interrogation room door.

Law, entering the room behind them, grasped Aqib's shoulders and forcibly propelled him down, tying a rope around his waist and the wooden chair so he couldn't move.

"Hi Aqib," Law said, standing over him. "You comfortable?"

"Fuck you!" He shouted, spitting in Law's direction.

"Well, that's not very nice, Aqib," Law replied, wiping the spit from his chin. "From where I'm standing, you are in no position to annoy me. But, if that's the way you want it, mate, I guess that's how it's going to be."

Law held the back of the chair.

"Get his legs," he said to Bradford.

Both men tilted the chair over, and Law placed a dirty cloth over his mouth.

"What do you want to say now, Aqib?"

Bradford snagged the container of water that was sitting in the corner and stood over Aqib.

"Hit him!" said Law, as his fellow agent poured a mass amount of water over Aqib's face and watched him fidget.

Aqib tried to speak through the rag. He was struggling to breathe and couldn't manage to get the words out. He dipped his head left, then right, trying to inhale air into his lungs while the agent followed his movements with the pitcher.

"How about now, Aqib? We know you sold Yellowcake to the Russians, you piece of shit!"

"Hit him again!"

Aqib's face began to turn a dark blue as Bradford filled his throat with the rest of the ten-liter jug. Not able to inhale, he began to convulse violently, trying his hardest to break free from the chair.

Agent Law pulled the chair back upright and raised the cloth from Aqib's face as he took in a gasp of air.

"What we can't figure out is why. Why would you sell that shit to Russia?"

Aqib didn't breathe a word. He only stared back at the two agents with utter contempt.

"You don't want to answer?" Law asked, punching Aqib in his face with a gloved fist and causing his head to snap back. "What about now, huh?"

"Go to hell!" Aqib replied, blood oozing from his lip as he faced forward, spitting a mixture of blood and water from his mouth.

Agent law balled up a fist and struck Aqib on the other side of his face, watching him wince in pain.

"I can do this all day, Aqib.," said Law. "If you don't answer me, this is not going to end well for you! Again, why are you selling nuclear materials to the Russians?"

Aqib stared Agent Law directly in his eyes. His hatred for the West was written all over his bloody face.

"We will get answers from you, sooner or later, Aqib," Law added. "What we do next is up to you."

∽

Back at Langley, the CIA machine had been working on overdrive. American Intelligence officers had just received a top-secret cable notifying them of the SAS raid on the INM in Niger, as well as the capture of their leader, Aqib Amir. Amir hadn't even been on the agency list until now.

The American Vice President, in a move he'd never done before, was on a visit to gather information that he could take directly back to the White House. Cash's Administration was antsy. They had yet to discover just how deep Petrov's nuclear plans went. They welcomed any assistance they could get.

"Where we at?" Vice President Mark Harris asked Sylvia. "Give me some good news."

"Well, Mister Vice President," she said. "We've received news from London that the stuff is definitely from Africa. MI6 Agents are grilling the man as we speak."

"Good."

"But," she continued. "So far, Amir isn't talking."

"Oh, I am sure they can get him to talk," he added. "in the meantime, we'll send a hellfire missile and level that place."

"You think that's wise, sir?"

"I don't see why not," he asserted. "The compound is in the middle of nowhere. Nobody lives anywhere close by. Besides, we have full discretion. And, they're a threat, not only in Russia's game but the rest of Africa and the whole of the world as well."

"Yes, sir."

Across the room, CIA Analyst Jenny Montgomery was occupied at her cubicle, analyzing satellite imagery of the IMN compound in the vast Sahara Desert. They'd gotten detailed analysis, as well as high-resolution interior images of the complex from UK intelligence.

"Boss? "She called out to Sylvia.

Sylvia stepped toward the desk, gripping Montgomery's chair, the Vice President behind her.

"What you got?"

"This is where they found the yellowcake, boss," Jenny said, pointing to a detached square building off to the side of the compound. "All fifty barrels of it. But, there's no telling how much of it is already in Russian hands. Part of the building burned down in the raid."

"But not all of it?" Asked Harris.

"Just the main building, sir," she said. "The yellowcake is still intact."

"The stuff needs to be destroyed," the Vice President replied. "I have already spoken to the director. You have full approval."

The American President had recently given unprecedented authority to the CIA to expand its drone program, with the capacity to launch strikes from anywhere in the world, without public disclosure or permission from the Pentagon. This gave the agency full control over targets of opportunity. They no longer had to wait for final approval and risk targets getting away before they had the chance to launch.

"I'll contact our people in Africa, sir," Sylvia replied as she went back and seized the secure phone from her desk.

Sylvia was referring to a secret CIA drone base located in the middle of the Northern Sahara Desert, fifty kilometers from the Libyan border, that nobody outside of the agency knew existed. The station was used to strike targets in Africa, as well as the middle east; Most notably, Afghanistan and Syria.

"Angel-1-1?" She said into the phone.

"Go for Angel-1," the drone pilot responded after a brief pause.

"I have a target for you, Angel-1. Stand by for coordinates."

"Copy that," he replied.

"Roger, Angel-1. Coordinates are 15.777426, 11.091221. I repeat, 15.777426, 11.091221. Please confirm."

"Roger," the pilot said. "Coordinates confirmed, 15.777426, 11.091221."

"That's a good copy, Angel-1-1. You're cleared hot."

"Roger that," the pilot continued. "Stand by for launch."

The group stood fast in front of the large monitor positioned at the center of the office, where they could observe the action in real-time from the pilot's drone camera.

"Commencing launch," the pilot said, their eyes fixated to the screen.

The roar of the drone take-off could be heard through-out the office as it rose from the runway and quickly gained altitude.

"On target in ten mikes."

"Copy that, Angel 1-1."

Vice President Harris and the rest of the team watched as one of the agency's many drones soared through the sky at lightning speed. Ten uneasy minutes pass by as they wait for the target to come into view. Finally, the outline of a set of buildings down below as light in color as the desert sands.

"I've got the target in sight," the pilot stated into his mic. "One hellfire, coming up."

They observed as the hellfire sailed through the sky to the compound below. Like hell raining down on earth, the entire place went up in a gigantic ball of fire as the missile struck. There was absolutely nothing that could have survived such power and devastation.

"Target destroyed," he said.

"Confirmed, Angel-1-1," Sylvia replied. "Target destroyed."

The Vice President got up from his chair after view-ing the building on the monitor screen burn ferociously under a dense cloud of black smoke towering high into the desert sky.

"Well," he said. "At least now I have some real news to give to the President."

A little good news was better than none. But, the American Government had absolutely no idea how much of the Yellowcake had been produced. Nor had they yet to uncover how much of it was actually in President Petrov's possession. That little detail was one that had been keeping President Cash and the CIA Director up at night. Perhaps MI6 could procure more information from their IMN prisoner.

CHAPTER 13

THE KREMLIN
MOSCOW, RUSSIA

PRESIDENT PETROV SAT furiously in his office chair, puffing a cigar and cracking his knuckles against the hard surface of the wooden desk.

He was infuriated. The bodies of his deceased Spetsnaz soldiers had been found late the night before. Now, he understood he had an unwanted guest in his country. Petrov was determined to find out who the perpetrator was. He was confident it was an American due to his recent threats toward the American president But, he'd left zero evidence behind.

The President stared aimlessly at the ceiling, pondering what he was going to do next. Whoever was attempting to thwart his plans, they no doubt knew what was in those metal barrels. An intelligence nightmare had been set in motion in Russia.

Petrov picked up his office phone and began dialing, anxiously waiting for the man to pick up.

Ten rings later—

"Nikolai?" he answered in Russian. "How are you, Nikolai?"

"I'm a little busy right now, quite honestly," Nikolai replied in a deep voice. "What do you need?"

Nikolai sat in his meager one-bedroom flat, cleaning his rifle and dressed in a black jumpsuit and hood, perfect for blending into the night. An assassin by trade, Nikolai didn't need a fancy place or an expensive car. Though he could afford it. He lived by the gun. To him, that was the one and only true testament of a man's worth.

With the President on the line, Nikolai finished wiping down his Dragunov SVU Sniper Rifle and placed it into its carrier, Zipping up the bag securely.

"I need a hunter, Nikolai," the President replied. "Why else would I call you?"

Petrov hesitated for a brief moment, waiting for Nikolai to answer him.

"Who's the target?" Asked Nikolai.

"I don't know who he is, yet," the President said. "But, I have a feeling he's trying to fuck up our ambitions. Nikolai, I just need him dealt with!"

"I see," Nikolai returned.

"I am sure you can flush him out," added Petrov. "That's what we pay you for, isn't it?"

Nikolai, known affectionately as the wolf by those who

knew and feared him, wasn't big on formalities. He never
addressed Petrov as Mister President. But, Petrov put up
with it because he didn't know a better killer and tracker.
The Russian President needed Nikolai. And, Nikolai knew
it. The man operated, sanctioned by the Russian government, anywhere he needed to be. A master of deception,
he could fade into the dark, or blend in with the crowd.
Mother Russia was his home, killing his calling card. Like
a wild cat in the bush, he liked to play with his prey before
killing them.

With no family to speak of, Nikolai was a loner. He'd
lived by himself for many years. He preferred it that way.
Nikolai never had to explain his line of work to anyone.
He could return home and kick his feet up on the sofa as
if nothing happened.

"Yes," replied Nikolai. "I can take care of that for you.
Just let me finish this drink first. Today's my birthday, you
know? I'll find him. Just give me unrestricted access and
I'm on it."

"Wonderful," said Petrov. "You got it, Nikolai. You
deal with this piece of scum and keep me far away from it."

"Don't worry. It will be done."

Nikolai hung the phone up and drank the rest of his
bottle of Stolichnaya. Flinging the bottle onto the table, he
inserted the eighteen-round magazine in his SR-1 Vektor
pistol and jammed it into the black hip holster at his waist.

"I guess my birthday will be postponed this year," he
said to himself.

Nikolai snatched the rifle bag from the floor next to

the sofa and strapped it to his back, exited the door to his flat, and headed down the stairs toward a 90's model four-wheel-drive Lada SUV he had parked at the end of the long walk.

Nikolai set the rifle carry bag on the passenger side seat of the vehicle and sparked up a Prima cigarette. Exhaling a white ring of cigarette smoke, he gazed at himself in the rearview mirror, the deep knife scar showed on his face stretching from his right eyebrow down to the lower half of his cheek.

As his dark brown eyes stared fiercely back at him, Nikolai had but one thing on his mind; death and the suffrage of those who dared to cross his homeland. Nikolai snapped the vehicle into gear. He flew out of the parking lot and down the highway, on a mission for Russia.

Meanwhile, Roger sat on the bed of the nondescript first-floor hotel room, fifty kilometers outside of Moscow. He'd been bouncing his leg nonstop and continually eyeballing the clock on the wall as it ticked down, second by restless second.

It was the scheduled meeting place he was told. But, he had no idea when the SAS team would arrive. He'd heard from Weber that morning regarding new intel that the British had passed along to UK intelligence after the raid in Niger. They, in turn, shared that information with the agency. Apparently, the Russian security threat was more significant than anyone had imagined. Now they were in a partnership with a known extremist group with unlimited access to stolen nuclear materials This wasn't just a problem for the United States, any longer. It had become a substantial concern that either or both countries could be targeted.

Roger walked near the sink and splashed cold water on his face to wash the edge away. As he unfolded the towel to dry himself off, all of a sudden, he heard a sound coming from just outside of the small room. Roger walked to the window, cracking the blinds open somewhat.

Three figures in civilian clothing appeared out of a dark, plain-looking Nissan Maxima, headed straight for the front entrance to the hotel. One of them carried a large, black briefcase.

"Is this the contact?" Roger wondered.

Not a minute later, the sound of steps gradually got closer and closer to the hotel room entry from down the long hallway. Shadows were cast under the doorway from the hallway light. Swiftly, a loud knock. Roger cracked the door open and saw a fit-looking guy standing there, grinning from ear to ear, and the other two directly behind him.

"Chris Hughes, I assume?" he asked, stretching his hand out for Roger. "May we come in?"

"Sure," Roger said as he stepped out of the way and closed the door behind them.

"Nice to make your acquaintance, mate," he said, shutting the door behind them. "I'm Captain Price, SAS. These two bloody blokes over here are Sergeant Maxwell and Sergeant Hall."

"Nice to meet you guys," Roger responded. "You made sure you weren't followed, correct?"

"Of course, lad. We aren't amateurs."

'Good," answered Roger.

"The word on the street is you could use some help over here, mate," Price added, patting Roger on his shoulder. "So, you former Special Operations or what?"

"I was an Army Ranger," replied Roger.

"Great," Price added. "I'm sure you know what you're doing. But don't worry. You can still run the show. My team and I are just here to lend you a hand."

"Roger that, Captain," he remarked as Price put his briefcase across the bed and opened it, revealing a treasure trove of weapons and gear.

The Captain sat next to Roger on the bed, fumbling through his gear. He holstered his Sig-Sauer P229 pistol on the inside of his khaki trousers.

"We look like a bunch of bloody tourists, don't we?" Price said, snickering.

"You can say that again," replied Roger.

"That's the idea, isn't it?"

The Captain leaned on Roger's shoulder as he inserted his combat knife into the sheath under his black polo shirt.

"So, what you think, mate?" he asked. "Do a little reconnaissance?"

"I need to get this American out of prison before they kill him," Roger answered. "He's not a mission priority. But, I believe the Russian President is trying to use him as leverage—something of a pawn that Petrov could utilize to keep the American Government at bay I'm worried that if I don't spring him soon, Petrov will have him bloodied and battered on Russian television."

"So," Captain Price continued. "Let's go get him, then."

Roger, rubbing his hand against his chin, glanced up at the Captain with a sneer.

"You think we can manage it?" he asked.

"Like I said, mate," the Captain added. "You aren't dealing with amateurs, here. Besides, four is much better than one. Isn't that right, Sergeant Maxwell?"

"Bloody right, sir!"

"Well, in that case," Roger said, banging the magazine into his MP-443 pistol. "What the hell are we waiting for? I have intel on his location"

"Let's go then, lads."

Captain Price snatched up the rest of his gear, secured the briefcase, and proceeded to the hotel room door, swinging it open.

"After you, mate," he said to Roger. "Let's go get the poor bastard."

The four of them headed to the parked car as the sun was beginning to disappear below the clouds. The Captain hit the gas and aimed the vehicle straight for the two-lane road in front of the cheap hotel and veering out to the main highway.

Fifty-five minutes went by, and the prison came into view just up ahead in the thick evening fog.

Price swerved the compact car into an abandoned

building site that was overgrown with trees and grass and put it into park.

"This ought to do," he said, jumping out and promptly stepping to the rear of the vehicle.

The Captain popped the trunk as the other men stood around him. He seized four black balaclavas and tossed one to each of them.

"Thanks," Roger stated, pulling the mask over his face, only his eyes shown through.

As Price slammed the trunk closed, the group got down low just on the outskirts of the foliage. The Captain retrieved a pair of small, pocket-sized binoculars from his pants and put them to his face.

"What do you see?" Roger asked.

Price zoomed the binocular lens.

"I see two guards by the front gate. One in each of the four towers and two patrolling. There's no telling how many inside."

The Captain handed the binoculars over to Roger.

"Yeah," Roger said as he took a glimpse. "I see them."

"So, you have a plan?" Asked the Captain.

Roger folded the binoculars back up and returned them to Price.

"Well," he replied. "The way I see it. We snatch one of these guards up with a piece to his head and make them hand him over. Either that or, we bust in with rifles and shoot everyone."

"I prefer option A," Price said.

"I thought you would," Roger continued. "Here's my

plan. We'll sneak over there, and one of us will dispatch a single guard while the other grabs his friend. The rest keep an eye out for any prison guards who are feeling brave."

Captain Price nodded his head as he glanced back at his two men.

"What do you guys think?"

"I think we have an American to save, sir," Sergeant Hall replied.

"Right behind you, then," the Captain said to Roger. "Let's just hope his buddies actually give a fuck about the guy, or it'll be a bloody prison shoot out. But, hey, nothing we can't handle."

"In that case," Roger added. "Follow me."

The men moved across a square patch of grass beside the prison, in a single file low to the ground to avoid being detected. The sun was barely peeking over the horizon as the light began to fade away, hiding their silhouettes in the shadow.

His suppressed gun aimed forward; Roger dropped one of the guards with a single gunshot to his head. Watching him hit the concrete hard, his friend glanced over and jumped backward, startled.

"What the fuck?" he said in Russian, kneeling down beside the other guard and noticing blood spilling from the hole just above his ear.

Before the guard could pick up his radio to notify his friends, Captain Price dashed toward him, tackling the man to the ground and getting a hold of his arm.

"Oh, no, you don't!" Price shouted to him.

He picked the guard up forcibly from the ground, pistol pressed tightly against his temple. Sergeant Hall, grasping the dead guard's shirt, pulled him back into the brush.

"Now," the Captain continued. "You'll do exactly as we say. Get it?"

Roger gave Price an unusual look, not knowing he was fluent in Russian. The guard didn't utter a word, so the Captain pistol-whipped him hard against the side of his head.

"Who in the hell are you?" the guard returned in Russian.

"Who we are isn't important for you to know.," Price said as he glanced at his name tag. "But, Yahontov, you will do as we say. If not, I'll shoot you right here. You understand?"

"Yeah!" The guard yelled back. "Just don't kill me, please. I have a family!"

Captain Price held one arm around the guard's throat, and the other gripped the pistol against his face. He moved in closer to the man's ear.

"Then, if you want to see them again," he said, jostling the man forward. "Move!"

Roger led the way while Captain Price followed by his side, the rest of the team close behind and watching the rear. As they made their way closer to the prison door, another guard spotted them through the window, running out, pointing his AK-47 at the team.

"Don't shoot!" Yahontov screamed. "Get back. They'll kill me!"

The men halted in front of the door, and Roger pointed his handgun at the armed guard.

"What's the code?" Price asked in Russian.

The guard remained silent. Roger snatched the rifle from his trembling hands and put it on his back.

"Give us the code!" The Captain continued as Roger held the barrel of his weapon against his temple.

He held his hands high in the air.

"1, 5, 8, 0, 2, 1, 4," He replied in Russian.

Captain Price and his men moved in closer to the door.

"You get all that, mate?" Asked Price.

"I think so," Roger answered. "My Russian is a little rusty."

"Let's make this fellow enter the code," the Captain added. "I am sure he'd oblige, seeing how my weapon is ready to splatter his head all over this dirty wall."

Roger removed the AK from his back and struck the guard with the rifle butt, causing him to fall hard against the prison wall, knocking him out.

"I got it," continued Roger. "Let's move."

The men marched rapidly across the prison room toward the secured door that led to the cells on the other side. As Roger entered the code with his non-firing hand, Captain Price had a steady hold on the captive guard.

"Don't you even think about trying to run, mister," he said. "You won't make it three steps."

Roger opened the door, and they advanced through to the prison block.

"Don't shoot!" The guard yelled, his voice repeating against the concrete floor.

The guards wandering past the cells hurried to see what was going on, their rifles aimed at the men.

"Don't even think about firing!" Price shouted in Russian. "Or, your man here is dead!"

The prison filled with noise as the inmates began to howl and cheer. Roger, moving his weapon around tentatively toward each guard, prepared to fire on a moment's notice as Maxwell and Hall followed suit.

"Drop your weapons!" Price ordered them as prison inmates started to howl and cheer from their cells. "We will kill him if you don't!"

Roger, Maxwell, and Hall, each aiming for a different guard, glared at the men.

"Drop them now, or we will start shooting! The choice is yours."

One by one, each Russian guard began to drop their AK's to the hard, floor, hearing the metal and wood clank as they fell.

"Sergeant Hall," Price called out. "Kindly remove their weapons."

"Roger that, Captain."

Hall sprang up the metal stairs and began recovering the rifles from the ground while the rest of the men progressed forward. But one of them refused to comply.

"Fuck you!" The guard shouted, holding his rifle at his hip. "You are in our country! We don't have to listen to you!

The guard brought his index finger over the trigger just in time for Roger to send a round flying toward him, penetrating his neck, his bloody body dangling over the metal railing above them and dropping his AK47 to the concrete floor with a loud crash. Sergeant Hall dashed down the steps to retrieve it. One of the guards cautiously backed toward the wall and pushed the bright red panic button, causing a loud alarm to ring out through the halls of the prison and deafening their ears.. Roger rushed toward the man and struck him in the head with the butt if his rifle.

"Asshole!" He yelled out as the guard hit the floor. "We need to hurry! I don't think we have much time!"

"Ok, Mister Yahontov!" Price shouted. "Now that that's over, where's the American prisoner?"

"They will have my ass if I tell you that!"

Captain Price hit the guard on the side of his face.

"You have bigger problems right now, mate," Price continued. "This is the last time I'm going to ask. Where is the American?"

Roger took the gun in his right hand and struck Yahontov across the face with it, leaving a bright red mark on his cheek.

"Answer him, or I will kill you right now, you son of a bitch!" Said Roger.

Not wanting to waste time, Roger was beginning to lose his patience. He aimed his rifle at the guard.

"Now!" Roger said. "This is your last chance!"

"Ok," the guard said to Price. "Ok! He's down in the basement!"

The Captain glanced back at his other two men.

"You lads stay here and guard these men. Don't let them fucking move! We'll be back in a minute."

"Got it, sir," replied Maxwell.

Captain Price released Yahontov, and he and Roger went for the basement door.

"Don't you fucking move!" Maxwell said as he got a grip on the guard.

Roger and Price continued down the steps that led to the bottom. The pungent odor of blood, sweat, and urine filled the air in the large, dusty room.

"Ugh, smells bloody rotten in here," said the Captain.

As the pair turned the corner, there he was, the American. The unlucky fellow was sagging from that chain. Still, his feet hardly touched the ground. He had urine stains on his filthy pants and caked blood all over the front of his body. They had no idea how long he'd been hanging there. But the man was too weak to talk, only spouting the occasional gibberish.

"Come on," Roger said. "We need to hurry and get him the hell out of here."

Roger directed the business end of his pistol and shot the chain in half, causing the prisoner to fall feet first to the ground.

Roger hoisted the man's skinny body over his shoulder, and they rushed through the basement door toward the front of the prison. There was no time to lose. The Russian guards would certainly notify their superiors as soon as the men left their sight.

Hall and Maxwell, the guards AK's over their shoulders, followed Roger and Captain Price to the waiting car as snipers from the towers began to fire at them. One by one, bullets ricocheted off the ground beside their feet as they dashed for the vehicle.

"Come on!" Roger shouted over the sound of bolt-action rifles cracking as he tossed the man into the back of the vehicle.

Before he could position the young guy all the way in, a round struck him in the lower leg, leaving a walnut-sized hole in his calf. Everyone else ducked low into the car seats.

"The package is secure!" Roger said into his radio. "I repeat, package secure!"

Captain Price hustled into the driver's seat as a high-powered sniper bullet pierced and shattered the rear glass of the small car, barely missing Maxwell's head and ripping a hole in the seat cushion in front of him.

"Go, go, go!" Roger continued.

The Captain hit the accelerator hard, spinning out and kicking up dirt as they bounced off the curb and into the road. They needed to get to a safe place, fast.

"How bad is it?" Price asked Roger.

"It's pretty bad!" He yelled back as he tore a shred of cloth from his shirt to use as a tourniquet, wrapping it tightly around the wound. "But no major arteries hit, as far as I can tell. I think I can stop the bleeding!"

"Good!" Price yelled. "Make sure nobody's following us!"

"Hall!" Roger said. "Hold this over the wound!"

"Got it!" Hall replied, pressing the cloth tightly over the man's injured leg.

Roger grabbed a rifle from the floor of the vehicle and pointed it through the broken rear windshield.

"I don't see anybody back there," he said, pulling his balaclava low around his neck. "I think we're clear!"

The American was in awful condition, barely able to talk. The guards had obviously roughed him up really bad. They would find out what happened to him soon. But, first, he needed to recover enough to be intelligible. There was absolutely no question that, if the poor guy had been held much longer, he would have most definitely been near to his death. Roger and the SAS team got there just in the nick of time.

CHAPTER 14

RAINFALL BEGAN TO blow through quickly as the Nissan Maxima came to a rolling stop on the dark, deserted street alongside the CIA safe house just on the outskirts of town.

Roger and the SAS team had driven all day and night to finally arrive in the former Soviet Republic of Belarus. They were exhausted. They hadn't heard a peep from the former prisoner in almost a day. The man was weak and couldn't talk. But, at least he was breathing.

Roger and the Captain prepared to take the American inside and get him ready to be transported.

"The package has arrived," Roger said into his radio as he exited the vehicle. "I repeat, the package has arrived."

Roger and Price each took opposite ends of the rescued American and carried him up the walkway to the entrance to the tiny flat. One arm nestled around the guy's leg;

Roger put his fist against the door. But, before he could knock, it suddenly cracked open.

"Been expecting you," said the man on the other side. "Hurry, come in."

As he closed the door and secured it behind them, Roger and Captain Price lugged their human cargo to the living area and sprawled him out face up on one of the sofas, putting a pillow under his head and elevating his injured leg.

"How is he?" the man asked.

"He'll live," Roger answered. "He took a sniper round to the leg. We got the bleeding under control, so he should be ok. The poor guy has been through hell. We need to get him out of here ASAP."

Roger removed the blood-soaked bandage that was wrapped around the wounded leg and replaced it with a clean one.

"I'm Agent Cameron, by the way," the stranger said. "Agent John Cameron."

"Chris Hughes," Roger answered. "This is Captain Price, Sergeant Maxwell, and Sergeant Hall of the SAS."

"Nice to meet you, mate," said Price.

"Don't worry, they have clearance to be here," Roger told him.

"Not worried in the least," replied Cameron. "HQ contacted me before you guys arrived."

Roger walked over to the coffee pot in the kitchen, snatching a few cups from the cabinet.

"Man, I need a boost," he stated. "You guys want some?"

"Sure, I'll take a double espresso with whipped cream," Price joked.

"How about black?"

"That's what I really wanted," he answered.

Roger poured four cups of black coffee, no sugar or cream, and gave the team three of them.

"Thanks, mate," said Price. "So, Mister Hughes, what's next, then?"

"What's next is," he said. "I am going to sit here and rest a while. It's been a long couple of days."

"Bloody right, mate," Price replied, barely able to keep his eyes open.

It was the middle of the night. The four of them sat still in total quietness for a few minutes, taking periodic sips from their coffee mugs. The lack of rest was starting to get the better of them. One by one, each man drifted off in a haze.

For the next three hours, Roger slept upright in the chair, dreaming of his family back home. The image of his son riding his horse in circles was flashing through Roger's mind as if he was still there. But, he wasn't, not yet, anyway. This was his reality. Roger was doing it for his country, the country that he and his family loved. In time, they'd understand his reasoning.

It was the first time Roger had the chance to relax in a while. But it wouldn't last very long. Suddenly, as the dream began to dissolve into the background, Roger was awakened to a faint mumbling sound. His head popped up, not sure of where the noise was coming from, or if he was dreaming it.

He titled his head to the side, and Roger saw the man on the couch, one eye partly opened and uttering something that he couldn't readily comprehend.

"What was that?" Roger asked as he sprang from the chair and stooped beside the man. "What did you say, partner?"

"He-is-after-you," the man murmured into Roger's ear.

"Who?" Asked Roger. "Who is after me?"

But, before he could answer, the man passed out again.

Roger glanced behind, noticing Captain Price staring at him. He'd clearly guessed from the look on Roger's face that something was amiss.

At the same time, Agent Cameron had opened the door to check on a sound he'd heard coming from the front of the building. He peeked around the corner of the doorway. As if it occurred in slow motion, Roger gazed up just in time to witness a stream of blood pour from Cameron's neck as he fell back against the open door and plunged to the ground.

"Sniper!" Roger yelled out.

He bolted toward the front of the flat to pull Cameron's body away from the entrance and slammed the door shut, bolting it.

"What the bloody hell?" Sergeant Hall asked as he woke and rolled out of his seat. "What's going on?"

"Get your ass down!" Price said as Hall and Maxwell hit the deck. "There's a sniper out there."

"How did they fucking know where we were?" Asked Roger.

"Don't know, mate," Price replied. "But, they're here now, aren't they?"

Roger crept his way forward in a low stance toward the window, cracking the bottom of the blinds somewhat so he could get a look.

"That's definitely where I'd be," he said, moving back into cover behind the wall. "Top of that building way down there. Must be seven-hundred meters away."

"We have to deal with him fast."

"Damn right, we do," said Roger. "He'll have us pinned in here if we don't."

Roger and the Captain each put on a Kevlar vest and snatched Kalashnikov's from the metal gun cabinet in the corner and proceeded straight for the back door.

"Hall, Maxwell, you two stay here and guard him," Price said. "And, for God's sake, stay down. We'll handle this. No need to give 'em more targets than we have to."

"Roger that, Captain."

Locking the door behind them, they advanced down the long, dark alleyway to the corner of the building, touching the apartment wall.

"Ok," Roger said. "Head for those cars over there. I'll be right behind you."

One at a time, they raced for cover in the parking lot, not wanting to give the shooter an easy target. As Roger dove behind a yellow Volkswagen, another shot rang out and cracked as it bounced off the side of the vehicle, barely missing his head.

"Damn it!" He shouted. "This guy is pissing me off!"

Roger gave Captain Price a hand signal, and the Captain did a five-second rush for the next pair of vehicles. Now, It was Roger's turn. He got down as low as he could, rifle in hand, and sprang toward a station wagon parked on the opposite end from the Captain.

As Roger prepared to move, another bullet hit two inches from his hand, causing him to jump back as the crack from the enemy rifle echoed against the surrounding buildings.

"He's fucking playing games!" Roger shouted to Price.

Roger glared up in Price's direction, getting ready to spring into action again. Preparing to move, Roger spotted the Captain as he went around the corner of the vehicle, falling backward onto the wet ground.

"Bloody hell!" He sounded.

Roger sprinted in the Captain's direction, aware that at any moment, it could be lights out from a single shot. Reaching Price's position, he slid along the ground on his knees.

"Where are you hit, Captain?" he asked loudly as he examined around the front of his body for an entry wound. "I don't see any blood!"

Captain Price rolled his hand along the front of his tactical vest, feeling a large, bullet-sized hole directly above his chest. Roger pressed his finger into the gap, feeling a fragment of metal stuck inside.

He started removing the Captain's vest and noticed the tip of the bullet distending from inside his front plate.

"Oh, you lucky bastard," he said to Price. "A little higher, and it would've hit you right in the neck."

Roger removed the mangled 7.62 round from the hole, fastening Captain Price's vest back together and helping him up into a sitting position.

"How do you feel?" he asked.

"I'm ok, mate," he said. "It just stings like hell."

I bet it does," Roger replied as they both pressed themselves against the vehicle beside them.

"Come on," added Roger. "We need to move now. Are you sure you are good?"

"Yeah, mate," Price said. "I'm good. I'll be right behind you."

Roger lifted his rifle and began firing from his position into the structure. However, he couldn't see him and had nothing to really aim at.

"Ok," Roger continued, tapping the bottom of his weapon magazine to make sure it was secure. "Follow me. We're going to sprint as fast as we fucking can to that wall over there."

Price patted the back of Roger's vest, letting him know he was ready.

"Ok, I'm making a run for it!"

Roger held his AK-47 tight to the front of his body as he ran as fast as his legs would take him to cover behind the long, rock wall, Captain Price trailing a couple of meters behind him while one bullet after the other pinged from the solid ground next to them.

"Shit!" Roger yelled. "That was close!"

"You're telling me, mate."

As they hugged the side of the wall, Roger glanced slightly over the top to get a look at the building a couple of hundred meters ahead.

"Ok, listen," Roger stated. "We're almost there. One more dash, and we take this bastard out."

"Roger that," the Captain said. "You're on point."

Roger and Price continued low to the ground, shuffling along and made it to the end of the wall. He turned to glance at Price and nodded his head. Roger took off running toward the side of the building, his weapon bouncing up and down as they rushed for the door.

He stacked the entry, Captain Price, directly behind him. Roger reached for the doorknob and turned it with a slow, fluid motion. As it opened just wide enough for them to enter, they started moving silently down the hall and to the stairs at the very end. Roger stopped, pointing upward into the stairwell.

They quickly climbed the steps, approaching the third and final floor of the abandoned building and turned the corner, rifles at the ready. Roger and Price began searching every room that faced the safe house. But, as Roger made it to the fourth flat and opened the unlocked door, the only thing he saw was an open window, and a table shoved up against it.

"Captain!" Roger called out.

"What you got?" Price asked as he entered the room.

Roger pointed to the window.

"Look," Roger said. "This is obviously where he shot from."

"Obviously."

Price moved to the table, noticing the total lack of evidence left behind.

"Well, Chris," he said. "Whoever the hell he is, he's gone now."

The sniper faded into the night as fast as he'd appeared. Roger and the Captain had a feeling that the shooter was just having fun with them. But, they had no idea how right they actually were. Ending them was his mission. Though, he'd enjoyed the hunt even more than the killing. A killer like him was a pain in the ass to deal with. It's what he lived for. Both men figured that it wouldn't be the last time he'd cross their paths.

Still, for now, their mission was to get the American student the hell out of the area. And, that was exactly what they were going to do.

CHAPTER 15

BELARUS FOREST
SAME DAY

THE HELICOPTER HOVERED over the forest clearing as Roger and Captain Price brought the weak body of the American student to the edge of the tree line. The surge from the spinning rotor blades caused the surrounding trees to wave rapidly in the wind as the chopper started to touch down in the tall, wavy grass.

"What?" he said as he awoke from the deafening racket and gazed up at them. "What… what's going on? Who are you guys?"

The man clearly couldn't recollect a thing, most likely due to repeated strikes to his head by the Russian prison guards.

"You're going home, mate," answered Price.

"Yeah, buddy," Roger said. "I'm sorry we never got your name."

"Michael," he replied, groaning in agony. "Michael Preston."

"Well, Michael Preston. You get to see your family again. Just hang in there. You're almost home."

An innocent man, the poor guy, didn't ask for any of that. He'd only been in Russia to see the sights. He had no awareness of the government conspiracy that had been taking shape in Moscow. He, like many others, only wanted to live his life. And, like many other people, he was oblivious to the real danger that it possessed. It had assuredly been a rude awakening for him. But, he was finally headed homeward.

The men carried Michael toward the helicopter as the crew stood by, waiting to get him loaded. They placed the young man's body onto the gurney as two men prepared to hoist him up.

"Good to go!" The crew chief yelled over the rumbling sound as they raised the gurney and settled it into the helicopter. "We'll take it from here! This man is fortunate. You guys are heroes!"

"How can we be?" Roger responded emphatically. "We were never here!"

"Roger that!" He replied, settling into the chopper to prepare for take-off.

The student's family would never be made aware of who rescued him. All they knew was their son had been unjustly confined in a Russian prison. That's all they needed to know. America and the UK were not officially operating in Russia.

"The package is en route, Charlie 1. Out, copy, over!" Roger shouted into his radio.

"That's a good copy, Charlie 1-3."

Roger and the SAS team departed away from the bird as it rose high into the dense, morning fog. They'd succeeded in rescuing the American student. His family could rest easy now, knowing he was finally safe. Roger had received news that they were to meet him in London, then head back to the United States.

They knew the American press would have a field day with him when he got home. But, at least he could no longer be used as a puppet in Petrov's crooked game. Now, Roger and the team could concentrate on the mission at hand. There was little uncertainty that the Russians would be gunning for them after this; No doubt whatsoever. But, they'd been careful to assure that nobody had seen their faces.

"So, Mister Hughes," Captain Price said as he bent against the vehicle and took a long drag from his cigar. "What's next on the agenda?"

"Destruction," Roger answered boldly. "Fucking destruction. We're going to bring President Petrov's little house of cards crashing to the ground. Then, we're going to burn it to ashes."

"That's what I'm talking about," Maxwell said. "Best part of this job!"

"Well," the Captain continued, smirking at Roger. "What are we wasting time for, then?"

"Exactly," Roger added as all four men hopped into the car.

They'd switched vehicles a little while ago, before leaving to drop off Mister Preston. Roger opted for something a little more off-road, knowing that a Nissan Maxima just couldn't handle some of the terrains they would, without doubt, be traversing through.

Roger steered the hard-topped jeep back in the direction of Moscow. As the vehicle bounced over the large rocks in their path and out into the roadway, Roger had their recent attacker in mind. How did he find them? Who did the shooter work for? And, most importantly, who in the hell was he?

What Roger didn't realize—a killer like that only misses on purpose.

He had begun his game of cat and mouse. A game that Roger and company were about to witness firsthand. They were embroiled in something that wasn't fully understood yet. However, they would realize that soon enough.

Cruising down the highway at eighty kilometers per hour, they approached the border with Russia just in time to see the thick haze evaporate into thin air.

As they gradually rolled up on the porous border, Roger swung the vehicle onto a dirt road that led through a wooded grove to the other side of the invisible boundary line. Belarus had been chosen for a reason. It was the perfect strategic location for agency involvement in Moscow. There was virtually no border control where the Belarusian border met Russia, allowing them to cross between the two with relative ease.

As they made their way farther into the country and back onto the main road, Roger received an encrypted message on his cell phone.

This is an agency priority target, the text read.

We've just received intel that there is a large shipment of plutonium headed to an unknown location, traveling to the north of you along the same route. A convoy of five vehicles. Two gun trucks, a couple of personnel vehicles, and the target truck. You are to follow that convoy to wherever it is going and carry out surveillance. We do not want you to get in a gunfight out there. We're sending you the coordinates now. They are currently only ten kilometers from your location.

Roger slid his hands over his eyes.

We've been in contact with Stirling Lines, the message continued.

You and the SAS team are now part of Task Force X-RAY. They will be with you for the duration of this operation. Report back once it is complete.

Roger paused for a brief time. He put the radio away and continued pushing on as Captain Price glimpsed over at him.

"What is it?" Price asked.

"We have a target to find," he answered as he veered the jeep to the left.

They continued, driving for the next few kilometers and made a right turn onto an isolated road out in the middle of nowhere. Ahead, Captain Price spotted taillights in the faraway distance, pulling out onto the roadway in front of them.

"That must be the target convoy ahead," he said as he covered his face and raised his binoculars. "Yep, that has to be them. I spot two armored vehicles with heavy machine guns."

"Roger that," answered Roger.

The rest of the team slid their balaclavas up as Roger pursued the convoy from what he believed was a safe distance. They resumed following the group of vehicles up and down hills, around curves, and over a two-lane bridge.

Then, without warning, the convoy came to an abrupt stop in the middle of the road. The turret mounted to the top of the rear gun truck began rotating toward the jeep as its bulky rear hatch opened up, revealing a group of Spetsnaz soldiers inside as Roger hit the brakes and drove off the edge of the roadway.

"Holy hell!" He shouted. "Dismount!"

Roger and the team abruptly sprang from the vehicle, taking cover behind the trees of the forest that lined the side of the road.

"There's been a slight change of plans, Charlie 1!" Roger said into his radio.

"What do you mean, Charlie 1-3? Is everything ok?"

But Roger was a little busy for pointless chatter.

"Charlie 1-3, what's going on, over?"

He'd made that radio call just in time to hear the fixed machine gun on top of one of the Russian gun trucks open up and begin to rip into that jeep with devastating firepower.

The tremendous force from the .50 caliber gun tore through that vehicle with immense power as it sent glass and metal fragments flying all over the place. Suddenly, a massive explosion shook the trees around them. The four-wheel-drive they'd just been driving had blown to bits in the middle of the road.

"Damn, that was close!" Roger yelled. "Why the hell did they fire at us? We were at least three-hundred meters away!"

"Someone must've tipped them off, mate," Price replied. "They wouldn't have shot at us unless they knew who we were. The real question is, who?"

"We'd better find out," Roger said. "And soon!"

"Roger that."

Roger and the men continued further into the woods to get ready for a fight. It was no use trying to use that vehicle as cover. It was nothing more than a piece of scrap metal scattered all over.

Roger and the other's got down low as they heard men surrounding the area they'd just left. A group of Russian soldiers in camouflage uniforms began to slip into the woods between the shrubs, shining flashlights as they infiltrated into the shade.

"Find the bastards!" Their commander shouted in Russian. "I want to know who they are before we kill them!"

Roger and the men hid in the shadows, waiting for the Russians to pass them by. Hugging a rotten tree log spread across the ground, Roger began to hear footsteps crackling over forest debris. Glancing upward, he spotted the silhouette of a soldier standing above him.

He gripped the long knife that was rested against his waist and gently began removing it. As the soldier stepped over the log, Roger reached up with one hand and yanked the man down by his shirt, using the other to insert the knife into his neck and watching blood spurt out from the gaping wound. His lifeless body went limp as Roger removed the blade and wiped the blood on the fallen man's pants and rolled back over.

The team could hear the Russians vague chatter getting closer as they held their positions behind the forest cover. Roger bounced upward against the tree in front of him, taking a quick glance and spotted the outline of an unknown number of soldiers headed their way through the gloom.

Roger tapped on Captain Price's shoulder and pointed forward.

"Spread out," Price whispered to his men as they each crept their way to different locations behind the dense brush.

The soldiers kept a constant momentum, getting closer to the team while Roger held his suppressed weapon at the ready.

"Come out, you assholes!" The Russian commander yelled. "Come out and face us!"

Captain Price gazed over at Roger; his finger held firmly on his pistol trigger.

"That's bloody close enough," he said, raising the iron sight to his face and aiming at the one closest to him.

Roger bowed his head back at Price, and they simultaneously began to fire on the approaching Russian soldiers. Sergeant Hall and Sergeant Maxwell, each on opposites ends of the formation, followed their Captain's lead and began firing into the gaggle of Russians, dropping two of them face down on the forest floor.

"Light them up, comrades!" the Russian commander screamed.

The soldiers countered quickly and began sending 7.62 rounds from their AK-47's flying into the team's location. They could hear loud recoil from their rifles and the sound of bullets as they whizzed by and lodged into and fragmented the hardwoods surrounding them. The light started to give way to the darkness from above, and only the bright flash from rifle muzzles gave away the Russian's positions.

As the team continued firing from behind cover, they knew they were in for a long fight.

"Come on, you assholes!" Roger yelled.

There was no use in remaining silent, anymore. The Spetsnaz were already aware of the team's position. The only thing left to do was to exterminate them.

Across the world in Langley, they'd been monitoring the operation from above through a satellite link. After the radio communication they had received from Roger, they were concerned the mission had been shot. Getting into a firefight with the Russian military was never part of the program. Now they were worried.

"We have a problem," Weber's assistant, Gloria said as she charged into his Langley office. "We have a big freaking problem."

"What is it, Gloria?" he asked. "What's the problem? You seem flustered."

Gloria placed a secure laptop on the desk in front of him.

"I am. The team just received fire, here," she said, pointing to a section on the satellite map.

"What?"

"Yeah," she continued. "The convoy fired on them from a good distance away. And, now they're in a firefight in the middle of the woods."

"Any friendly casualties?"

"Not yet, sir," she replied. "But, why would they initiate fire unless they knew they were being followed?"

"That's a damn good question," he said. "Damn, good question."

Before Weber could say anything else, his office phone began to ring.

"Weber," he said as he picked it up and placed it to his ear.

"Is what I have heard true?" Cabot asked into the phone. "Are my analysts correct?"

"That depends on what you have heard, Mister director."

"Come on, Richard," the director answered. "Don't bullshit me. You know damn well what I am talking about. Answer me. I have no patience for games!! Did they, or did they not take contact?"

"Yes, sir," said Weber. "It is true."

"So, they got into a gunfight on the edge of a Russian village?" Cabot asked. "We are trying to prevent war, Richard! I can't go to the President of the United States and tell him to prepare for World War Three because our people have itchy trigger fingers! This is a complete debacle! "

The CIA Director was furious. It appeared to him that their guy in Russia was acting without authorization.

"You all recruited him," he continued. "And, now we have an asset out there doing whatever the hell he wants! This is on you. If you don't fix it, you'll be working security at the mall!"

Weber attempted to swallow the lump in his throat as it went dry. It was the first time the director had ever shouted him down the telephone or in-person for that matter. And it made him a little nervous.

"But, sir," Weber added. "He didn't fire on them first."

"Wait. What did you just say?"

"I said the team didn't initiate contact with the Russians!"

"That means… "

"Exactly, sir," Weber added, already convinced of what the director was thinking.

There was a minute of silence on the phone as Weber waited for the director to proceed. Both he and Cabot realized one main thing. Somebody had compromised the team.

"That changes the whole game now, doesn't it?" the director added.

"I would think so, sir," Weber answered. "But, after the incident at the warehouse, any American is liable to be a target."

Cabot didn't want to go to the President with that information prematurely. President Cash was known to be an unpredictable guy when he was nervous. He had a lot on his plate as it stood.

"I'll contact Stirling Heights and inform them of the situation," Cabot said. "What about the cargo?"

"I am not sure of where it's going, sir."

"Well, we need to find out," Cabot replied. "Get on it!"

Weber and the CIA Director just hoped that the Russians didn't know the team's real identities. That would make moving around the country freely extremely problematic for them, as well as ruin the operation before it really got off the ground.

The CIA was reasonably sure they knew what the plutonium was being used for. However, they needed eyes on to confirm. They counted on Roger and the team making it out of there in one piece. The swift reaction of Russian forces only serves to prove how volatile the Russian President had become. He knew that his nuclear ambitions were causing severe unrest in the United States, as well as the rest of the West.

"Keep me updated, Richard," the director added. "Notify me of any changes, however small."

"I'll do that, sir."

As Richard slammed the phone onto the receiver, he had a sick feeling in his gut. He could imagine the outing of their assets in Russia displayed all over the International media. It would make for good television. But it would be a complete nightmare for them.

Weber just hoped that he had made the right call and that Roger was as talented as they deemed him to be. They couldn't afford any mistakes. Errors in that line of work could turn deadly quickly. And, for an entire nation, it would be a high price to pay.

CHAPTER 16

DOBRIN, RUSSIA
TWO HOURS LATER

ROGER HUNCHED DOWN under the towering forest canopy in the dirt next to Sergeant Hall, raising his shirt to get a good look at the gunshot wound he'd sustained to his right leg. Now he was lying face up, gaping at the stars between the branches as he groaned in pain. With a small pair of tweezers, Roger removed what was left of the bullet fragment from just inside the hole.

"How is it?" Sergeant Hall asked.

"Well," Roger said. "I think you'll live."

"You sure know… how to make a guy… feel better," Hall stammered.

He'd been hit with AK fire toward the end of the two-hour-long clash against the attacking Spetsnaz soldiers. They'd been outgunned and definitely outnumbered. Pure grit saw them through to the end of the bloody ordeal.

"Ugh, Jesus!" Hall cried out as the adrenaline in his

body started to wear off, exposing his real pain. "Bloody hell, that fucking hurts!"

"I know, buddy," replied Roger. "No bones or major arteries hit. All things considered; it could have gone a lot worse."

Bodies scattered the dirt around them as Roger reached into his MOLLE and snagged a large dressing from his pouch. With an alcohol wipe, Roger wiped the dirt and grime from the bleeding wound and began wrapping a bandage around it, applying pressure to the top with both hands.

He held his palms flat on Sergeant Hall's leg for a couple of minutes.

"There," he said. "The bleeding has stopped."

"Yeah, lad," Captain Price added as he held Sergeant Hall's gloved hand. "You'll be as good as new in no time! Just thank your lucky stars you weren't shot in the head."

"Yeah, yeah," he said.

Sergeant Hall winced as he sat up in the dirt.

"What I really need is a bottle of Laphroaig whiskey," he said as Roger helped pull his pants back up and over the wound. "That's better than any damn painkiller."

"Right you are, lad," Price said.

In a moment of amusement amid a nasty situation, they all laughed at him.

"Well, for the time being," Roger said. "We need to find a way out of here before someone sees our blown-up vehicle and calls the police. I don't feel like dealing with Russian cops right now."

Roger seized the radio from inside his tactical pants as he sagged against the tree beside him.

"Charlie 1, this is Charlie 1-3, over," he said into the mic.

For a time, all they could hear was static on the line.

"Charlie 1, Charlie 1-3, do you read me, Over?"

"Roger, Charlie 1-3," Weber answered. "Where the hell have you been? We lost contact, and our satellite feed went down. What the hell happened out there?"

"Been a little busy, Charlie 1. You know, getting shot at and stuff?"

"What's your status, over?"

"Ten Russian Special Forces KIA and one friendly wounded. He's shot, but stable."

"Roger that, Charlie 1-3. Stand by. I'll get you an evac!"

"Negative, Charlie 1," Roger answered. "We've got it covered."

"You sure, Charlie 1-3?"

"That's affirmative," Roger added. "Charlie 1-3, out."

Roger clipped the radio to the inside of his pants pocket. He rose to his feet to search the corpses of the dead Spetsnaz soldiers. Continuing forward with his bright mag light shining, he discovered one of the downed men twitching as he reached for an object beneath his uniform top. Roger retrieved the suppressed weapon from his holster. As the gravely wounded Russian glared up at him, Roger looked him right in the eyes, pointing the gun at him. With a single movement of his finger, Roger squeezed the trigger, and the soldier's head fell back onto the ground.

"That's for shooting my friend, asshole."

He bent over to look inside the pockets of the dead Russian commander lying next to him. Reaching into his blouse, Roger's hand grazed a folded-up piece of paper and recovered it.

Roger, nor any of the other men understood much Russian.

"What you got there?" Price asked, seeing the mystified look on Roger's face as he wandered near him. "What is it?"

"I'm not sure," Roger remarked as he unfolded the note. "But it looks important. We need to find someone who can translate this."

"Good idea," Price said. "I think I know of just the guy we can call on, too."

Captain Price began helping Roger search the remainder of the dead, not finding anything more of significant value.

"Come on, mate," Price continued. "We need to get some new wheels."

Captain Price began backtracking to the roadway where their destroyed vehicle sat.

"You good to walk?" Roger asked Sergeant Hall.

"Yeah, I'm good, mate," Hall answered.

"Good," Roger said, clutching his hand and pulling him to his feet as they followed behind the Captain.

The men waited at the edge of the woods, faces covered, while Captain Price lifted the weapon from his pants and marched to the middle of the street.

"What are you doing?" Roger asked.

"Trust me, mate," Price replied.

A couple of minutes pass by, and the Captain spotted headlights coming over the hill three-hundred meters away. As the black Audi approached, Price stepped forward, pointing his handgun at the windshield. Frightened, the smell of burned rubber filled the air as the lady skid in the middle of the road holding her hands high.

Captain Price neared the driver's side door and opened it.

"Sorry, miss," he said. "I need your vehicle."

The woman shouted something in Russian that they didn't understand. Frantic, she got out of the vehicle screaming at Captain Price.

"Yeah, yeah. Lady. I'm really sorry."

Price hopped into the driver's seat as the rest of the team followed. The Captain put the gear into drive, and the car squealed away, leaving the poor Russian lady standing confused in the dark, alone by the side of the road.

"That woman has no clue what just happened," Roger said.

"We needed a ride," Price replied as he snatched the black balaclava down over his neck. "We do what we must, mate."

They drove into the night, the moonlight being the only thing, aside from headlights, that lit the Russian countryside.

"Where we headed?" Roger asked.

"We're going to see an old mate of mine," the Captain

answered. "A man who knows a great deal about the Russian government, probably more than he should. Let's just say that he used to work for them."

For the next hour, there was unbroken quiet in the car until the Captain turned left onto a long dirt driveway that led to an old log home situated on a plot of land that was cut out of the vast Russian forest, secluded from the highway.

"Who the hell lives here?" Roger asked as he took a look around.

"Don't worry," Price said. "You're about to meet him."

The team exited the Audi as the yellow porch light suddenly came on. The front door was opened, and there stood a shadow of a figure, clad in flannel clothing, boots, and using a walking stick. He was an old man, with a gray crew cut, wrinkly skin, and tattoos up and down both arms.

"Are my eyes deceiving me?" the Russian man asked in well-spoken English as he walked halfway down the steps. "William? Is that really you?"

"It sure is," Price replied, shaking the man's hand with a firm grip. "How are you, Maxim? It's been a long time, mate."

"I'm still getting around," he answered. "A lot of work to be done around here."

"I can imagine," Price said.

Maxim took a quick glance at Roger and the other two.

"So, who are your friends, William? I am assuming this isn't a social visit."

Maxim knew all about the Russian nuclear business. He understood what had been happening to the country he'd called home his entire life. He didn't like it. But it was the reality of the situation. Maxim figured he knew what they were doing there, without the Captain having to say a word.

"Oh, my apologies, Maxim," the Captain said. "This is Chris Hughes. He's in charge of the operation. That man over there is Sergeant Maxwell, and this one is Sergeant Hall. Guys, this ugly old chap right here is Maxim Oblonsky."

Maxim glanced at Hall for a moment.

"What happened to you, my boy?" he asked, noticing Sergeant Hall's slight limp and the hole in his dark, blood-soaked pants.

"Fucking Russian military," Hall replied. "But we got the bloody bastards. Every last one of them."

"Russian military?" Asked Maxim.

"Something like that," he replied.

"Wait, hold on a second," Roger stated as he pointed to Maxim. "I don't even know who this guy is. Can we trust him?"

"Chris," Price replied. "Let's just say that he is a former employee of the Russian government and he knows where all the bodies are buried. I wouldn't have brought you here if we couldn't trust him, believe me. He's shared a lot of useful info with us in the past. Maxim has been an informant for years now."

"Ok then," said Roger. "I'll take your word for it."

Maxim walked further down the wooden steps and onto the ground.

"So," he continued. "Why is the Russian military after you?"

"Well, that's sort of why we're here," Price said. "I'm sorry to be all business, Maxim. But we were pursuing a convoy of Russian military trucks suspected of transporting a batch of weapons-plutonium when we were attacked. They turned out to be a group of Spetsnaz soldiers guarding it. I was hoping maybe you could shed some light on the subject."

"Yeah," Roger said. "Same thing when I was surveilling a warehouse that was supposedly used by the Russian government to store things they didn't want to be on the record. That was before Captain Price and his team joined the party."

Maxim lit a cigarette and gave the men a curious look. Captain Price, who'd known the man going on ten years, had no idea what he was going to say next. It seemed everything that ever came out of his mouth was unpredictable.

"Come with me," said Maxim. "It is best if we talk inside."

Maxim escorted them to his living room and pointed to the sofa.

"Please, sit," he continued as he walked toward the bar and poured them all a drink.

Maxim placed four tall glasses on a tray and set them on the wood coffee table in front of the men.

"This is the good stuff," he added. "One hundred per-cent pure Russian. Enjoy."

"Thanks, Maxim," Price said.

"My pleasure…" he replied. "So, to what do I owe the honor?"

"Well, sir," Roger said, reaching into his pocket. "First off, we were wondering if you could translate this for us."

Maxim snatched the piece of paper from Roger's hand and put his glasses on. As he examined the note, the team watched in silence, eager as to what it would say. Whatever it was, they hoped it would reveal something useful.

"Oh my," Maxim uttered. "Mother of God."

"What?" Roger asked. "What does it say?"

Maxim removed his reading glasses and sank deeper into his chair. At that instance, he'd wished that he could somehow go back in time, never having read the letter. As he glimpsed back up at the men, Maxim had a confused look on his face.

"Come on, Maxim," the Captain added. "Spit it out. What is it?"

"It is a letter from the Russian President's office to the Spetsnaz commander," he said. "It says that the Uranium is to be delivered to the rail yard for delivery to delta site. It seems they are abandoning their previous idea of a submarine launch and opting for a long-range ICBM instead, one that could very well reach any city in the United States."

"Bloody hell," said Sergeant Hall.

"Go on," Roger stated. "What else does it say?"

"It further states that they are aware of American plans to disrupt their goals," continued Maxim. "If they spot anybody attempting to follow, do not hesitate to destroy them."

Maxim folded the note back up and gave it to Roger.

"So," Maxim said. "How would they have this information?"

"I have a good idea of who is behind it," Roger replied. "We also have this other asshole after us. But, nothing we can't handle."

"You have any idea where this nuclear facility is located, Maxim?" Captain Price asked.

"Yes, I do," he answered. "If I recall correctly, It's the Semipalatinsk test site in northeastern Kazakhstan. It's an old Soviet missile testing site. It is supposed to be closed."

"Maybe Petrov had other ideas," Roger said. "If the place is supposed to be closed down, it could be the ideal way for them to conduct research and testing in secret."

"So, it seems."

Captain Price drank the rest of his drink and rose to his feet.

"We appreciate your time, Maxim," he said. "Sorry to drink and run, mate. But we have work to do. I'm sure you understand."

"Yeah," Roger added. "Thank you, sir. It was very nice to meet you."

Maxim got out of his chair to shake Roger's hand, leaning in close to his face and looking right into his eyes.

"I must warn you," he told him. "President Petrov has

eyes and ears everywhere. You must tread carefully, my friend. Assume nothing is what it seems. But, remember, you did not hear that from me."

"I understand, Mister Oblonsky. Thank you."

"Thanks for the hospitality, mate," said Sergeant Maxwell, gripping Maxim's right hand.

"Sure," he replied. "As you say in the West, don't be a stranger."

The team bustled through the door and right to the car as Maxim watched them from the doorway. They had a new mission in mind.

"We need to get to that site as soon as possible," the Captain said as he put the vehicle into gear and tore down the drive.

"We will," Roger answered. "But, first, I have a fucking weasel to deal with."

❧

Twenty minutes later, the black Audi spun into the parking lot in front of the safe house Demetri had set up on the outskirts of Moscow as the clock struck two o'clock in the early morning. Roger had been fuming on the roughly hour and a half drive back to the point where it all began.

Roger was confident that Demetri was the one who talked. The way he'd been acting since he'd arrived was anything but stable. Roger trusted in his instincts. It had to be him. There was no other person that Roger had associated with.

He had no clue what he was going to do once he faced the man. But, whatever it was, it wouldn't be pleasant.

Captain Price stopped the car in a parking space directly to the front of the walkway that led to the door on the ground floor. He pulled the latch and pushed the door slightly, stopping as Roger grabbed his arm.

"No," Roger said to him. "I'll handle this one alone. No need for you guys to be involved with him."

"You sure, mate?" Price asked.

Roger loosened the grip on the Captain's arm.

"I'm sure," he replied. "Just wait here. I won't be too long."

Captain Price slammed the door closed.

"I guess you know what you're doing. We're here if you need us."

"Yep," Roger said casually as he climbed out of the car. "Be back in a few."

Roger made his way up the walkway to the door. He paused for a moment, his hand on the gripping of the Sig Sauer pistol hidden under his shirt. He glanced into the window, but all the lights were off. The place was utterly calm. It appears as though nobody was home.

He marched around to the back and tugged on the sliding glass door. To his surprise, it opened. Roger proceeded forward in the darkness, weapon in hand, and softly tip-toed through the living area and into the hallway.

"Demetri?" he called out. "You here?"

With his left hand, Roger reached for the light switch

and flicked it upward. But it wouldn't turn on, as if some-one had messed with the breaker box.

Cautiously, Roger rounded the corner into the bed-room, his handgun and attached tactical light illuminating forward as he held it straight with every shift of his body.

"Demetri?" Roger continued, raising his tone. "Come out wherever you are. We can talk about this, Demetri. It doesn't have to be this way!"

Roger knew that something was up. Demetri had to know that Roger would find out about him sooner or later. He was waiting to be attacked. Roger just knew that Demetri would be hiding, waiting for him somewhere in the house.

But, as Roger rounded corner after corner, checking in each room, under and behind every crevice, he was nowhere in to be found.

"Maybe he just left," Roger thought to himself.

He headed back to the doorway to meet Captain Price in the parking lot. But, as he pushed the door closed, Roger caught a glimpse of something or someone moving toward the back of the building.

As Roger swiveled his head to the left, Demetri bounded for him, smashing against his body and tackling him to the ground.

"What the fuck are you doing, Demetri?" Roger asked as Demetri punched him in his side. "I knew there was something off about you! You picked the wrong side, you bastard!"

"Wrong!" Demetri screamed as he struck Roger in

the face, causing his lip to bleed. "I choose my country, Mother Russia! You are the American imperialist pig who tries to destroy us! But you will not succeed! I will make sure of that!"

Demetri slid a large knife from the back of his trousers and swiftly lunged it downwards for Roger's head. In a reflexive reaction, Roger elevated his arms and caught Demetri's wrist mid-swing.

"Die, you dog!" Demetri screamed.

Roger began pushing the knife back as hard as he possibly could, straining as he attempted to match the bodyweight that Demetri had used to hold him down. Pushing the knife slowly away from him, Roger let go of his left hand and stretched his arm out for the gun he had dropped behind him in the struggle.

"No, you don't!" Demetri added, kicking the pistol across the concrete with his right foot.

But, in a split-second decision, Roger let go of him, thrusting a finger from his free hand into his left eye and causing him to drop the knife. Roger snatched it up with his other hand and instantly jumped on top of Demetri. Not a second later, he brought the blade down and into the right side of Demetri's chest, putting his weight into it as he lodged the knife between Demetri's ribs. His arms fell limp against the cold, cement floor.

As he lay still, blood oozing from his body and coughing up blood, he attempted to speak.

"Ill-see-you-in-hell…"

Roger knelt over Demetri, watching as the life wholly drained from his body.

"I knew you were playing us, you piece of shit!" Roger shouted.

He sputtered one last time and then drew his final breath, his head leaning to one side as the blood pooled beside him on the ground. Roger wiped the blood from his hands on the man's pants, reached out to grab his handgun from the floor, and stood up.

"You'll see your dear leader in hell, you fucking asshole," he said, standing over Demetri's body as he holstered his firearm.

Roger rushed in to grab the gear and the rest of the weapons he'd stashed there and shoved them into a large, Army green duffel bag. He left Demetri's corpse where it fell and hurried to join Captain Price and the team. As he hopped into the passenger seat of the car, Price glimpsed over at him

"That sure was a ton of racket, mate." said the Captain. "What the hell happened? I was about two-seconds from rushing over if you hadn't told me not to!"

Roger buckled his seatbelt and adjusted his clothes.

"Let's just say he isn't a problem anymore," he answered. "And I won't be returning here. This safe house is compromised."

"Well, ok then," Price added. "Then we continue on, yeah?"

CHAPTER 17

LANGLEY, VIRGINIA

VICE PRESIDENT HARRIS stormed into Director Cabot's Langley office while he sat at his desk, going through his morning routine of reading an inbox full of emails and enjoying his morning cup of coffee. On that day, however, that routine would be short-lived. As he quickly glanced up from his computer, startled, the Vice President leaned over Cabot's desk.

"What part of covert doesn't make sense to you, director?" the Vice President asked, taking a seat in front of Cabot. "We are trying to fuck up Russia's nuclear ideas, not make them worse for us! This is still a clandestine agency, isn't it?"

Sipping from his cup, Cabot calmly set the mug down and folded his hands on the desk.

"I'm sorry, Mister Vice President," he answered. "But, you'll have to be a little more specific."

"Ok, let me be clear, then," he said, placing a laptop

onto the desk and turning it so Cabot could read it. "Is this clear enough for you, director?".

As the CIA Director glanced up at the headline, his facial expression abruptly changed. The article was from a Russian News Agency, translated into English.

Russian special forces involved in massive shoot out with an unknown force in the Russian forest, not far from the Capitol of Moscow. There were reported to be numerous soldiers killed in this act of violence. The Russian Government is attempting to locate the perpetrators of this hostile act. Anyone with any information should promptly report to their local authorities. This type of vileness against the Russian military or Government will not be tolerated. These criminals will be caught and prosecuted to the fullest extent of the law. Reporting from Moscow, this isNatalia Bykov, RT News.

"You get it now, director?" Asked Harris. "We can't have assets running around a country like Russia, getting into shootouts with the Russian military. Now, this shit has made the Russian media!"

Vice President Harris collapsed the laptop and put it back into his bag.

"We are handling it," Mister Vice President, said Cabot. "The man just outed a double agent, the one who is believed to be responsible for the leak. I've been in direct contact with our man. He has his orders. We have things under control, sir."

"You'd better," replied Harris. "We are supposed to be preventing Russia from starting an all-out nuclear war, not provoking one. More importantly, we have innocent American citizens to think about. Your job depends on it, John! Is that clear?"

Cabot understood that it wasn't Roger's fault that they'd been exposed. He also conceded that they never should have involved Demetri, in the first place. He'd been found and approached by undercover CIA Officers hiding out in Estonia after deserting his Spetsnaz unit. He had all the signs of a defector.

Demetri seemed like a man who'd grown frustrated and weary of his home country and the path it was taking. The agents believed they could turn him. And, for a while, it seemed as though they had. He'd provided valuable intelligence about Russia's military and inside information on his highly secretive Spetsnaz unit.

However, as it turned out, he wasn't as dedicated to overthrowing President Petrov's regime as they had believed him to be. Perhaps he was faking it all along.

"Yes, Mister Vice President," Cabot answered. "Crystal clear, sir."

"Good," Harris added. "Don't make us look like fools, John. The world is watching now. Remember that."

"Understood, sir."

The Vice President rose to his feet in time to see Richard Weber rush through the door.

"Mister Vice President," he said, nodding at Harris as he approached Cabot's desk.

"What's the matter, Richard?" Asked the director. "Busting into my office like this. What is it?"

"Well, sir," he said as he glanced over at Vice President Harris. "I have good news and bad news."

"Ok," Cabot replied. "I'm listening."

Weber glared back over at Harris once more, hesitating to speak in front of him.

"Well, sir," he said anxiously.

"Anything you have to say to me you can say in front of the Vice President," he told him. "Come on. I don't have all day."

"Ok, sir," Weber answered. "Demetri is dead."

"What? When did this happen?"

"Late yesterday, sir," Weber continued. "The team returned to the location, and he attacked the asset and was consequently killed in the struggle. That is the good news."

"What's the bad news?" Asked Cabot.

Weber paused for a moment, taking a deep sigh as he stood in front of the director.

"Well, sir," he said. "Somebody is definitely after them. We don't know who he is yet. We aren't sure whether they are aware of the team's identity, either. We do know they took sniper fire from an unknown gunman just outside of the safe house. They did get the hostage out in time"

Director Harris had a troubling look on his face.

"That means they knew where the location was."

"Correct, director," said Weber.

"But how did they have that information? More importantly, what else do they know?"

"We aren't one hundred percent certain because he didn't give up much before he was killed. O'Neil is quite convinced that it was Demetri, sir."

The Vice President pulled his chair closer to Cabot's desk and scowled at Weber.

"Are you telling us this operation is trashed, Mister Weber?" the Vice President asked. "The agency didn't vet this son of a bitch?"

"Mister Vice President," Weber said as he leaned against the desk. "That is all we know right now. Demetri has been dealt with."

"But, you don't know what information he leaked, do you?"

"Mister Vice President," Cabot interjected. "He was never given much, to begin with. We never fully trust a foreign asset. They are never given more information than we need them to have. Let my people get back to doing their jobs. You will know if there is more intel on this mission. Now, is there anything else, sir?"

Vice President Harris got up from the chair and went for the door. As he jerked it open, he looked back at director Cabot one last time.

"Cabot," he said. "You better be on top of this mess. Your job depends on it. The United States is the most powerful country in the world. We can't afford to be rash. Got it?"

"Yes, sir," Cabot replied. "I got it. May we get back to work now please?"

"Don't be a smart ass," replied Harris. "The world hates a smart ass."

Harris slammed the door shut as the director looked up at Weber.

"Asshole," he mumbled under his breath. "Next time he decides to interject his bullshit I'm going to lose my fucking temper."

Weber gave the director a half-smirk.

"Richard," Cabot said. "Listen. I'm not going to micro-manage you or insult your intelligence. These damned politicians have no idea about what it is we do. They don't understand. Just handle it. And, make sure you keep me updated at every step. We don't need surprises anymore."

"Copy that, sir," Weber replied.

Vice President Harris was mixing politics and intelligence, which never belonged in the same room together. He was micro-managing, and Director Cabot didn't like it one bit.

Vice President Dick Cheney had done the same thing during the Iraq War, hovering over agency analysts when they were looking for Weapons of Mass Destruction in Iraq that didn't exist.

Director Cabot wouldn't put up with it much longer. He had trust in his people. He surely wasn't going to sit there and allow anyone to undermine their competence or professionalism. That just wasn't his style.

❦

A couple of hundred miles away, at the United Nations Headquarters in New York City, the President of the United States had just left a meeting with the UN General Assembly. They'd been discussing ways they were planning to put pressure on Russia to disarm, or significantly reduce their nuclear stockpiles.

Russia's spokesperson had been conveniently absent from the meeting. That was no surprise to anyone in attendance. Russia, more specifically President Petrov, felt threatened by the international community. That tends to happen when a country isolates itself and threatens nuclear war.

The meeting had dismissed, and the American President left assured that he had world leaders' support in his endeavors against President Petrov's Russia.

President Cash, along with many secret service agents and staff, exited through the big, glass double doors of the tall building in mid-town Manhattan and went straight for the Presidential limo parked right in front of the circular drive and in the center of the motorcade.

Circling him, the agents remained close, protecting the President's body as they were trained to do. As they reached the President's car, one of the agents held the door open for him, the rest going for the other two vehicles to the front and rear.

Cash took a step forward off of the curb. With one leg on the floor of the vehicle, he braced his arm on the inside of the door. As he pushed himself into the back, there was a crack of a noise that seemed to repeat against the surrounding buildings.

The agents' eyes focused on a group of buildings far down the street. As he glanced downward, he spotted a mass of blood coming from Cash's suit coat.

"The President's been hit!" Senior Secret Service Agent David Downes yelled into the radio mic clipped to his uniform shirt. "I repeat, the President's been hit!"

President Cash's body had fallen hard, crashing against the door before his head hit the pavement. Agent Downes wrapped his arm around the President's waistline, lifting him up high enough to shove him inside. He wasn't going to wait for an ambulance.

"Where is he hit?" Agent Martin asked as he ran from the last vehicle.

"In his chest!" Downes yelled, placing a bandage over the wound and applying pressure to stop the bleeding. "We need to get him to a hospital now! Counter-sniper teams, locate the shooter!"

"Copy that," one of the team members said over the radio. "We're on it."

The secret service, in a move they'd routinely performed, had sharpshooters placed throughout the area, in anticipation of a long-range attack. However, none of them had seen where it came from. It was hard to tell, with the sound of the shot bouncing off the city buildings, which direction it originated.

The President's motorcade hastened around the circular driveway and bounced out into the city street pointed right for the closest hospital, New York University Medical Center, in Manhattan.

"Step on it!" Downes yelled to the driver. "Go around the traffic. They'll get out of the damn way when they see this presidential seal!"

Agent Downes gripped President Cash's hand as he lay across the back seat, wailing in pain. He'd been hit in his left lung.

"Keep your eyes open, Mister President! We're almost there! Just a couple more minutes!"

"I… ugh… I-can't-breathe."

The President was having difficulty speaking. His lung had collapsed. The convoy had made it to the hospital emergency room, which, luckily for them, was just down the street from the UN building. The vehicle sped into the ER drop off point, brakes shrieking as they came to a stop.

"Somebody help!" Agent Downes screamed as he rushed into the emergency room entrance. "The President has been shot!"

For a moment, every person in the ER waiting area had a bewildered look on their faces, as if they thought it was a prank.

"I'm serious!" He added. "The President's been hit!"

Nurse Gonzalez, the triage nurse on duty, hurried with Downes through the double doors to the waiting limo.

"Oh, my God!" She said. "You are serious!"

"I told you!"

The nurse dashed back into the ER and quickly

snatched a stretcher from the corner of the room and ran back out with it.

"Come on!" She continued as Martin, and the rest of the agents rushed near them to lend a hand. "Let's get him loaded! He's going right into a room!"

Agent's Downes and Martin clutched the President's limp body and loaded him onto the stretcher. Nurse Gonzalez pushed the gurney into the building. The group hurried down the hallway through the entrance to the interior of the hospital.

Doctors and nurses gathered around as they wheeled Cash into the room and shifted him to the hospital bed. A crowd had begun to appear just outside of the door to the hospital room.

"He has an open pneumothorax!" Doctor Watson said as he rushed to his bedside. "We need to insert a chest tube, right now!"

Nurse Gonzalez hurried to one side of the bed to assist the doctor in inserting the tube to relieve pressure from the President's collapsed lung. Doctor Watson made the tiny incision, and they pushed the long tube into his chest. The nurse prepared the machine for drainage and put an oxygen mask over the President's face.

"He's going to need a thoracostomy," said Doctor Watson. "Nurses prep the OR (operating room) for me now! Everyone else, get out, and give us some room, please!"

The American, as well as international media, would inevitably hear about this news soon. The question on everyone's mind was, who would be bold enough to attempt an assassination of the American President in such a busy place as New York City? It could have been anyone, any person with a background in long-range marksmanship. The hunt for the shooter had begun. In the meantime, President Cash was being treated at one of the best hospitals in New York.

CHAPTER 18

THE CHOPPER APPROACHED low, touching the ground momentarily to allow Roger and the SAS team to hop out in the middle of the night in an open field, five kilometers outside of Kurchatov, Kazakhstan.

A moonless night, the team, outfitted in all black clothing and black Kevlar helmets, began making headway under complete darkness, a few dozen kilometers from the Russian border. Their mission was to find and identify any nuclear materials located at the site.

"Good luck, 1-3," the pilot said over the radio as he propelled further away from the LZ. "We'll be standing by for extraction, over."

"Roger that," replied Roger. "Charlie 1-3, out."

Roger and the team started moving their way across the tall, grassy meadow that was fed by the Irtysh River to the edge of a dirt road that bordered the water on the other side. As they advanced closer to the roadway, Roger held a fist and stopped the formation just at the outer edge of the field.

"Get down," he said. "A car is coming."

The last thing they needed was to be discovered and reported to the local authorities. If anyone had gotten wind that the team was coming, this mission would turn into a complete failure before it ever started.

They kissed the dirt under the thick vegetation and waited for the vehicle to pass. Lying perfectly still on the earth, headlights beamed past them as the car drove by not two meters from the team's position.

"They're gone," Roger continued as he came to his feet. "Come on. We need to get away from this road."

One at a time, they passed the roadway and down a rugged embankment toward the slowly moving water below.

"Looks like we're going to have to cross," said Captain Price. "Fucking A, this water looks bloody cold."

"Got that right, sir," Maxwell added.

"Well, let's get it over with," Roger said.

They entered and began crossing over in a gaggle, weapons held just above the murky water.

"Fucking hell, this water is bloody freezing!" Hall said.

"Just suck it up, lad," Price replied. "You're a member of the best fighting force on earth. Surely a little cold water won't bother you."

"Small price to pay for being the world's elite," Roger added.

As they exited, water dripping from chest to toe, the team followed the river down to a walkway cut into the earth that led up the slope just outside of the town limits.

The region was rocky and desert, with only the occasional green patch. It certainly didn't give much in the way of cover or concealment, which made timing very important. The team couldn't afford to prolong this mission far into the morning and risk being spotted. They needed to be out of there before the sun came up.

They started the five-kilometer trek toward the objective, over a flat, sandy piece of land a couple of hundred meters away from the blacktop. Their wet clothes began to dry off fast as they force-marched their way closer to the area in the muggy heat of the desert night.

After a forty-five-minute walk, they finally reached the hilltop observation point overlooking the old Soviet Nuclear site, Semipalatinsk. The place seemed abandoned. As the team settled in, Roger placed his .300 Winchester Magnum sniper rifle, bipod extended, onto the ground beside him, and pulled out his night vision binoculars.

"See anything, mate?" Captain Price asked as the rest of the team laid down in the prone beside him.

Roger scanned toward the front gate, then left to the buildings that ran along the road inside of the perimeter. The site was surrounded with high chain-link fencing topped with razor wire and barbed wire, guard towers in every corner, and a massive, steel-reinforced gate at both entrances.

"I don't see a damn thing," Roger answered as he caught something moving around the lights just outside of the front gate. "Just bats."

"They are neutral, mate," Price joked. "No need to shoot them."

The men waited there on that hill for what seemed like a couple of hours. The area around them was peaceful and calm, except for the occasional animal sound.

Suddenly, as they listened to the noise of light wind hitting the mound beside them, something emerged down the roadway.

"I got headlights, sir," said Sergeant Hall. "They are coming this way."

Roger placed the binoculars to his head again.

"I got 'em," he said as he observed a convoy of gun trucks and a cargo truck, painted in desert colors, down the road until they came to a halt in front of the guardhouse.

"That looks like the convoy that attacked us, doesn't it?"

"It sure does," replied Price. "And, I bet I can guess what their cargo is."

The truck pulled up, and a single guard from inside the small building approached the vehicle. Roger watched as the driver handed the guard a set of documents. The convoy was waved through, and they proceeded to the center of the complex, swerving into a large warehouse three hundred meters to the front of the team.

As they laid on that hillside, they watched as the gang of uniformed Russian soldiers exited the structure where they'd parked their vehicles and approached another group waiting just outside of the building. One of the men, in particular, got Roger's attention. Dressed in a camouflage jumpsuit, his face covered, and a Dragunov sniper rifle slung over his shoulder, he definitely stood out from the others. But the long gun was the main attraction.

"Could this be?" Roger thought to himself.

He kept his eyes focused on the man. But, as he peeped through the glass, the suspicious figure turned around, eyes focused toward the team's position as if he could sense they were there.

"What the fuck?" Roger said, releasing the binoculars to the dirt.

As Roger had observed the man, it was a disturbing feeling that he appeared to be looking right at him, like it was a sniper's sixth sense.

"What's wrong, mate?" Price asked.

Roger picked the binoculars back up and gave them to Captain Price.

"You see that man, the one with his face covered?"

"Yeah, I see him. Why?"

"I think that's the guy who shot you," said Roger.

"You think so?" Price asked as he watched the man talking to the soldiers' leader. "I don't know."

"I think it is him," Roger added. "He just looks off from the rest of them. He definitely doesn't appear to be a soldier."

Captain Price gave the binoculars back over to Roger. But, as he took another look, the man had disappeared from view.

"What the?" he said as he glanced around the rest of the complex. "Where the hell did he go?"

Roger knew they couldn't focus their efforts on a single individual. So, the team kept monitoring as the Russians began offloading the cargo truck with forklifts onto flatbed trucks just outside of the warehouse. Leaving the semi-trucks where they stood, the soldiers got back into their armored vehicles and went the way they'd come in.

"Let's go," Roger said. "We may not have much time before they move it."

The team, each pulling balaclavas up to their eyes, followed Roger down the hillside and to the boundary fence of the launch site. Retrieving a pair of wire cutters from his vest, Roger began cutting a hole wide enough for them to crawl through.

They entered and made their way to the building they'd been watching, staying close to the walls as they moved to the corner. Roger glanced upward, noticing a security camera pointing toward the interior of the base. He raised his weapon, shooting and disabling it so they could move.

Roger took a quick look around the wall.

"Clear," he said. "Let's move. Watch those security cameras."

The men continued down the wall to the front of the warehouse, the flatbed trucks sitting idle only 50 meters to their front. As he took a glance around the corner, Roger spotted two soldiers talking, rambling along the roadway.

"Hold one," he whispered.

The team held a position in the dark, waiting for the two men to pass.

"Clear," Roger said again.

They followed Roger to the front of the warehouse and prepared to collect evidence. Roger climbed his way to the top of the trailer and raised the heavy tarp that was spread across it. As he looked inside, Roger's eyes got wide.

"Damn," he said. "I was afraid I was right."

But, before he could say anything else, a lone soldier walked out of the darkness toward the team. Captain Price, Hall, and Maxwell knelt, securing every angle as their weapons pointed in different directions. The Russian soldier moved in closer, looking up in Captain Price's direction as he froze, aiming his AK47 straight ahead.

"Who are you?" the startled soldier asked in Russian.

Instead of answering, Price aimed his suppressed MP-5 at him and squeezed the trigger, watching him fall face-first onto the ground with a 9-millimeter sized bullet hole in his head.

"That was bloody close," he said, grabbing the soldiers' dead body and dragging him into the dark building.

Captain Price left him there and marched back toward Roger's location.

"You won't believe this," Roger said to the Captain.

"What?"

"Fucking nuclear warheads, that's what!"

"You're shitting me," Price replied.

"I wish I was, believe me."

"Hurry up and tag them, mate," replied Price. "Don't want to be around that shit for longer than you have to."

Roger tossed the GPS tracker into the large box, peeled the tarp back over it, and leaped down from the trailer.

"On me," Roger continued. "Let's move."

The men headed right for the missile silos that were located on the other side of the facility, moving against the buildings to avoid being detected. But, as they entered an open area between the launch site and the multitude of structures lined in a row, abruptly, every light inside the base came on.

"Fuck," Roger said. "Hit the dirt!"

The team was now completely exposed, in the prone on the open ground. The alarm began to sound, and Roger and the team knew the mission had just been compromised.

"How the hell did they know we were here?"

"I don't know," Price said. "But we have to get out of here, Chris! They'll be on top of us any minute."

The team picked up and raced for the fence line as a large group of soldiers emerged from inside the buildings. It was as if the whole place had just woken from a deep sleep, now lit up like a Christmas tree.

"Hurry," Roger told them as they crept their way through the opening in the fence. "At least we tagged the target. The silos will have to wait!"

They advanced as fast as they could back toward the

hill to call for extraction as the gaggle of Russian Soldiers searched for them around the edge of the perimeter.

"Falcon 6, Falcon 6," Roger said into the mic as they darted across the sands. "This is Charlie 1-3. This mission is compromised. I repeat we are compromised! Need extract time now, over!"

The team had only just made it back into the cover of night. Roger and the men weren't out of danger yet. As they made their way up the sandy hill, a single shot burst through the thin, desert air.

"It came from the East!" Roger yelled.

Roger glanced behind him and saw a splash of blood, turn Sergeant Hall's vest bright red. He fell backward onto the dirt, his lifeless eyes staring up at them.

"Shit! Sergeant Hall!" The Captain shouted as he lowered beside his body.

"Fuck!" Maxwell yelled.

Captain Price placed a single finger against Sergeant Hall's carotid artery. There was no sign of life.

"Damn," he said, dropping his head over his team sergeant's body.

"He's gone, man," Roger said to Price as they heard the group of soldiers getting closer by the second. "Come on! We need to get him out of here, now!"

"Falcon 6, we have one KIA and a large group of soldiers pursuing us! Where you guys at?"

Roger and the rest of the team wanted to get the sniper badly. However, with a large number of Russian soldiers chasing them, and carrying a team member who was KIA, the only thing they could do was move and shoot.

"We'll be on your location in two mikes, Charlie 1-3," said the pilot. "We're coming in hot!"

The Captain lifted the body of his dead team member over his shoulders, and they hustled down the other side of the hill to flat ground as the Russians continued following their tracks in the sand.

The men approached the designated LZ and pointed their weapons in the direction of the advancing Russian soldiers. Spreading Sergeant Hall across the ground, Captain Price took a knee, and the team started firing into the oncoming soldiers as they caught the whipping of helicopter blades getting closer to their position.

"Hold them back!" Roger yelled.

He started firing his M4 into the group, dropping two of them to the dirt.

"Approaching your location, now," the pilot said over the radio.

As the helicopter hovered over the sandy terrain, kicking up a massive amount of dust, the door gunner opened fire with the mounted minigun into the group of Russians. The gunner held them at bay while Captain Price loaded the body of Sergeant Hall into the helicopter.

"What happened to him?" the crew chief asked over the sound of rotor blades and machinegun fire.

"Bloody sniper!" Price replied.

Roger and Sergeant Maxwell sprang into the chopper,

and it took off under small arms fire from the ground as the machine gun resumed ripping into the group of soldiers.

"Hurry up!" Roger yelled. "Get us the hell out of here! This thing is a God damned bullet magnet!"

As the helicopter started to peel off, Roger spotted smoke coming from down below.

"RPG!" He shouted.

The pilot did an evasive maneuver, the rocket barely missing the tail rotor.

"That was close!" Roger said.

"Bloody right, mate!"

Captain Price glimpsed back down at his deceased team member as they zoomed over the barren desert.

"Poor Sergeant Hall," he said, shaking his head in disgust. "He was a hell of a soldier. Being in the Special Air Service was a dream to him. He was one of the good ones! I can't believe he's gone!"

"Me either," Sergeant Maxwell added. "He was a good teammate and a good mate. We went to selection together, straight out of our Army unit. He'd never give up. We trained for it together. Hall is the one who pushed me to make it through. I never would've been picked up if it weren't for him."

"We'll get him, guys," Roger told them. "Don't you worry about that. He'll get his due."

CHAPTER 19

GREENWICH
LONDON, ENGLAND

THE TEAM HAD flown back to the UK to escort the body of Sergeant Hall from RAF (Royal Air Force Base) Brize Norton in Oxfordshire, to his hometown in the London Borough of Greenwich.

As a sign of respect to his fallen team sergeant and his family, Captain Price wanted to notify Hall's spouse personally. Roger had accompanied them to England to pay his respects to his fellow warrior.

Sergeant Hall had a wife and three little kids at home. The life of a Special Operations Soldier was fraught with hazards. That was no secret. And, every family knew that it was always a possibility in that line of work. Nobody ever really expected it to happen to them until it did.

The British flag flailed in the strong gusts as Sergeant Hall's casket, union flag dressed over it, lay ready to be lowered into the ground. Many family and friends were in company, even some whom Hall had never met. But, one of them stood out from the rest. Hall's widow, Maxine, was dressed in all black, with a dark veil over her face. She'd been in utter shock since the death of her husband. Maxine wanted answers. But the team couldn't give her any. She knew that. And it clearly didn't help to ease her pain.

As the Sergeant's coffin gradually sank below the turf, Maxine had broken into tears. Roger glimpsed at her, a tear rolling down his cheek, and began to think of his own family and how they'd react if he were ever killed in action.

"I feel so awful for her," Roger whispered to Maxwell. "I couldn't imagine what my family would do if they had to bury me especially my son, Patrick. It would destroy him. I wish I could call them right now."

"I bet you miss them," Maxwell whispered back.

"Every single day," Roger said. "You have family?"

"Nope," Maxwell answered. "Just my mum. My dad died a few years ago. Cancer got him. Hall was the closest thing I ever had to a brother."

"I'm sorry. He was a good man, and a good teammate. I am so sorry."

"Me too."

The pair continued watching as Maxine began to sob uncontrollably. It was an emotional and moving event, and he felt immense sorrow for her. She stood at that graveside completely helpless, gripping her children and doing her best to comfort them as her husband disappeared into the earth.

Suddenly Maxine thrust herself forward, trying to

jump into the pit, knowing it would be the last time she'd ever be this close to him again.

"Maxine, no!" Her father, Jacob, yelled from behind, holding the back of her dress and tugging her backward.

He squeezed her tightly while she balled uncontrollably, tears causing her makeup to run as the crowd began to part. They had given her a crisply folded British flag as well as a posthumously awarded Military Cross for her late husband. Though, none of that would bring him back. As the team, along with Supervisor MI6 Agent, Jennifer Holloway looked on, they couldn't help but feel terrible for her.

"I'm going to go talk to her," Captain Price said.

As Price neared Maxine, Roger glanced to his left and spotted an unfamiliar person leaning against a tree and gawking at them from a distance. Roger stood by, watching the man out of the corner of his eye.

"Maxwell," he uttered. "You see that?"

"See what, mate?"

"That guy over there to the left."

Maxwell glanced past Roger.

"Yeah, I see 'em. What the hell is he doing?"

Roger glimpsed over at Price and nodded to get his attention.

"I don't know," he added. "But something isn't right. We have to get these people out of here, right now. We need to do it carefully, though. We don't want to cause a panic out here."

"Roger that," replied Maxwell.

Roger had proven himself to Captain Price on more than one occasion. Trusting his abilities, the Captain left Maxine for a moment to see what was going on.

"What is it, mate?" he asked.

"Don't look now, Captain," Roger said. "We're being watched."

"Where?"

"That guy behind me about two-hundred meters," Roger continued. "Between those trees. He must have followed us here."

Captain Price caught movement through his peripheral vision.

"Ok, mate," he said. "Bloody hell, come on."

Agent Holloway gripped the Captain's arm tightly.

"Are you sure about this, Captain?" She asked.

"Something is off," he answered. "And we are going to find out what it is. Better elsewhere than here, you agree?"

"Fine," she said, letting go of his forearm. "But, try not to get into a firefight in the city."

"I can't make any promises," he continued.

The team advanced toward the crowd calmly, not wanting to incite too much confusion.

"Guys," Price said. "We want you all to remain calm. We have an urgent situation, and we need you to quietly vacate the premises, please."

"Are you blokes serious?" A family member asked. "This is a funeral!"

"Listen," Roger added. "We wouldn't ask unless it was

extremely vital. Now, please exit the cemetery. Trust us. We don't have time to explain."

The gathering of people casually started to make their way to their cars, parked on the street that ran along the edge of the cemetery plot.

"Come on," Roger said as they pulled back to a silver Range Rover parked only a few meters away from Hall's gravesite. "Let's see what this asshole wants."

As they entered the Rover, Roger glared back up in the direction where the fellow had been standing. But, he'd seemed to have gone.

Roger looked behind him and noticed a silver BMW leaving the scene.

"I think that's him!" Roger said. "He went right!"

Captain Price stepped on the accelerator and turned the vehicle right onto the roadway just outside of the cemetery, facing downtown London.

"You see anyone yet?" Price asked.

"Not yet," Roger answered as he took a look behind them. "Where in the hell did he go?"

"He made us cut Sergeant Hall's funeral short," Price added. "I want to have a little chat with this bloody asshole, whoever the hell he is!"

The Captain shot through the intersection as the light turned yellow. Suddenly, a black BMW with dark, tinted windows emerged behind them from out of a side street.

"Hold up a second," Sergeant Maxwell said. "I think

I got something back here, Captain. This car is right on our ass!"

Captain Price took a quick glance through the rearview mirror. The unknown figure didn't seem to be making an attempt to hide the fact that he'd been following them. He was trailing the Range Rover rather closely, which made the team a little uneasy.

"Ok, then," he answered. "Let's take this chap for a little ride, shall we?"

The Captain increased his speed. He began weaving in and around traffic as the BMW almost stuck to their every move.

"He's still back there," Maxwell said.

Price made a sharp left-hand turn. The stranger remained on their rear, a car coming dangerously close to clipping his tail end as he veered into the left lane behind the team. He wasn't wavering in the least, doing everything to get their attention except blaring the horn at them.

The Range Rover progressed right down Regent Street to the center of Piccadilly Circus. They entered the circle next to Barclay's Bank, and Captain Price hit the brakes, coming to a rest beside the pedestrian walkway as a group of locals and tourists walked by them.

"What are you doing?" Asked Roger.

Captain Price observed the BMW through his side mirror with his hand on the door latch.

"I'm going to go see what our friend wants," he replied.

"Wait," Roger told him. "I'm coming with you."

They exited the vehicle, the mystery man sitting in his

car as still as a statue a few meters behind them. Roger and the Captain marched toward the car as the man behind the tinted glass followed their every move.

Approaching the driver's side door, Roger tapped lightly on the window. The man casually rolled the window down and glanced up at the two of them standing on the roadway. As cigarette smoke filled the air around them from the man's vehicle, Roger glared down at him.

"Why are you following us?" he asked.

The man didn't utter a word. Captain Price grabbed him by his shirt collar.

"We'll ask you again, mate!" He shouted. "Why the bloody hell are you following us? Are you responsible for our friend's death?"

But, he still remained quiet.

"I've had enough of this!" Roger said.

He pulled the door open abruptly and snatched the guy out of the BMW, shoving him hard against the side of the car and causing the cigarette to tumble from his lip.

"We aren't going to ask you again!" Roger yelled. "Now, answer me! Why in the hell are you following us?"

"I am afraid you have it all wrong, my friend," he answered in a sharp Russian accent. "But, if you let me go, I will be glad to explain."

"Fine," Roger replied.

He released his grip on the man, watching him adjust his clothing as he lit another cigarette.

"You better start talking!"

"I can't talk here," he added. "This place is too busy. How about some tea? I'll buy."

The team followed the man to Itsu, a sushi restaurant just down the street from the center of Piccadilly Circus. As they entered the building, he led them to a corner table overlooking the large bay window that faced the street. The place was quiet enough, with only a couple of patrons on the opposite side of the room.

"May I help you, gentlemen?" the waitress asked as she approached the four-person table.

"Yes," replied Price. "I'd like a spot of tea. What about you, guys?"

"Four tea's, please," the stranger said to her.

"Four teas coming up, sir," she replied before returning to the rear of the restaurant.

"So, mystery man," Roger said as his eyes met the strangers. "What exactly is it you want? Why are you following us all over London?"

The team wasn't prepared to let their guard down, not just yet. They had no idea who this man was or what his intentions were.

The gentleman had a fierce look about him as if he'd lived a harsh life. He had a few scars on his face, and his thousand-yard stare appeared to cut right through them. His bushy, blonde hair hung low over his brows, and they couldn't see his eyes behind the dark sunglasses he was wearing.

He glimpsed around the ceiling of the establishment, seemingly looking for surveillance cameras in the vicinity.

"My name is Alexander Sokolov," he said. "I am a former FSB Agent of the Russian Federation. Now, I am more of a freelancer. I left the agency a couple of years ago and never looked back. I didn't much care for our President's hard stance on nuclear weapons. He's been trying to bring the Soviet Union back to fruition. It's no good. They have tried to track me down and assassinate me two times. But, both times, I got away."

"That still doesn't answer our question, Alexander," Price said. "If that is even your real name. Why have you been following us? More importantly, why did you show up in the middle of our mate's funeral service?"

The waitress appeared in the middle of the conversation. She placed a tea on the table in front of each man before turning to leave.

"Yes, it is my real name," he answered, taking a sip from the cup. "And I have followed you here to London to warn you. I have become somewhat sympathetic to western ideals as of late."

"Warn us of what?" Roger asked, holding a teacup in his hand.

"I felt obligated to inform you of the dangers you face, mister…?"

"Chris Hughes," Roger answered.

"Well, Mister Hughes," he said. "You and this team of yours are in grave danger."

"How so?"

"They know who you are," Alexander continued.

"Russia will not stop coming after you. Does the name Nikolai mean anything to you?"

"I've heard the name, yes," Roger replied.

Alexander hesitated for a second, glancing at each of the team members.

"He's the man they call the wolf," he added. "He's good at sniffing people out, no matter where they are. There is no doubt that he is the one who killed your friend. And, he won't stop until he kills all of you. I know this man. That is why I am here, you see? If you wish to catch him, you have to beat him at his own game."

Roger looked up toward the restaurant entrance and spotted Agent Holloway walking through the door.

"Gentleman," she said. "Everything ok? I got a little bothered when you left in such a hurry."

"Everything is peachy, Agent Holloway," Price answered. "Meet our new friend here, Mister Sokolov."

"How do you do, sir?" She asked.

"Madam," Sokolov said as he nodded at her.

"Listen, guys," Holloway continued. "If there is any-thing you need, don't hesitate to ask. You know where to find me. I'm very sorry about the death of your friend."

"Thanks, Agent Holloway," Price answered. "We'll do that."

The Agent retreated back to her car that was parked along the curb in front of the restaurant. Roger peeped at Alexander, who'd remained silent during Holloway's brief presence.

"So Mister Sokolov," Roger said. "Anything else we should know about?"

"Yes," Alexander replied. "You need to be very cautious. Trust no one. There is nothing they won't do to get to you. Messing with President Petrov's nuclear program is a suicide mission, Mister. If you are still intent on carrying it out…"

Roger interrupted him before he could finish.

"We have to," he said. "He's threatening to nuke the United States, and no telling where else. We can't just ignore it!"

"I understand that," Alexander replied. "Believe me, I know how crazy this man is. That is why I defected. But, I am warning you, if you do not stop the wolf, he will pick you off one by one! As you can see from the day's events, it has already begun. You don't have much time before he surfaces again."

Roger rose to his feet to shake Alexander's hand.

"Thank you, I guess," he said as he gripped his hand tightly. "How do we contact you if we have more questions?"

Alexander glanced back as he headed for the door.

"You don't," he responded. "I just wanted to warn you. Now I have."

Alexander disappeared through the crowd of people outside. As the team marched back to where they'd left the Range Rover, Roger was a little uncertain, wondering where this mission was going to lead next. Wherever it was, they'd better be on top of their game, for Sergeant Hall's sake.

Stopping Petrov from launching his nukes was the priority. If they could avenge their dead comrade in the process. Then, so be it.

CHAPTER 20

THE TRAIN SCREECHED to a stop on the tracks next to the base as many armed Russian soldiers holding AK47's stood guard on the platform at the station in the Siberian wilderness of central Russia.

Spetsnaz Commander, Colonel Abram Abdulov, watched as his men prepared to offload its fragile cargo into the enormous warehouse behind him.

"Hurry up and get this unloaded," He shouted. "We don't have much time!"

The base was one that the Russians had been successful at hiding from western intelligence. Disguised as a regular train depot, its real purpose was hidden under the high cliffs circling the complex. Four missile silos dotted each corner of the base, buried beneath enormous camouflage netting and hidden from aerial view.

The flatbed train cars were packed with pallets containing

bulky canisters of weapons-grade uranium that the Russians scientists had been working on around the clock. Inside, loads of nuclear materials were all lined up in a row, covering the majority of the space inside the impressive structure.

The forklift operator jammed the metal forks into the center of the wood pallets as the Commander observed. One by one, he carried the large metal containers inside and offloaded them to the ground as the scientists conducted their work.

On the other side, another group of nuclear scientists were adding the finishing touches to an experiment that had been ordered by the Russian President himself. They were on a tight time schedule. President Petrov was due to arrive any minute.

As scientists carried out the final checks, a large white aircraft came into view over the horizon.

"Right on time," Colonel Abdulov said to himself.

The Presidential aircraft had actually arrived early. Petrov was never late for anything. And, his people had gotten used to the idea that they'd better not be, either.

"It is time, men," the Colonel shouted. "Report to the flight line to meet comrade, Petrov. Move now!"

The company of Russian special forces soldiers hurried to greet the Russian President. They got into formation just as the plane began to land, white smoke rising from the tires as it touched down.

The aircraft came to a stop at the end of the runway. The door lowered down, unveiling a set of steps that led to the ground. As President Petrov exited the plane, he made his way down, his security surrounding him. The Russian Commander gave a salute as his men followed suit behind him.

"We are honored to have you here, Mister President," the Colonel said.

Petrov shook Abdulov's hand as he lowered his salute.

"I trust there are no problems, Colonel, "Petrov said.

"We have no issues, Mister President," he replied. "Everything is in order."

"Good," Petrov added. "I would hate for this to turn out poorly for anyone involved."

Colonel Abdulov didn't say a word in response. He knew what the President meant. Letting him down wasn't in the cards for the Commander. He valued his job and his life far too much to make stupid mistakes. And, he expected the same perfectionism from his men. For them, everything, good or bad, always rolled downhill.

The Colonel escorted the President to a car parked at the edge of the flight line. He opened the door for the President, and they settled in for the five-minute drive out to the observation area.

"Go!" Abdulov yelled to the driver.

This missile was the one, the one they'd been trying to perfect for a year of constant bickering between the Russian and American Government. It was the one that the Russian President planned to use to get the United States to back off and to make Russia a world superpower once again.

It was his golden ticket, the thing that he knew would

strike fear into the hearts and minds of western politicians. And, the Russian people knew he wouldn't hesitate to use it. Petrov demanded that the West stay out of Russian affairs. But, with a rebirth of Soviet power looming over them, that was something they just could not do.

As the vehicle pulled up to the observation post, Colonel Abdulov escorted President Petrov up the steps to prepare to witness real Russian power; the power that the Russian President said would help to restore old communist ideals.

"We are ready," the Colonel said into his radio. "Initiate the countdown!"

"The clock is ticking," the voice on the other end replied. "T-minus five minutes and counting."

Petrov stood ready; his eyes glued to the launch site through the high powered binoculars.

As the minutes counted down, the Colonel remained enthusiastic and trusting that all would go as planned, for everyone's sake.

"T-minus, 5... 4... 3... 2... 1."

Smoke began to rise as the loud rumbling from the silo shook the ground beneath them. Petrov's eyes got more intense as the tip of the warhead appeared from below ground. The missile immediately shot up, and a massive ball of fire propelled it upward with a sudden jolt, pushing it higher and faster as it drew higher and faded above the clouds above.

A team of nuclear scientists and engineers monitored the missile from the control room, watching to ensure that the flight path went according to plan. Time seemed to move in slow motion as President Petrov waited for word that the ICBM had landed at the designated point.

A few minutes later, Colonel Abdulov had gotten word from the Russian engineers that the missile had successfully landed at the missile testing range in Russia's far east.

"Victory!" The engineer said over the radio. "The eagle has landed!"

The group applauded loudly at their glorious achievement. President Petrov was all smiles, now that he had a competent team to carry out his orders. Every new development had seemed to eventually be butchered by incapable people who couldn't make a nuclear weapon if their lives depended on it.

"See, Colonel," he said as he placed his hand over the Abdulov's back. "Proficiency does pay off. For you, and for Russia!"

"Yes, sir," the Colonel replied confidently.

After all, he had nothing to be nervous about anymore, as long as the Russian President was satisfied. As Petrov retreated back to his transport, Colonel Abdulov breathed a sigh of relief.

In Washington, Vice President Mark Harris approached the podium to address the nation concerning the most recent news about his boss, American President Larry Cash.

His feelings turned to worry as his friend lay in the hospital's intensive care unit, uncertain of what the outcome of his condition would be, or if he would ever make it out of there. Although they were friends on the same side of the political spectrum, Harris was much more of a hardliner than President Cash was. He took a much stricter stance on countries like Russia.

Harris surely never thought it would come to this. As he stood there, his head filled with both ideas and sorrow, his eyes met the camera.

"Ladies and gentlemen," he said. "I come to you this morning with a heavy heart. The President, currently at an undisclosed hospital, is literally fighting for his life as I speak to you today. I urge his supporters to pray for him as we do not know what the result will be. President Cash required emergency surgery yesterday and is surrounded by close family and friends at his bedside. Please, join me in a moment of silence…"

Vice President Harris paused for a minute as he looked at the camera.

"I will be taking over his duties as president beginning today," he continued. "I will update you as news comes in. Thank you, and God bless."

The American public was surely stunned by the news. It had been a long time since an attempt on a president's life had gone that far. What nobody could understand was how it got past the Secret Service.

The Vice President departed from the camera and headed back down the long hallway toward the oval office. As he closed the door behind him, he noticed CIA Director Cabot sitting in the chair, leaning on the desk.

"Been waiting long, John?" Harris asked him.

"Just a few minutes, sir," Cabot replied.

The Vice President took a seat at the oval office desk, glancing up at the director as he poured himself a drink.

"Care for anything?" he asked.

The director only shook his head.

"Bad business what happened to the President," said Cabot. "I hope they can find the son of a bitch responsible."

"Come on, John," Harris answered. "You know who's responsible. It's that damn Russian maniac of a president. We just can't prove it yet. But, we will. However awful, I know you didn't come here just to discuss that. What's really on your mind?"

"I have an update for you, sir."

"I'm listening."

"Task Force X-ray was attacked on a mission in Kazakhstan. One of the SAS members was killed as they were pursued by an unknown number of Russian Spetsnaz. It seems they were expecting them, sir."

"Demetri was the guy you all trusted? It seems as though Ivy League schools don't always breed competence, huh?"

"Yes, sir," Cabot replied. "I get your sarcasm. It was a mistake of epic proportions.

"You think?"

"But," Weber continued. "He's since been eliminated by our man on the ground."

"And?" Harris asked. "Are you telling me this operation is toast? I don't need more bad news right now, John."

"I don't think so, sir. They now know the team is operating in Russia, which makes this mission a lot more complicated. They've sent Russia's best killer to hunt them down. He's the sniper who killed the SAS team member, according to our man. We are coordinating with MI6 right now to remedy the situation."

"Good," Harris replied.

The President's Press Secretary, Isabelle Jenkins, came walking through the door as if it was urgent.

"I'm sorry to just bust in like this, sir," she said as she pushed the door shut. "But, have you seen this morning's article in the New York Times?"

"No, I haven't, Isabelle. I haven't had much time to read lately. Why?"

She tossed the paper face-up onto the desk in front of him.

"What the hell is this?" he asked as he picked it up, a picture of President Cash displayed across the front page. His mood turned to anger as he glanced up at the article's headline.

United States President Larry Cash shot in protest by an unknown armed American citizen amid Russia controversy.

The Vice President only got halfway through the one-page article before he stopped reading it.

"This is bullshit!" Harris shouted in anger as he crumpled up the newspaper and tossed it into the garbage can. "The investigation isn't even completed yet. The papers can't get anything right!"

"Right, sir," Isabelle answered. "What would you have me do?"

"Tell them to print a retraction! All this crap does is fuel an already explosive situation. And, it tells the world that the American public is out of control. We don't need that kind of publicity! We all know who is responsible for this! We don't want the international community to think that President Petrov can control our people!"

Isabelle nodded her head to the Vice President.

"I'll get to it right away, sir."

"You do that, Isabelle. And, keep pressuring them until they agree."

As Isabelle left the room, Harris glanced back over at Director Cabot.

"Listen, John," he said. "I don't give a damn what it takes. I have been in contact with the British Prime minister. We have their complete support."

"I understand, sir," the director said.

Suddenly, Cabot's cell phone began ringing in his coat pocket.

"Excuse me a moment, sir," he said.

"Sylvia?" he answered. "This better be important. I'm in the oval office right now."

"Are you sitting down, sir?"

"Yes, why?" he asked as he glanced up at Vice President Harris.

He knew that whenever she talked like that, it usually wasn't good news.

"Russia just successfully launched its newest ICBM, sir. It landed at a missile range in the far east of Russia just over an hour ago. We're working it right now. But we have no idea where the launch originated. It's an intelligence black hole. Satellite imagery hasn't even revealed anything."

As Director Cabot sat, listening, his look turned upside down.

"Wherever it came from, sir, it wasn't any of the known Russian nuclear facilities. We're doing our best to track it down, but we are in the dark here."

"Ok, Sylvia," Cabot said. "Keep on it."

The director hung the phone up and placed it back into his pocket. His face turned as white as a ghost as he looked back up at Vice President Harris.

"What?" Harris asked. "What is it, John?"

Cabot waited a moment before answering.

"You've heard of the new missile that the Russian Government has been boasting about, sir? The one that they claim has the range capability to reach Washington?"

"Yeah," Harris replied.

"They just conducted a successful launch, sir. And, we have no idea where it came from."

"Well, find out, John. That's what you get paid for!"

"Yes, sir," Cabot replied. "We'll contact our non-official cover operative in Russia, see if he and the team can locate it. That's our best and probably our only option, currently."

CHAPTER 21

ALEPPO, SYRIA

A GROUP OF sand-colored Syrian Army vehicles sped down the dusty two-lane road on the outskirts of the war-ravaged city as Syrian military helicopters buzzed overhead. The sound of gunfire and mortars exploding could be heard in the distance as Syrian Army soldiers fired from their posts atop an ancient fort overlooking the town.

Every building around had been destroyed in the fighting, Most were nothing more than mounds of brick rubble on the side of the street.

The Syrian Army commander, Colonel Abdi Hussain, was on his way to meet up with the General in charge of Russian Spetsnaz units that had been battling the Free Syrian Army and ISIS alongside Ali Abdullah's military forces. As they rolled down the roadway, the region was almost completely deserted. Civilians had fled the devastation in droves. Some sought refuge in neighboring countries. Most of them ended up in Europe.

Of course, Russia stood by the Syrian authoritarian regime. And why wouldn't they? Both had a similar ideology. With the United States backing the Syrian Kurds and the Free Syrian Army, Abdullah needed an ally like Petrov. But, they didn't just trade information and military power. Abdullah's regime was a favorite nuclear arms dealer to enemies of the United States. Russia was no exception.

The military convoy turned left onto a sandy road that led to a Russian checkpoint of a combat outpost ten kilometers away from the city.

"Halt!" The guard yelled in Russian. "State your business!"

Colonel Hussain's interpreter translated into Arabic for him.

Hussain was a die-hard regime supporter, and one of Abdullah's most esteemed senior officers. He hated America and the West and would have done anything to maintain the fabric of Bashar's government, including killing Syrian civilian protestors.

"The Colonel is here to see the commander," the interpreter told the guard. "We have an appointment with the General."

The guard held a hand up and made a radio call to his headquarters further down the road. Receiving the all-clear from his command, the Russian soldier waved the convoy of trucks through the guard station.

As they neared the parking area, Colonel Hussain and his interpreter hopped from the vehicle. The General had been expecting the Colonel and proceeded from the command tent to greet them.

"Al-Salaam Alaikum," he said in the traditional Muslim greeting while putting his hand to his heart.

Colonel Hussain spoke to his interpreter in Arabic.

"The Colonel says it's very nice meeting you, again, General," the interpreter told him. "But, we must get right down to business."

The Colonel's translator, Abbas Aziz, was a Syrian born scholar who spoke five languages. Unlike many others, he was also a supporter of the regime. He'd graduated from Damascus University a few years prior. But, the only job he could seem to get in his war-torn home country was being an interpreter for Russian military forces.

"Very well," Chernov replied. "Follow me."

Colonel Hussain and Abbas followed the General into the headquarters tent and took a seat at a large table in the middle of the room.

"Would you like some tea, Colonel?" the General asked in Russian. "Or, maybe some of our world-famous Vodka?"

Abbas translated into Arabic. Colonel Hussain just shook his head.

"The Colonel doesn't drink, General. "

"All business, huh?" Chernov replied as he pulled up a seat next to them. "I like that."

Colonel Hussain leaned in closer to the General. "So, Colonel," said Chernov. "What is your proposal?"

Hussain uttered something into Aziz's ear.

"Colonel Hussain, on orders from the President himself, would like to request that you deal with a group of American special forces operating in our area. He has become tired of American military presence in our country, General. We are looking for a speedy conclusion."

The Colonel suddenly had the General's undivided attention.

"They have become a problem and need to be eliminated," said Aziz. "In return, we will deliver the shipment of plutonium to you once the job is complete."

The Syrian war had very much become a pay to play system. President Abdullah's government would only transfer goods if Russian forces helped them to eliminate particular threats to their objective.

"Interesting," replied Chernov. "And, all we have to do is kill a bunch of Americans, you say?"

Aziz once again translated for the Colonel.

"That is the deal, General. Take it or leave it."

"Well," General Chernov answered. "Since you put it that way, Colonel, how could I possibly refuse?"

The General Pushed the talk button on the radio mic clipped to his camouflage uniform top.

"Colonel Belov," he said into the radio. "Your men are clear to engage the American team."

Hussain snapped to his feet, giving the General a swift Syrian military salute.

"May we emerge triumphant, General!" He yelled in Arabic.

∽

In the town of Tel Shegheb, close to Aleppo, a special forces team was on its way to meet an element of the Kurdish Peshmerga at their unit outpost in a captured ancient fortress on the outskirts of Aleppo, overlooking the city from a high hill.

The Islamic State had always been the target. The Kurds had been successful at pushing them back and allowing many of the surviving civilian populace to escape. That success came at a considerable cost. Peshmerga had suffered several casualties during the lengthy battle with IS fighters.

Conventional American forces had been ordered out of Syria following the nuclear threats made by Russian President Boris Petrov. However, small teams of American Special Forces, Navy SEALS, and Delta had been left behind to support and train Kurdish militias in the country.

Up to that point, the United States and Russia had remained neutral in their fight against their common enemy, ISIS. They'd refused to engage one another or even operate in the same area. But, now, the Islamic State fighters had been mostly killed or driven out of Syria and Iraq.

A new target had been identified. The Syrian regime had contained its hatred for America. Now, they wanted all US forces out of their country. And, they had nuclear warheads. It was an evil partnership between the Syrian and Russian regimes, to say the least.

The A-GMV (Army Ground Mobility Vehicle) zipped down the desert road, assault packs, and rucksacks strapped to the sides. Staff Sergeant Kyle Harris, the team weapons sergeant, scanned their surroundings with the 240B (240-Bravo) Machine-gun mounted to the top of its tubular metal frame.

They had a meeting set up with the local Peshmerga Commander, Colonel Aman Abdella. But, this meeting wouldn't go quite as planned. As the team sergeant, Sergeant First Class Mark Owen swung the vehicle right, and down a sharp decline, a group of three Russian military vehicles obstructed the path in front of them.

"What the fuck?" Team Officer, Captain Jenkins said as they made their way closer to the roadblock. "What the hell is this?"

They hadn't been used to the Russian military being outside of their own area of operations. And they sure didn't seem as if they were there for a friendly chat. The transport came to a sudden stop a couple of hundred meters in front of the sitting convoy.

A standoff initiated briefly as the Russian unit began to stare down the team. Suddenly, all seemed to move in slow motion as the Russian commander held his arm up high.

"Fire!" They heard the officer shout as their gunner swung his NSV machine-gun toward the special forces team's position.

"Go!" Jenkins roared as rounds began to pound the side of the truck. "Get us the hell out of here!"

Small arms and machine-gun fire hurled toward them as Owen slammed on the gas, whipping the vehicle around in a cloud of dust off the road and into the open desert.

The team Captain instantly jerked the radio from its receiver and pressed the talk button on his mic.

"Charlie 7, this is Charlie 3-3. We are currently being engaged by an unknown force of Russian Army pursuing behind us. Please advise over!"

"Charlie 3-3, that transmission was garbled," the voice on the other side said. "Say again your last, over."

"I said we are being attacked by a convoy of Russians, over!"

All of a sudden, a shot punctured the driver's side door of the team vehicle, barely missing Sergeant Owen and ripping into the truck's radio.

The voice on the other side of the line fell silent.

"Fuck!" Jenkins yelled, throwing the mic down on the seat.

Harris swiveled his gun to the rear and began exchanging fire into the pursuing Russian Army vehicles.

"Why are they engaging us?" Sergeant Ramsey asked from the back seat as he and team medic, Staff Sergeant Chris Harley fired M-4's through the rear windows.

"I have no fucking idea!" Owen sounded over the bursting sound of gunfire.

The exchange between both sides created mass confusion. Civilians from the surrounding village dashed for cover inside their homes as the vehicles raced past, leaving a trail of dust in the air behind them.

"Aim for the grill, damn it!" Sergeant Owen continued. "Stop those fucking trucks!"

Suddenly, a bullet struck the Russian gunner in the

face, blowing half of his head off as blood splatter dotted the top of the vehicle. But the convoy kept up its relentless pursuit, trailing close behind and gaining momentum as the team led them over open desert roads and sandy dunes in their speedy attempt to lose them.

It appeared the special forces team wouldn't be able to lose the convoy that was quickly closing in behind them. But then, as swiftly as a sandstorm erupts, the Kurdish Peshmerga unit, with its five vehicles and numerous troops, appeared over the sands. Once, the Special forces team was greatly outnumbered. Now the odds were even.

With Colonel Abdella at the helm, the formation of Peshmerga began sending AK-47 and Dshk Machine gun fire bursting into the convoy's location as the Russians, now outnumbered, attempted to flee back the way they'd come from. Sergeant First Class Owen slammed on the brake as the Kurdish unit continually moved forward. He quickly turned the vehicle around.

"Fire!" He shouted to Sergeant Harris as they joined the Kurds in engaging the Russians, trying to flee for the hills. "Pound them into the fucking dirt!"

The wall of incoming bullets began to overcome the Russian convoy. The Peshmerga had caught them completely by surprise. No longer the aggressors, the Russian commander knew they needed to get out of dodge before they were utterly obliterated. But it was too late.

Struck by a bullet to the head, the Russian Officer fell back, blood soaking the seat behind him behind a shattered windshield. One by one, each man began to fall beneath the crumbling weight of a superior force.

Following a rain of heavy gunfire, the last Russian soldier alive tried to escape through the wreckage of his now stationary vehicle. Sergeant Harris opened up with his heavy machine gun, sending pieces of his body flying everywhere in a bright red mist and almost cutting his body in half as he fell forward against the glare of the sun, dead.

Owen paused for a bit, trying to get his breath.

"That was close!" He said to the team. "What the hell was that all about?"

"I don't know," Captain Jenkins replied. "But we're going to find out!"

The Captain hopped out of his bullet-riddled truck and approached the front vehicle of the Peshmerga unit.

"Al-Salaam Alaikum," he said to the Kurdish commander, placing his hand to his heart. "I don't know what we would've done if you hadn't shown up, Colonel. Thank you."

"You are most welcomed, Captain," Colonel Abdella said in near-perfect English. "These Russians have occupied our land long enough. It is time for us to send them back to where they came from!"

Jenkins glanced momentarily back at his team.

"What we can't understand, Colonel, is why they attacked us. They are supposed to stay in their own AO."

The distressed look on the Colonel's face hinted that maybe he knew something the team didn't.

"You haven't heard, Captain?" he asked.

"Heard what, Colonel?"

Colonel Abdella stepped toward his command vehicle and retrieved a briefcase, pulling a single paper from a large stack of documents and gave it to Jenkins.

"This is a piece of intel we came across after a long battle with a small Russian special forces team a few days ago," said Abdella. "It isn't good news for America, I'm afraid."

However, a non-Arabic speaker, the Captain couldn't read it. He gave the paper to his weapons sergeant, Harris, who was completely fluent in the language.

"Translate this for me, Sergeant," said Jenkins.

Sergeant Harris looked down at the document. As he began to read, his expression turned to a look of concern.

"This is an official document from President Ali Abdullah's office to the Russian commander," he said. "It states that the President appreciates the collaboration of President Petrov and his armed forces to finally expel the American aggressors from his country. In return for their faithful devotion to duty as an ally against the West, he will continue to trade Syrian nuclear stocks, warheads, missiles, and technology with the Russian government."

"Jesus!" Owen said to the Captain. "This is no good! What do you want to do with this, sir?"

Captain Jenkins snatched the document from Harris, folding and gently placing it into his cargo pocket.

"We need to report this up now," he replied. "This

thing is much bigger than any of us! I have a feeling the CIA is going to want to get their hands on this."

Captain Jenkins reached his hand out for Colonel Abdella.

"Thank you for your assistance, Colonel," he said. "And thank you for this. You may have found something here that could completely change the course of this conflict."

"It is my pleasure, Captain," replied the Colonel. "Those Russian bastards will get what is coming to them, that is for sure. May God watch over you and repel those disgraceful pigs, inshallah!"

"Inshallah, Colonel."

CHAPTER 22

BALVI, LATVIA

"ANDREI?" ROGER CALLED out in rage as they busted through the door of the small flat located just on the edge of the tiny town in the former Soviet Republic.

Two CIA paramilitary guys, those who were tasked with safeguarding the former Russian scientist, approached Roger and the team from the living room of the tiny house.

"I need to talk to Andrei," he told them. "Where is he? It's urgent."

They both knew that Roger was a non-official cover operative. Neither man desired to cross him.

"He's in the back," one of them remarked.

Roger and the guys marched straight down the hall to where the bedrooms were located.

"Andrei?" Roger called again. "Come out! I need to speak to you."

Andrei, not instantly recognizing Roger's voice, peeked around the corner through the doorway.

"Chris?" he said in his Russian accent.

"Yep," Roger replied as he seized Andrei by the neck and shoved him back into the bedroom and up against the dresser. "You have about ten seconds to tell me the fucking truth, Andrei!"

Captain Price and Sergeant Maxwell stood and watched as Andrei's face turned red with Roger's hand around his throat.

"I... can't... breathe..." Andrei said achingly.

"Tell me what is going on!" Roger yelled. "I don't have time for games!"

"Please-let-go-of-me..."

Roger momentarily related his grip on Andrei.

"What are you talking about?" Andrei asked, hunched over, and struggling to take in air.

"What am I talking about?" Roger asked. "You haven't seen the news?"

"No," Andrei said. "I haven't watched much TV lately. Why?"

Roger unfastened the pack that was resting on his back and dropped it to the floor. He pulled out a medium-sized agency tablet from one of the interior pockets. Holding it to Andrei's face, Roger pressed the video play button, showing a recorded satellite feed of Russia's recently successful launch. They both knew what the next step might be.

As Andrei viewed the content unfolding in front of him with complete shock, he bowed his head in regret.

"Ugh... Petrov," he grumbled.

"So," Roger said to Andrei. "Why can't we find this

place? It's completely off our radar. As a Russian nuclear scientist, you must know where it came from."

"I do know," Andrei answered. "Or at least I am reasonably sure. But you guys are not going to like it."

Captain Price moved in front of Roger.

"Like what, mate?"

Andrei glimpsed left and right at the both of them.

"Ok," Andrei said. "I'll tell you. But, don't say I didn't warn you."

"We're listening," said Roger.

"That place," Andrei continued. "If my premise is correct. And I am rather sure it is. It hasn't been in use in decades. It was the major nuclear base between 1960 and 1985. The Soviet Union used it during the Cold War stand-off with America. It's fortified, probably better than any base you have ever seen. Besides the usual defenses, it is naturally protected by the environment. The mountains surround it on three sides."

"Bloody hell," Sergeant Maxwell said.

Roger and the Captain instantly glanced at one another.

"Go on," said Roger.

"There is only one way in and one way out," Andrei added. "The region around it is protected by SAM (Surface-to-Air-missile) sites on all sides for one hundred kilometers. So getting an aircraft in there is out of the question."

Andrei grabbed a pen and a piece of paper from the bedside table and began jotting down the location of the secret base.

"Here," he continued.

"Why didn't you tell us about this place before, Andrei?" Roger asked as he jerked the note from Andrei's hand.

"Because," Andrei replied. "I only started working for the government in 2005. It was never in use when I was there. And I had no reason to believe that it ever would be. Although, knowing our President, I guess I should have suspected. That base remained abandoned for decades."

"I guess they had other plans."

Roger seized his bag from the floor and strapped in back onto his back.

"Thank you," he told Andrei. "Sorry, I doubted you. I don't want to sound jaded, but you learn to trust very few people in this business."

"I understand," Andrei answered. "I am just glad I could help. Russia is no longer the country I remember. It's a shame, really."

As Andrei followed them back out into the hallway, he had a severe concern for the direction things were taking.

"Listen," he said to them. "Be very wary if you do decide to go to that place. Petrov will spare no expense to ensure that it is extremely well protected. Once you are in there, there will be no way for you to escape."

"Thanks for the warning," Roger said.

"By the way, Chris, now that we are on good terms again, who are your friends?"

"Oh, my apologies," Roger continued. "This is Captain Price and Sergeant Maxwell, SAS."

"Good to meet you, mate," Price said. "I only wish it could have been under better circumstances."

"Yeah, well," Andrei replied. "Such is the way of the world."

"I suppose so. Bloody shame."

Roger led the team back through the living area with Andrei following them.

"Guys," Roger said to the two CIA paramilitary sitting on the living room sofa. "He'll be with us for a few. There is something we need to talk about. Don't worry, we won't let him out of our sight."

"Roger that," one of them replied. "Don't keep him long."

The team made their way through the door of the house, down the gravel drive to the street a short distance away. Roger took the pack from his back and tossed it into the back seat. He folded the paper that Andrei had given him and put it into the back pocket of his beige cargo pants.

"There is just one more thing we need to discuss, Andrei," he said. "This agent of theirs, the one we are sure killed one of Captain Price's men."

"Yes, you must be talking about Nikolai," Andrei replied. "The wolf, they call him."

"What do you know about him?" Captain Price chimed in.

When it came to his team, Price wasn't playing around. Both he and Roger wanted this man. But, they'd need to find him first.

"I want to put a hurting on this man for killing one of the best SAS Soldiers I have ever commanded. When we find him, I'll make him beg me to kill him. Tell us what you know!"

"Easy," Roger told the Captain, holding his arm out to keep Price from losing his temper. "We will get him, brother. Just calm yourself."

The Captain shrugged his shoulders and took a step back as Roger leaned against the car door.

"So," he continued. "What do you know, Andrei? Nobody else can seem to help us find him."

"That's the problem," Andrei answered.

"What is?"

"He finds you, not the other way around. Why do you think they call him the wolf? He's President Petrov's go-to man."

"That's what people keep telling us."

"I don't even know what he looks like, only his reputation," Andrei added. "He's like a ghost, always there but never seen."

Andrei snagged a pack of Prima cigarettes from the front pocket of his jeans and put one between his lips. As he flicked a large, old school metal lighter and placed the flame to the tip, a familiar sound reverberated through the air. Everything seemed to move in slow motion as the team ducked for cover behind the doors of their vehicle.

The look on Roger's face was one of pure terror as the 7.62 millimeter bullet struck Andrei square in the neck. The shot completely severed his brain stem, instantly killing him and causing his body to fall straight to the cement.

"Andrei!" Roger yelled.

But Andrei was no more, his corpse lying in a pool of blood and his head just about severed off. Roger and the men had hit the ground hard, not wanting to give the sniper more targets to shoot at.

"Damn it!" he added. "This man is trying my nerves!"

Roger pushed one half of Andrei's body off the side of the car and hopped into the driver's seat as fast as he could.

"Let's go, guys!" he yelled. "We need to get the hell out of here!"

"What about him?" Captain Price asked as he dove into the passenger seat.

Roger hit the accelerator, burning rubber as he bounced off the curb and into the roadway.

"Nothing more we can do for him!" he said.

Roger had his foot thrust tightly against the floor, doing his best to drive that old Soviet Lada as fast as those wheels would take them. White lines dotted the highway as the forest to their right and left flew by in a flash.

"See anyone back there?" he asked.

"No!" Shouted Maxwell. "It looks like we're in the clear!"

But, Sergeant Maxwell may have spoken too soon. As Roger glimpsed into the side mirror, he spotted a red motorbike speeding over the hill and gaining on them quickly from behind.

"Shit!" he yelled. "He's coming up fast. Take that bastard out!"

Price and Maxwell stuck their heads out and began discharging their rifles through the door windows as the bike swerved quickly to both sides, the rounds barely missing him and bouncing from the pavement.

"Aim for the tires!"

As soon as they pointed their rifles back through the windows, the bike driver pulled a UZI Submachine gun from his overcoat. He started sending 9MM bullets flying at the team at six-hundred rounds per minute, blasting the windows and covering them in shards of broken glass.

"Fuck!" Roger yelled. "Is everyone ok?"

"Yeah, mate," Maxwell answered from the back seat. "Other than the fact that I got pieces of bloody glass in my eye and can't see a fucking thing!"

"Hit the floor!" Captain Price said to Sergeant Maxwell as he aimed his assault rifle over his head, through the fragmented back windshield at the pursuing bike.

The team could not see the man behind the dark visor of his helmet. Nor did they need to. Even though none of the men had ever seen his face, they all knew who he was.

They weren't sure how he was getting his information or how he knew where they were going to be. Roger had killed the double agent, Demetri. Was there someone else? They didn't know for sure. All they knew was the man was good, maybe too good. He would be a thorn in their sides and a detriment to the mission as long as he was alive. That is one thing they were very confident about.

The firefight continued as they sent rounds, hurling back and forth. Somebody was going to be seriously hurt or killed before the day was over.

All of a sudden, as Roger weaved side to side to evade

incoming bullets, they heard a loud pop. The car began to sputter and vibrate vigorously as he increasingly started to lose control. A front tire, then a back tire exploding with compressed air, and the vehicle began to veer toward the right side of the road.

Roger tried to regain control, mustering all of his strength to yank the steering wheel to the left and back onto the road. But it was no use. The Lada pulled abruptly to the right as the men approached a bridge that ran over a river beneath them. Roger and the Captain immediately glimpsed at one another, mentally preparing for what was about to happen.

Suddenly, the car rammed violently into the guard rail and tumbled over the top, plunging thirty feet down to the steep embankment below. The harsh noise of metal slamming to the hard ground pierced through the air as the car came to a rest upside down, the hood submerged in five feet of dirty water.

As Roger dangled there, barely alert, blood spilled from the side of his head onto the dashboard below him. His vision was going in and out. He was concerned for his team and attempted to reach out to them.

"You... guys... ok?" he asked, barely able to speak a word.

All he heard in response was his team moaning in pain as they both lay in a pool of blood only a couple of feet from him. Roger couldn't see their injuries, let alone his own. However, as he glimpsed uphill to the bridge so many feet above them, he noticed a chilling sight.

The man on the motorbike sat there, idly watching the car from above. Perhaps he chalked them up for dead. But, as quick as it had appeared behind them, the bike disappeared down the street, the powerful zoom of its engine becoming fainter the more distant it got.

CHAPTER 23

YOU COULD HAVE sliced through the tension in that office with a knife. Richard Weber sat silently in the corner while Director Cabot typed away on his office computer. He hesitated to open dialogue.

Weber had been called on almost daily to give the director regular updates on the situation in Russia. It had become more turbulent by the day.

What was supposed to be a covert operation had become anything but pretty early on. It had endangered innocent people as well as put Roger's team in a terrible situation. Not only were they trying to prevent a nuclear war. They were being hunted. And, it seemed as though the hunter was playing a game of sorts.

"Ok, Richard," the director said as he looked up from his computer monitor. "You come storming into my office as if there's some kind of emergency. So, spit it out. What is it?"

"I was waiting for you to finish what you were doing, Mister director."

Cabot tossed a piece of paper into the garbage can and leaned over in his chair.

"I can multi-task you know? I've been at this job for more than a day."

"Sorry sir," Weber said to Director Cabot as he sat in the brown leather office chair in the corner of the director's office. "It has been confirmed, sir. The Russian Nuclear scientist is dead."

"Damn it!" Cabot yelled from across the room. "How in the hell did that happen? Wasn't he being guarded?"

"We are still trying to ascertain that, sir. We aren't entirely sure yet."

Weber bounced his leg anxiously while scratching the top of his head. He was apprehensive, knowing that the CIA Director was looking for explanations that he couldn't give. Cabot could be a handful when he didn't receive the answers he was seeking.

"How did they even find him?"

"We don't know, sir," answered Weber.

"Ok," the director said. "So, the team was there, and then they just went offline. Do you know what happened to them?"

"Not yet, sir," replied Weber. "We are still looking into that. We lost radio contact shortly afterward."

"So, you don't know who killed him. You don't know

what happened to the team. Tell me what you do know, Mister Weber!"

"Sir," Weber replied, clearing his throat. "We know that Russia has launched its latest long-range ICBM successfully. We know that the task force's presence had been leaked by a so-called CIA informant, a man who's history was all but verified. Now, the only asset we had who was knowledgeable of Russia's nuclear weapons program is dead, and the team is being hunted all over Russia and surrounding countries. That is what I know, sir!"

Director Cabot frowned up at Weber with an intense stare.

"Are you suggesting that we didn't do our due diligence, Mister Weber?"

"As a matter of fact, sir," Weber continued in a moment of courage. "That is exactly what I am saying! If we hadn't been so careless and looked harder into Demetri's background, none of this would've happened. The mission wouldn't be compromised, and we wouldn't have lost friendlies in the process!"

"Well, Richard," Cabot said. "Thank you for that insightful observation. You know, we may be the foremost intelligence agency in the United States. But we are not perfect. We do our best with what we have to work with. Our people are the best in this business. But, occasionally, mishaps do happen."

"Sir, the agency cannot afford to…"

Director Cabot interrupted Weber before he could

finish. "Thank you for your feedback, Richard. You are excused."

Weber was distraught. It seemed to him that Director Cabot didn't want to admit that the agency had blundered and caused the death of an innocent person. But that is hardly the first time that has ever happened. What was one life in the international game of espionage? They called it collateral damage. All throughout the CIA drone wars in Afghanistan, innocents had been killed in the name of freedom. It was a reputation the agency had been trying to shed for some time.

Nevertheless, when mistakes begin to affect friendlies on the ground, that is an entirely different matter. They'd already lost one team member.

As Richard abruptly shot up and marched for the door, Deputy Director Riley came barging in, brushing up against him as he exited for the hallway.

"Morning, Richard," he said.

"Sir," Weber snarled as he continued through the door.

Riley proceeded into the room as Cabot began to pour himself a cup of coffee.

"Have you heard the latest?" he asked Cabot as he took a seat beside the desk.

"Heard what, Anderson?" Cabot asked. "By the way, would you like a cup?"

"No, I'm good, boss. Thanks," Riley replied. "We just received a piece of intel from Special Forces teams on the ground in Syria that suggests that President Abdullah has been selling nuclear warheads to the Russians for months now. It was given to them by one of the Peshmerga commanders near Aleppo."

"What?"

"Yeah," the deputy director continued. "Apparently, it was his way of thanking the Russian Government for sending troops to Syria to fight the Free Syrian Army. Those bastards had been doing it under our damned noses all along."

"And you trust this information?"

"I do, sir," Riley said. "The Peshmerga have never let us down."

"That isn't going to fly one bit," Cabot replied.

"My sentiments, exactly," Riley said. "The question is, what do you want to do about it?"

"Well," replied Cabot. "We need overwhelming proof, first. We find and destroy Russia's nuclear stockpiles. Then, we deal with Syria. They'll get what's coming to them. Everybody does, eventually. In the meantime, I'll brief the acting President on the situation, and see what he has to say."

"Right, boss."

In Latvia, the space surrounding the bridge was packed with white smoke as the vehicle leaned upside down at the bottom of the steep hill.

The team had been lying tangled in the wreck, motionless as the sun began to disappear into the darkness. Roger's eyes had come partially opened, the bright flash of sparks lighting up the corner of his right eye.

He tried to move his head, but the torn seat belt had wrapped tightly around it. With barely enough strength to move, he reached for the knife that was attached to the belt around his waist.

"Ugh," he moaned.

He drew the knife from its sheath and carefully brought the blade up to his neck. With a slow sawing motion, Roger began to cut into the fabric. Dangling by his neck and arm, the right side of Roger's body had gone numb. As the knife sliced through the remainder of the seat belt, his body fell hard against the dashboard under him as he came crashing down.

"Shit!" Roger bellowed as he landed against the side of his hurt limb.

Roger attempted to push himself upward, but his injured arms just couldn't support the weight of his body. As he lay on his back against the damaged seat, he peeped upward, spotting what seemed like an explosion waiting to happen as sparks shot up from the front of the hood-less vehicle.

"Have to get out of here," He painstakingly grumbled.

Roger glimpsed over at his team, unconscious beside him in the car.

"Guys," he said as he shook Captain Price by the shoulder. "Wake up!"

"Ahhh," Price replied, barely coherent as he tried to roll over.

"It's going to blow," Roger continued. "We have to get out of here."

"I can't bloody move, mate," the Captain replied as he tried to nudge Sergeant Maxwell.

Roger, with the only reserved strength he had, braced himself against Captain Price's body and kicked the partly broken driver's side door open.

Sergeant Maxwell had barely woken, and Captain Price was tugging on his shirt.

"Come on, mate," he said. "We have to get out."

Roger, his right arm numb, slithered through the opening on the left side of his body. On his knees, he reached through and cut Captain Price's seat belt off.

"Come on!" he said, clutching the Captain with his left hand.

Captain Price snagged their weapons from the back of the destroyed Lada and shimmied his way through the open door as the pain from his head began to set in, dragging his kit behind him.

"Bloody hell," he said. "I think I cracked my head."

As the Captain lay on the ground just outside of the wreck, he called out for Sergeant Maxwell.

"Come, sergeant!" he said as he reached out for him.

"I can't feel my fucking legs," Maxwell said.

The Captain took both of his arms and began pulling him through the vehicle.

"Come on, sergeant!" he said as he struggled to drag his body through the wreckage. "Let's get you out of there!"

"A little more!" he continued as Sergeant Maxwell pushed against the inside of the vehicle. "Almost there!"

The Captain struggled to pull him through, and Maxwell laid face up on the damp ground, not able to move his hurt legs.

Captain Price resumed dragging Sergeant Maxwell from the car, rifles on his back, across the ground as he and Roger hightailed it as far from the vehicle as they could, the bright sparks only getting higher with each passing second. Suddenly, without warning, a massive blast shook the hillside as debris from the wrecked Lada blew high into the air and dotted the area surrounding them.

"Damn!" Roger yelled out. "That could've been very bad!"

"You're telling me, mate!" Price replied, blood and sweat streaming down the side of his face. "That didn't help my bloody headache, one bit!"

Not a house around for kilometers, Roger was confident that nobody had heard the explosion on that secluded stretch of road. Meanwhile, Sergeant Maxwell was trying to sit up, his body asleep from the waist down.

"How you doing, Sergeant?" Roger asked as he worked to cut Maxwell's pants to access the damage to his body.

"I can't feel my legs!"

"Let's see what you got going on, then," Roger replied.

With minimal bleeding, it wasn't immediately apparent what injuries Maxwell had. Roger ran his fingers along the edges of his legs, looking for signs of broken bones. But, when he lifted his shirt up, he was in for a shock. A tiny piece of metal was protruding from the lower part of the sergeant's back.

"Damn," Roger said.

"What?" Maxwell asked. "What is it?"

"You have a piece of metal in your back. Just hold still, and don't move around too much."

"I don't feel a damn thing," Maxwell said. "Can you get it out?"

Roger gave Sergeant Maxwell a concerned look.

"I shouldn't even touch it, to be honest," Roger said. "It'll probably do more damage coming out."

"What do you want to do, then?" Captain Price asked.

Roger looked upward at the top of the hill overhead. They were in a very remote region of Latvia. He knew the man who'd caused them to crash would've been long gone by then. And his radio had been blown up in the debris.

"Captain, is your radio working?"

Price reached behind him and retrieved the radio from his waistband.

"It's a little banged up," he said as he turned the power knob. "But, yeah, it seems to be working, well enough."

"Good," Roger said. "We need to get Sergeant Maxwell out of here in a hurry. His injury is critical. We don't need to waste any more time out here."

"Roger that," Price replied. "I'll call it in, then."

Captain Price switched the radio frequency and put it up to his mouth.

"Raptor 1," he said into the mic. "This is Charlie 1-3 of Task Force X-RAY, need immediate evac of critical friendly casualty, over."

There was a brief pause on the line as Captain Price waited for a response.

"Raptor 1, do you read me? Over."

"Roger that, Charlie 1-3. What is your location over?"

"Hold one," he replied, snatching the handheld GPS from his bag and quietly thanking God that he'd remembered to pull it from the wreck.

The Captain studied the GPS for a moment, holding it out in the palm of his hand.

"Ok, Raptor 1," Price continued. "I'm sending you the location now, out copy, over."

"That's a good copy, Charlie 1-3. It may take us a bit. But we'll get there."

"Roger that!" Price answered as he tossed the radio onto the top of his bag.

The good news was that Sergeant Maxwell wasn't bleeding much that they could see. The bad news, they didn't know the full extent of his injuries. Had Roger simply yanked that piece of metal from his body, they could only guess the damage it would cause. Still, they had no idea if he was bleeding internally or not. That was something only the doctor could say.

As they remained on that hillside in the middle of nowhere, they could only hope that the medevac chopper would arrive sooner rather than later. The team still had to carry on with the mission, with or without Maxwell.

Roger knew they needed to find the culprit soon. The operation would be jeopardized until that man was no longer a threat. With the team laying on the side of that cliff, beaten up and bloodied, time was not on their side.

CHAPTER 24

THE INTENSIVE CARE wing at Royal Brompton Hospital in the Southwest London Borough of Chelsea had been eerily quiet, the only sound coming from occasional staff chatter out in the hall and the constant pacing beep from Sergeant Maxwell's heart monitor.

One of the busiest hospitals in London located in an affluent area, Royal Brompton, had a reputation for staffing some of the best doctors in Britain.

Fresh out of surgery, the Sergeant had been out for hours, lying on his back on the slightly slanted hospital bed, not making a noise except for the random snore.

"You know," the Captain said to Roger. "I never got your real name."

"My name is Roger."

"Roger, huh?" the Captain asked.

"Yep."

"That's a typical American name," Price replied, chuckling. "So, Roger. How'd you end up here?"

"I was minding my own damn business ranching on my land when the CIA showed up at my damn doorstep."

"No shit?"

"Yeah, seriously."

"Maybe they knew something about you that you didn't know," Price said.

"Maybe."

"So, where you from, anyway?" the Captain asked.

"Montana," Roger answered. "Bozeman."

"Nice," Price told him. "I'm from Brighton, originally. I have a wife and two daughters back home."

"Oh, yeah?" Roger asked. "What are their names?"

"Wife's name is Isabella. And my two teenage daughters are Candace and Rebecca."

"Pretty names," Roger said. "I bet they miss you."

Captain Price kicked his feet up on the end of the hospital bed.

"Probably not as much as I miss them."

Deprived of sleep, the two were struggling to keep their heads up Outside of the closed door, nurses and doctors shuffled between rooms, tending to their patients. In the corner, Roger and Captain Price had been sitting and restlessly staring at Sergeant Maxwell's vital statistics. They had been there all night and were anxiously waiting for news on the Sergeant's condition.

The night before, doctors had worked tirelessly on Maxwell's back injury from the very instant the medevac chopper had touched down. Concerned that the metal piece had severed a nerve, the Sergeant had been sent straight into emergency surgery. His long-time team Captain, Price, was concerned for Sergeant Maxwell's future in the regiment. He was more so worried about his wellbeing.

As Roger and the Captain, bandages of their heads began drifting off to sleep in their chairs, heads against the wall, the door suddenly swung open. Roger's eyes opened and noticed the doctor, black turban firmly over his head, approaching out of the corner of his eye.

"Good morning, gentlemen," Doctor Arjun Badal said in his Indian accent as he set his clipboard on Maxwell's bedside table.

The doctor had immigrated to England from Punjab, India, in the '80s to attend Oxford Medical School. A young, gifted student, Badal had graduated at the top ten percent of his class. He'd since became one of the most sought-after specialists in London and had had a remarkable medical career ever since.

"Has he awakened yet?" the doctor asked.

"No, sir," Roger replied.

"Who are you guys to him?" Badal continued.

"Just friends," Roger answered. "But we are the only family he has."

"Oh, I see," Badal added. "Well, He got a hefty dose of pain medication. So he may be out for quite a while."

Doctor Badal walked to the other side of the hospital bed to check Sergeant Maxwell's vital signs. As he looked over the Sergeant's medical chart, Roger popped up from his chair and neared him.

"Any idea of how this happened?" Doctor Badal continued.

Roger pondered shortly before answering him.

"Car accident," he replied.

Roger wasn't completely lying. But he couldn't exactly tell him the whole truth. The team's work was top secret. They took that very seriously.

"Were you all in the same car?" the doctor asked as he glimpsed at their bandaged heads.

"Yep," Roger added.

"Do you two need medical attention?"

"We're good," Price blurted out from the corner. "Just concentrate on our friend here, ok, doctor?"

"If you say so," Badal answered.

"So, what's the news, doc?" Roger asked. "Is he going to be ok?"

Doctor Badal placed the Sergeant's medical file back into its folder and put it on the desk. He strolled toward the men, arms folded in front of him.

"Well, he will be live," he told them.

"That's great news!" Captain Price replied.

"However…" The doctor added.

The look on their faces abruptly shifted. An intermediate comment like that was never a good thing. They anticipated something now coming that wouldn't be ideal. Roger and the Captain apprehensively waited for the doctor to continue, hoping they were wrong about what he was about to say.

"I am sorry to be the bearer of bad news," said Doctor Badal. "But, your friend is paralyzed from the waist down."

"What?" Roger growled as Captain Price lowered his head into his hands.

"The metal shard severed his sciatic nerve," the doctor continued. "We got it out safely. But he will never walk again."

"No!" Price roared.

Roger sat back down in his seat, staring at Sergeant Maxwell as he slept and wondering how he was going to take the news. His career in the Special Air Service meant everything to him. Roger knew this would most likely all but destroy him.

"I am very sorry, guys," Doctor Badal said. "I wish I had better news."

"Thanks, doc," Roger said as he shook his head.

"Fuck!" Price said under his breath as he hit the side of his chair. "Poor kid."

As the door closed behind the doctor, Captain Price received an encrypted message on his cell phone.

"What's going on?" Roger asked the Captain as he gaped down at the phone screen.

"It's Agent Holloway," Price replied. "She wants to see us in the car park."

The two immediately moved outside and marched through the double doors to the main hospital toward the lift that would take them to the parking garage.

"What does she want?" Roger asked.

"I don't know," Price answered. "She didn't say."

Captain Price leaned his hand against the inside of the lift as it began to lower.

"Damn it," he said. "This is all I fucking need right now."

Roger could see that the Captain was having a tough time thinking of anything other than his injured team sergeant. But there was nothing he could do or say to mitigate that pain. All they could do was assure that the one responsible would pay for what he had done. That was the only thing either man was sure of.

The bell dinged as the door to the lift slid open. There, leaning against the trunk of a black Jaguar only meters from them, stood Agent Jennifer Holloway.

As Roger and the Captain moved closer, Holloway extended her hand.

"Hello, gentlemen," she said. "I am sorry about your friend. Any news on his condition?"

"He hasn't woken up yet," Roger answered. "The doctor said he may not ever walk again."

"I'm very sorry, Captain," she added as she glanced over at Price. "It could have been a lot worse, though. I'm just glad Maxwell is still alive. I'm happy you all got out of there in one piece."

"That's optimistic," Roger replied. "Considering we've lost one team member, and another will never be out of a wheelchair!"

"I'm sorry, guys," she replied. "I didn't mean it that way."

Captain Price was standing by Roger, not really saying much at all. But he had one concern.

"Why did you call us out here, Holloway?" he asked. "My team Sergeant is lying in intensive care right now. I don't want him to wake up alone. We need to be with him."

Holloway paused for a moment.

"Well," she replied. "Because I have something, or should I say someone you may want to speak with."

The agent walked around the Captain and opened the back door.

"Please get in," she added. "This won't take long."

As Roger and Price climbed into the vehicle, they noticed the back of an unknown figure sitting in the passenger seat. Agent Holloway hopped into the driver's seat and slammed the door shut.

"Mister Hughes, Captain Price," Holloway said. "Meet Antoniy Chernoff."

"Hello, comrades," Mister Chernoff said in his strong Russian accent.

Chernoff had the looks of an old man who'd seen better days. His face was deeply scarred and wrinkled. And the bags under his eyes made it seem as though he hadn't sleep in a long while. He was missing a few fingers from his hands and had burn marks up and down both arms.

"Mister Chernoff has been in exile from Russia for two decades," Holloway told them. "He was tortured, burned, held captive, you name it. This man has been through hell, as you can see. He was granted asylum by the prime minister and has been living here under an assumed name ever since."

"We are very sorry, Mister Chernoff," Roger said. "But what does this have to do with us?"

"Because, Mister Hughes," Holloway replied. "We believe the same man who did this to him is the one you are after."

Chernoff's shaky hands pulled an old, grainy photo from his breast pocket and handed it to Roger.

"This was my family," he said, a single teardrop rolling down his face. "My wife and three daughters, all murdered by that monster."

Chernoff wrapped a heart-shaped locket hung around his neck through his fingers, a picture of his family inside, and kissed it.

"They never even found the bodies," he continued. "But I know it was him. The only reminder I have of them are the few things I was able to grab before fleeing. If I hadn't of left when I did, I have no doubt that I would not be sitting here talking to you right now."

Roger peeped down at the image. He certainly felt compassion for this man. Roger couldn't imagine what he would do if the same happened to his own family.

"I'm very sorry, Mister Chernoff," Roger said as he gave the photo back to him.

"Mister Chernoff is former KGB," Holloway said. "He spoke out against the regime and was held captive and tortured for two years before escaping. That's when his family was killed."

"They wished they had killed me too," Chernoff added. "I've been openly critical of the regime since I busted out. But they never could catch me. I always told myself that if there was anything I could ever do to get back at those who killed my loved ones, I would do it."

He removed an old, brown leather wallet from his pocket and snagged another photo.

"This is the one you're looking for," he added as he handed it to Roger.

Roger stared at the image of the man as Chernoff spoke.

"His name is Nikolai Alexeyev. He is one of the FSB officers who refused to give up his old communist ways. Many old KGB Agents are just like him. Same old methods, different name. These guys operate under the banner of democracy. But there is nothing democratic about what they do. People, those who are against the Russian Government, disappear all the time. But you will never hear about this in the Western media."

Roger and Price just glimpsed at one another.

"They like to play games before they kill you," he added. "To make people suffer. In some sick, twisted way, I guess it is amusing to them. The Russian Government does nothing to stop them. But, in fact, they condone it."

The men stared at the picture for a couple of minutes.

"This asshole killed one of my men and put the other in the hospital!" Captain Price said. "He tried to kill all of us. He failed!"

"That's why we are here, Captain," Holloway said.

Roger couldn't take his eyes off of the image. Nikolai

appeared to be the stereotypical idea of what a Russian assassin would look like. The man had no smile. He was wearing dark sunglasses with a scar across the face. He appeared as cold as ice. But, at least they knew who they were looking for now.

"You can keep the picture," Chernoff said. "But I caution you to tread carefully. Moscow has eyes all over. If you do find him, please make sure you kill him, for everyone's sake. This man has done enough damage to people to last a fucking lifetime, may my family rest in peace."

"Thank you, Mister Chernoff," Roger said. "And I am very sorry about your family."

"Oh," Chernoff added. "A little tip, Nikolai loves Vodka. You may find him in some of the many pubs around Moscow."

"Spasibo," Roger replied in Russian.

"But," Chernoff added. "I will warn you against getting into a shootout in the capital city. If you do, there will be FSB agents coming out of the woodwork. Plus, your typical military types. Russia is far too vast and remote for that, you know?"

Roger carefully put the picture of Nikolai into his pocket.

"Thanks," he said to Chernoff.

At least now they knew they were no longer being hunted by a ghost, but a man who, until now, had no face. The hunted were about to become the hunters.

"So," Agent Holloway said. "Now, you know. Use this information how you see fit. You know what you need to do. Do it for Sergeant Hall, Sergeant Maxwell, and all of the other innocent people whose lives have been wrecked."

First, they needed to tend to Sergeant Maxwell. They weren't sure how he would take the news once he woke up. Being an operator was his passion. He didn't really know anything else.

"Ok, guys," Holloway said. "I'll come to see Sergeant Maxwell once he wakes up. I have some business to handle. Just give me a call."

"Roger that," Captain Price said as he and Roger got out of the car and headed back toward the hospital entrance.

"I have an idea," Roger said to Price as they entered the lift.

"What's that?"

"Just give me a bit to work it out in my head," he said. "We need to beat this bastard at his own game."

Roger and the SAS Captain knew they had some planning to do. But first, they needed to make sure that Sergeant Maxwell would be ok without them for a while. They were sure that he would be traumatized once he received news of his medical prognosis.

The men were fiercely determined to make sure that Sergeant Hall and Maxwell's sacrifices would not be in vain. The time for playing games was officially over.

CHAPTER 25

FSB HEADQUARTERS
MOSCOW, RUSSIA

THE LONE AGENT settled on the bench in the hall just outside of the FSB Director's office, wiping down his suppressed Sig Sauer .40 caliber handgun and watching the passing time on his black military-style wristwatch.

Nikolai was livid, eyes twitching in nervous anger as he waited for the director to call on him. Always working alone, he didn't like to be on anyone else's time. The director had summoned him to his office on short notice. And he was less than thrilled about it.

Nobody had ever talked to Nikolai the way the director had spoken to him on the phone earlier that day. He'd been one of the Russian Government's most trusted assassins. But this time, there was a different manner coming from the director. Errors were not something to be taken lightly in that line of work, particularly with so much at stake.

"Nikolai!" FSB Director Mikhail Volkov roared in Russian through his partly opened officer door. "Get in here!"

Volkov had been a career politician in the old Soviet Government. He was amongst President Petrov's inner circle of trusted colleagues and was appointed to his position shortly after the Russian President rose to power. The director loathed the West as much as Petrov did. And he would give anything to see them languish as he believed Russia had after the collapse of Soviet communism.

Nikolai stepped into Volkov's office.

"Close the door behind you," he told him.

He shut the thick, wooden door and strolled toward the director's desk. Nikolai silently stood there, as stiff as a statue and staring over the director's head.

"Look at me, Nikolai," Volkov commanded.

The agent lowered his eyes, flexing his jaw muscles, and seemingly staring right through Director Volkov.

"Why am I here?" Nikolai asked in a flat, bold tone.

"Because I ordered you, Nikolai," Volkov replied. "Remember, you are not the one in charge here. I am."

Nikolai continued looking straight ahead. His fists balled up as if he felt like striking the director.

"Yes, sir," he grudgingly replied.

Nikolai was still the best and most feared agent Russia had. But he didn't exactly follow orders well. Perhaps it's what made him so lethal. Though many of the younger agents didn't understand, they weren't around during the days of the old KGB.

For the most part, Nikolai had always been free to

operate independently. That wasn't going to change now. But this time he spoke too soon.

"Your last target, Nikolai," Volkov stated before Nikolai interrupted him.

"What about them?" he asked. "They've been dealt with, as I told you."

"Are you sure about that?"

"Yes, I am sure," he replied. "What's the fucking problem?"

The director lit a cigarette and reclined back in his black leather chair.

"Did you see the bodies?" he asked, scowling back up at him with a hard look as white smoke filled the air.

"They went over a twenty-meter high bridge!" Nikolai answered. "Nobody could have survived that!"

"Really?" Volkov asked, switching on the television located on the wall behind him. "Then what in the hell is this?"

As Nikolai glimpsed up at the TV screen, he began to feel nauseous.

Passersby reported on a massive explosion that rocked the countryside of this tiny Latvian village. A vehicle drove off the bridge in what authorities suspect as a drunken accident. However, no bodies were found as emergency crews dug through the charred remains yesterday. Anyone with knowledge of this event or those involved are asked to report to their local authorities immediately.

Nikolai could feel the overpowering sense of anger run throughout his entire body. He felt as if his head was about to explode.

"How could this be?" he questioned to himself. "How could they have possibly made it out of that vehicle alive? The crash alone should have killed them."

At that moment, Nikolai began to realize that he may have made the most critical mistake of his life. He'd never walked away from a target without confirming the death. But this time he had. Crashing down a high cliff, he just knew they were dead and that one slip up may have cost him dearly.

"Now you know," the director said as he turned the television off. "The President is not happy with you, Nikolai. Neither am I. What in the fuck were you thinking?"

Nikolai, a man of few words, just gazed straight ahead.

"I hope for your sake and Russia's that you can rectify this situation, Nikolai," Volkov continued. "President Petrov is getting prepared to make his move on America. He is preparing to attack. We don't need any loose cannons running around right now! You understand?"

Nikolai couldn't look the director in the eyes without wanting to jump across that desk and choke him.

"I said, do you understand!?" the director continued loudly.

"I understand," Nikolai replied in his sharp Russian voice as he stood over the desk, desiring to kill director Volkov for speaking to him in that way.

"Good," the director replied. "If you fail again, you can expect a visit from the Russian President himself."

Nikolai's eyes remained glued to the director's. He didn't know who he felt the most contempt for, his enemies or those in charge. Nikolai hated politicians. On the one hand, he felt as if he was wasting his time in that office. He wanted to get back out in the field as soon as possible and as far from the Moscow elite as he could.

The other part of him believed that perhaps the director was right. Nikolai had failed. His entire sense of worth relied on his skills as an assassin. If he couldn't do it right, then maybe he didn't deserve to be there. Of course, he wasn't going to admit that to anyone.

"You are dismissed," Director Volkov told him. "We will not have this conversation again, Nikolai. You either return successfully this time or don't return at all. Now get the fuck out of my office!"

Nikolai squeezed his fists as hard as he could as he stepped toward the office door, slamming it behind him. He didn't know what to feel.

⋦

Along a highway ten kilometers outside of Moscow, the car cruised at eighty-five kilometers per hour as Roger and Captain Price raced in the direction of the Russian Capital.

Earlier that morning, they'd jumped from a British MH-47 Chinook Helicopter into the outskirts of a forest just over the Russian border from Estonia. With the whole of the FSB now aware of them, using commercial travel was simply not an option.

With an old Soviet Moskvitch that had been discreetly left for them in a remote car park a kilometer from the landing zone, the men directed themselves toward the FSB Headquarters building in downtown Moscow.

A *half-hour later*, as they donned their disguises and caps and placed their handguns into the fanny packs around their waists, they crossed over the Moscow City limits. The entire city was bustling with swarms of people heading for Moscow's Red Square, where the Russian President was getting ready to observe his country's annual Victory Day Parade. The duo had hoped that the excess of people traveling to Moscow to watch the event would make it that much easier for them to blend in.

It was an occasion that the President used to showcase Russia's best and newest military and nuclear weapons. But the men weren't there to watch any parade. They were there to track a target. They had gotten a tip-off on a meeting that Nikolai had that day at the Headquarters of the FSB. The tip came from an unnamed associate of Mister Chernoff, a man who was an active FSB Officer.

He wasn't a double agent, but merely a man who'd grown weary of his country's direction and wished to stop a disaster from happening. He didn't see it as treason but working for the greater good.

There were many Russian agents and government officials who were afraid for the Russian people and what would become of them in case of war. They feared President Petrov's quick temper. They were scared of what a nuclear war would do to their own country. And they were afraid for their families, and rightly so.

Then, there was the other side, the one Nikolai belonged to, who wanted war with America, no matter the cost. It was a dividing line. But, regardless of what anyone believed, they couldn't stop it. Petrov had far too many Russian nationalists on his side.

Neither Roger nor Captain Price wanted to trust the man. But, at that point, it was the only lead they had. They slowly drove past the downtown festivities, headed for the Lubyanka Building, FSB Headquarters, about a kilometer away. As they made their way to the edge of the street across from a bus stop, Roger put the vehicle in park.

"Here we are," he said.

As the pair reached the street corner across from the FSB Headquarters building, they left the car by the side of the curb. The men stooped on the bus stop bench and waited. Their eyes trained directly on the building's entrance as downtown traffic zoomed past them.

Minutes had gone by while the men sat, steadily waiting as a slew of people who were standing around them got on the bus and pulled away from the bus stop area. All the while, Roger's eyes hadn't deviated from the large door at the front of the complex. He held the tiny photograph of Nikolai in the palm of his hand. As he glanced down at it, as he had numerous times, a man suddenly appeared through the front door of the sizable structure, wearing dark sunglasses, a long black overcoat, and black patent leather shoes. But, the long scar across his face was the most significant.

"You see this guy?" he asked Price. "See his face?"

"Roger that," the Captain answered.

"I think that's him," Roger continued. "Time to make our move."

The men started to scurry through the crowd of people toward the street. As they hopped in, Roger whipped the car into gear, pulling out into the lane three cars behind him. He kept his distance, not wanting to give a hint to their presence. As they trailed behind Nikolai, he rounded the corner and headed down the road that led out of Russia's capital city.

"Where are you leading us, you bastard?" Roger thought to himself.

They maintained a constant speed for five kilometers, traveling with the steady momentum of highway traffic. But then, all of a sudden, Nikolai picked up the pace, veering around highway traffic as he went pedal to the metal at almost one hundred kilometers per hour.

"What the hell?" he uttered. "I think he made us!"

"Who gives a shit?" Price asked. "Don't lose that bloody bastard!"

Roger slammed on the gas, quickly passing every other car on the roadway. But as they got closer to their target, he abruptly changed direction and veered off and into the thick patch of grass of a large meadow at the side of the highway.

"Where the hell is he going now?" Roger asked out loud.

But he wasn't expecting an answer. Neither of them knew what this man was up doing.

"Be careful," Captain Price said. "It could be a trap!"

They followed the tire marks in the grass as Nikolai appeared to be gaining speed on them. But Roger was going as fast as he could, crossing through that field and swerving around trees that dotted the landscape around them.

Suddenly, they found themselves further into the edge of a forest, slowing speed as Roger tried to avoid crashing the vehicle into the brush. He gradually made his way through the wooded area, following the tire impressions as he swung the car left and right.

"Where the fuck is he?" Roger asked. "I don't see 'em!"

"I don't know, mate!" Price yelled as the car jumped a ditch and landed in the middle of a dirt road on the other side of the bush. Tire treads marked the earth on both sides of the way.

"Which direction?" Roger added.

"I have no idea," the Captain answered.

'Fuck!"

They sat quietly, trying to figure out which way to go. Roger hit the accelerator again, abruptly swinging the car to the left. Rear tires spun as they propelled forward, gaining speed once more. As they tore down the roadway, an unwelcome sight came into view in the distance. It was a roadblock. And they knew they had to get around it one way or the other.

"Damn it!" Roger yelled as the car came to a stop one hundred meters from the three vehicles blocking their path.

"I don't think they are police, mate!" Price said. "As far as I know, police don't carry sub-machine guns. What do you want to do?"

"Well," Roger said as he gawked at the men holding Ak-47's. "We can't go around them. There are too many trees everywhere. We'd be too slow on foot. We could back up. But they would just start shooting at us."

"What's the fourth option?" Asked the Captain.

"We go through them!"

"Ok, mate," the Captain replied, snatching his .45 Beretta from his waist and cocking it back. "Why the hell not?"

"Ok," Roger said as he took in a deep breath of air, removing his gun and setting it against the small of his back. "Follow my lead."

Price hid his pistol as they slowly got out of the car, hands held high in the air.

"We give up!" Roger yelled out to the group of armed men. "Don't shoot. We'll come quietly!"

Neither Roger nor Captain Price had any doubt that these guys were FSB Officers. It was a big gamble for them to believe that the gunmen would be willing to take them in alive. But as they stood by, as still as statues, the group started to walk toward them.

"Don't you fucking move a muscle!" One of the men shouted in Russian as they inched their way forward.

"My Russian is a little off," Roger whispered to the Captain as they watched the men move toward them. "How's yours?"

"It's a little rusty, to be honest," the Captain replied. "But I believe he said don't move."

"Not moving!" Roger yelled back to them.

As the men got closer and closer, Roger eyeballed them one by one. The four of them kept their AK's pointed ahead by the hip. If they could time it right, Roger believed they could take them down before they had time to squeeze the trigger.

"Ready partner?" Roger asked. "You get the two on the right. I got these."

"Roger that," Price mumbled.

As the armed men approached their positions, Roger and Price got ready to act. Two men neared Captain Price's location. The other two were on Roger's. They kept their hands up as their hands were taken and drawn down behind their bodies.

But as Roger caught the sound of the handcuffs unclipping, Almost at once, they each snatched the loaded handguns from their pants and quickly let off two shots from the hip, four bodies dropping to the ground on top of one another.

"Bloody hell," the Captain said. "I can't believe that worked!"

Roger stood over the bodies, squeezing the trigger and sending a second shot into each of their torsos.

"Let's search 'em," Roger said as he hunched over the two dead men. "Grab weapons, ammo, and whatever else you can find!"

Reaching into one of their front pockets, Roger retrieved an ID badge and held it up to his face.

"These guys were FSB," Roger said, showing the Captain the man's identification. "There's no doubt about it."

"This was a trap all along," Price responded as he slung one of the AK47's to his back. "That asshole lured us here on purpose."

"Yeah," Roger continued, looking over the dead FSB Officers vehicles and down the roadway. "And the slick bastard got away!"

As he finished searching the corpses, Roger tossed the AK into the backseat of the Lada. Captain Price continued rummaging through the pockets of the dead FSB Officers. As he reached into one of their pants pockets, he pulled out a folded-up letter.

"Chris, I may have found something over here," he said.

"What is it?" Roger asked as he walked to where Price crouched on the ground.

"It's an official correspondence from the Director of the FSB," he said. "My Russian is a little off. But from what I gather, he is ordering them to report to Mount Yamantau once the job is complete. It looks like they did anticipate us showing up."

"Mount Yamantau?" Asked Roger. "Could that be the same place that Andrei told us about before he killed him?"

"That's what I was thinking," Captain Price answered.

"I need to report this up," Roger added. "We need to get satellite images of the terrain, so we know what we're working with."

"I can get that from Agent Holloway," said the Captain. "It'll be much quicker that way."

"Good," replied, snatching the letter from the Captain, folding it up and placing it into his back pocket.

He knew they were on borrowed time. If those agents didn't report in, there was little doubt that the area would be flooded with officers very soon.

"Let's get the hell out of here," he told Price. "Moscow is only minutes away. I don't want to be around here when they send reinforcements!"

"Roger that."

CHAPTER 26

"THE GROUNDWORK IS almost complete, Mister President," the Russian Chief of staff said as he walked through the office door and stood over Petrov's desk.

The Russian President sat still, glaring over Chernov with intensity. He slammed two glasses onto his desk table, pouring a shot sized bit of Vodka into each one.

"Please, sit Ivan," Petrov said.

The President kept his eyes glued to Chernov as he took his seat, eyeing him as if he was angry at something. Petrov grasped the glass of Vodka in front of him and drank it with a single gulp while his Chief of staff followed suit.

"Let me ask you something, Ivan," the President said.

Chernov only nodded his head.

"Do you agree with what we are doing?" Petrov asked. "The goal we are trying to accomplish? Are you on my side?"

The Chief of staff thought about his answer for a second. But it was too long for the Russian President.

"What's the problem?" Petrov continued as his voice began to get heavier. "Are my reasons not clear enough for you, Ivan? Do you not understand that the United States has held us back for years? There's been nothing but sanction after sanction as America spouts to other nations about disarming their nuclear weapons! It's hypocritical! Do you not see that?"

"No, sir," Chernov answered. "It's not that. I am just concerned about retaliatory strikes. I am concerned for the Russian people, sir. That is all."

"That's all?" President Petrov continued while springing from his chair and getting into Chernov's face. "Let me tell you something. It's about loyalty, Ivan. Plain and simple! If you are not with me, you are against me! You understand me now?"

"Yes, Mister President," Chernov replied, quivering in his seat.

The Russian President had appeared to be losing his mind for a while. Everyone in his cabinet could see it. But nobody would speak about it for fear of what would happen to them if they did.

"Good!" President Petrov shouted in anger. "Now, get the hell out of here before I break your jaw just for the god damned hell of it!"

The Russian Chief of staff hastily rushed through the President's door and out into the hallway. He was fearful of what Petrov was becoming, and for the future of Russia. But, he would have to be scared in silence. Everything that happened in Russia always got back to Petrov. It wouldn't be the first time he'd made someone disappear.

President Petrov reached into his desk drawer and pulled out a large picture frame with an old, Polaroid image inside. As he glanced at it, he kissed the top and set its bottom down on his desktop.

"Rest in peace, comrade," Petrov mumbled to himself in Russian.

It was a picture of his old KGB boss, Mikhail Belsky, who'd died in a suicide bomb attack in Chechnya during the Second Chechen War in 2005. The blast had torn his body entirely in two, sending pieces of him flying in all directions.

"You always understood," Petrov continued, gazing down at the photo of the man posing on a mountain top in Nepal. "When nobody else did, it was always you. See you on the other side, comrade. It's too bad you didn't live to see me fulfill the promise I made."

Petrov poured himself more Vodka and raised the glass to eye level.

"To triumph!" he said, as he toasted to his dead friend. "Long live mother, Russia!"

Petrov tilted his head and swallowed the half a glass, slamming it back onto the table as his door suddenly came open.

"Were you talking to someone, Mister President?"

Senior Presidential Security Agent, Aleksandr Gorky asked as he stood in the doorway, decked out in a black suit and tie with matching shoes. "I don't want to intrude, sir."

"No," Petrov replied, slipping the frame back into the wooden drawer. "Come in, Agent Gorky. I was just reading over some notes."

The Russian President never wanted his people to see the emotional side of him, what little there was. To him, it represented weakness and vulnerability. And he couldn't show instability to the world.

"Thank you, sir," Agent Gorky said as he stepped in front of the President's desk. "The helicopter is ready whenever you are, sir. She's fueled up, guns checked, ready for the long flight, Mister President."

"Very well," President Petrov replied, snatching his briefcase from the white, tile floor. "Let's go, then."

The President locked his office door and followed Agent Gorky through the long corridor. They marched out to the helipad located in the center of the residence grounds as four other security agents accompanied closely behind them.

One agent held the helicopter door open as two soldiers proudly held their salutes. His staff already inside, President Petrov made his way up the short steps to the luxurious brown leather seating that sat adjacent to the shiny wooden presidential desk that extended out from the side.

The door to the chopper was secured, and they lifted off, soaring high above the skyline of downtown Moscow.

The Russian President sat in his chair, staring through the window at the city below as Defense Minister, Sergei Zorkin took a seat beside him.

The Defense Minister was in charge of GRU, the largest foreign intelligence agency in Russia that also commanded Russian special forces, the Spetsnaz.

"Is our plan working?" President Petrov softly asked Sergei.

"Yes, Mister President," he replied. "We have people on it as we speak."

The Russian President had a secret that he didn't want the rest of his administration to learn about. At least not until it was close to coming to fruition. He'd hidden it from everyone, even his closest advisors. Petrov couldn't get the old days out of his head. He remembered a time when he was proud of his country, proud of the power it represented. One bold action could restore his nation's honor. America would no longer be the world power it once was. All he needed was one more decisive chess move and it would be check mate.

He'd remembered how the Russian people had suffered following the Soviet Union's decline. He intended to keep the pledge he'd made to his old friend so long ago.

"Good," President Petrov said. "That's good, Sergei. We have them right where we want them."

"Yes, Mister President," the Defense Minister answered. "They won't even see it coming."

The President nodded his head as the two settled back into their cushy seats while the helicopter raced across the vast Russian wilderness below. Nobody said much on the ride to Mount Yamatau. But the tense atmosphere pretty much said anything anyone needed to know.

Some of them respected Petrov. Some simply coincided with him out of fear. But, he didn't care either way. To him, power was power, no matter how it was achieved.

∽

The chopper began to reduce altitude and hover over the helipad as the evening sun started to go down. The Russian President had an entourage expecting him. As the wheels met the deck and the helicopter door dropped to the ground, Petrov and his security agents descended down. Awaiting his arrival was the FSB Director, the commander of the secret installation, Colonel Bortnik, and various other installation officers.

The Colonel strolled toward Petrov, snapping a swift salute as the President returned it.

"Welcome, Mister President," Bortnik said. "We are honored that you chose to inspect the installation in person, sir."

"Good, Colonel," Petrov replied, giving him a firm handshake. "I assume everything is in order?"

"Yes, sir," Bortnik added. "If you'd follow me, Mister President. I will show you myself."

"Excellent, Colonel. Please, lead the way."

The commander escorted the Russian President and the rest in attendance down a long, metal walkway with metal railings that rose high above the ground over the underground missile silos. The silos had been intentionally left open to show President Petrov the huge nuclear-tipped missiles.

"Here we are, Mister President," said the Colonel. "As you can see, sir, four missiles all armed with the latest in Russian nuclear technology and engineering."

"That is just perfect," Petrov responded. "Excellent work, Colonel."

"Thank you, sir," the Colonel stuttered as his nervousness turned to a sigh of relief. That means a great deal coming from you."

The Colonel's reaction was a mixture of duty and fear. He was terrified of what would happen if they hadn't met the President's deadline.

"Thank you, Colonel," Petrov said. "Now, if you would kindly follow me."

"Yes, Mister President," the Colonel replied as he stood at attention, bringing his stiff hand back up to his brow. "Thank you, sir!"

Colonel Bortnik followed the President as he approached Director Volkov, who'd been standing behind him. Defense Minister Zorkin also listened in on the short exchange.

"Come," said Petrov. "We have much to discuss. You too, Sergei."

The three of them followed the Russian President to an unoccupied room in the center of the missile complex. His presidential security stood by the door, sub machine-guns held to their sides as Petrov and company entered the room.

"Have a seat," Petrov said to them as he leaned, both hands firmly placed against the large conference table in the center of the room.

The men knew why they were there. It wasn't a question of why, but when their plans would come to light.

"Listen," the President continued. "Our friends in Syria have delivered the goods. The package is on its way as we speak. It's been in transit for a couple of weeks, now. America will not take us as fools for much longer!"

They all just nodded their heads.

"Nobody, but those in this room will know about this," he added. "If it leaks, there will be hell to pay! Do you understand me? We cannot afford for western intelligence agencies to get wind of this! Got it?"

"Yes, Mister President," they all echoed.

"Good," the President replied. "The shipment is due to arrive any day now. Our man in the US will pick it up and load it onto a moving van. From there, it is out of our hands. Let's just hope he doesn't somehow fuck it up!"

"Yes, sir!"

"Remember, Colonel, your responsibility is simply a distraction," Petrov added. "Everything else will fall into place. Or, should I say, their heads."

"Got it, Mister President."

Suddenly, Director Volkov's cell phone began to ring in his coat pocket. He reached in and silenced the noise.

"Are you going to answer that?" Petrov asked.

"I don't want to interrupt our meeting, Mister President."

"Just answer the damn phone," the President replied. "It may be important!"

"Sir," Volkov said as he stepped out of the room for a bit.

"This better be fucking important," he said, as he brought the phone to his ear. "I'm in a meeting with the President right now!"

"It is, director," the FSB Agent on the other end said. "They're dead, sir. All of them!

"What are you talking about, Alex?"

"Those men," he answered. "The targets, sir. It appears they escaped, and four of our agents are confirmed deceased!"

"Damn it!" The director yelled. "Where in the hell is Nikolai?"

"I don't know where he is, sir. I can't reach him by phone. Either his phone is turned off, or he's just not answering."

"Well, find him!" Volkov shouted. "Tell him to contact me as soon as possible!"

"Yes, sir!" the agent answered.

"Fuck!" Volkov yelled to himself as he put the phone back into his pocket. "That's just what I need right now!"

The director turned around and grabbed the doorknob, entering the room as President Petrov glimpsed up at him, noticing the bewildered look on the director's face. He realized that he would have to inform the Russian President. If he found out on his own, there would be hell to pay.

"What's the problem?" Asked President Petrov.

The director leaned against the table, shaking his head in disgust.

"Some of my agents have just been killed," he said. "Both targets escaped. This is getting out of hand now."

"Out of hand?" Petrov said. "That's what you call it? Forget about arresting them. I want those assholes dead! I don't give a damn how you do it. I don't care if you have to fucking blow up an entire city block to get them. Get it done, or that will be the least of your worries!"

The director lowered his head. He didn't really know what to say to President Petrov. But, he felt his control slowly slipping away.

"Yes, Mister President," he said.

Deep down, he wasn't that certain. To him it felt like the Soviet Union all over again. But that's precisely what the Russian President wanted. And he would stop at nothing to achieve it. Director Volkov had no choice but to follow his President, or he and his family would never be seen again.

The director glanced up at the President, wanting to give the impression that everything was ok. But Volkov knew it wasn't. He'd imagined that it would only be a matter of time before Petrov imploded on everyone around him. The only thing Volkov could do to keep the Russian President's trust and save face was to carry out his orders.

"Ok, gentleman," Petrov continued as Director Volkov faked a smile. "Now that we got that out of the way. May we all have a celebratory toast once this is all over!"

"To victory!" Zorkin shouted.

CHAPTER 27

IN THE AIR

THE C-130K CLIMBED high and fast over Russian airspace, high enough to only see clouds underneath them. The aircraft was transporting the team to their mission objective at one of Russia's secret ICBM bases in the vast wilderness of the country.

Hours earlier, Roger had stood to the side, waiting as two SAS troops followed Captain Price out to the roof of the tall Headquarters Building of the 22nd SAS Regiment at Stirling Lines.

In the center of the rooftop stood a blue, unmarked, plain-looking helicopter that could have passed for a civilian aircraft. It was one of many disguised choppers that the SAS had used in operations all over the world. Without giving a clue to who the helicopter was transporting, it gave them the capacity to fly to any location incognito. But today's mission was to get them to the British Army airfield in a rush. They had a plane to catch. British intel-

ligence had been surveilling this mysterious mountain base
using satellite imagery. Now, they were going to find out
exactly what it contained.

Roger stood against the low wall at the edge of the
rooftop as the Captain approached.

"These are our new team members, Chris," Price said.

"This chap right here is Sergeant Bailey. And that
funny looking chap over there is Staff Sergeant Dixon."

"Good to meet you guys."

"Likewise," Dixon returned.

Now, the team readied themselves as the snow-capped
mountain peaks came into view under the dense clouds
that surrounded them.

"One minute!" the pilot said into the mic.

"Roger that," Roger replied into his earpiece.
"One minute!"

The back ramp of the plane began to drop, and each
man, parachute on his back and gear hanging from his
front, positioned his body to run for it. They pulled their
night vision goggles over their heads as they got ready to
make a flying leap.

As the aircraft reached the mark and the red light
turned to green, each man, one by one, leaped from the
back opening. Roger monitored their altitude on the
altimeter attached to his arm as they soared their way
through the clouds.

"This shit never gets old!" Roger shouted to Price as he
and the rest of the men sailed to him, their arms and legs
extended above their heads.

"Right, mate! Takes my breath away every single time! Only crazy men jump from a perfectly good airplane!"

"Ha, ha!"

The team parted from one another, diving straight toward the ground at high speed. A nighttime HALO jump was precarious. But it's one they'd each done many times before.

Reaching five thousand feet, Roger yanked his chute open and began steering it toward the designated landing zone, only a few kilometers from the site as the others followed behind him. The earth came up fast, and Roger rolled his body as his feet hit the dirt, the remainder of the team landing a short distance away.

"Good luck, guys," said the pilot.

Roger unsnapped the parachute rig from his body and bent on one knee, examining the terrain on the satellite image under his green-tinted flashlight.

"Which way, Chris?" Captain Price asked.

"West," said Roger, pointing to a spot on the map. "We follow this direction around the curve up ahead to the gate. It should be roughly five kilometers."

Roger and the rest of the team dropped the rucksacks from the front of their bodies. They strapped them to their backs, rifles clipped to the front of their tactical vests.

"All right, men," Roger said. "We have a little hump ahead. Let's move."

Under cover of night, the team hiked over the rocky and hilly ground toward the end of the mountain road that led into the only entry to the secret base. Not able to gain access from either side, the single direction they could go was ahead.

Roger stretched his body across the dirt, peeping through the scope of his sniper rifle as the others got into position around him just off the main road. Captain Price retrieved his binoculars from his vest and slid up next to Roger.

"I got two guards at the gate entrance," Roger said. "Two more in each of the front towers."

"I see 'em," the Captain replied.

"I can't see a damn thing past that," Roger added. "The place is too big. We need to get in there."

Suddenly, the men heard a rumble coming from behind them.

"Hug the dirt!" he continued. "Someone's coming!"

As the team planted their bodies against the ground, they spotted a military transport truck move past them toward the base entrance. The vehicle passed, and they popped their heads up to get a look.

Roger glanced through the scope again as the truck pulled up next to the guardhouse.

"Looks like they're just transporting troops," he said, waiting for them to pass through the guard post.

He watched as the front gate guard waved them through the checkpoint.

"OK, they're gone," Roger said. "We have to deal with these guards. But we need to leave one breathing. At least until we can question him."

"Roger that," Price replied.

"Bailey, Dixon," Roger continued. "You two stay back here and stop anyone who might surprise us. Call if you need help."

"Will do," Bailey answered.

Roger and Price pushed in closer to the entrance to the base, holding three hundred meters shy of the gate. Lowering themselves to the ground, Roger looked through the scope again.

The Captain removed the suppressed L115A3 sniper rifle from his back and unfolded the bipod, bringing the butt of the weapon firmly into his shoulder.

"Ready when you are, mate," he said.

"I'll take the one on the left, you get right," said Roger.

"Roger that."

As Roger rested the tip of his finger on the trigger, he settled the crosshairs center mass of the guard's chest, running through his tactical breathing. He squeezed a round off, and the Captain followed just a millisecond after the first shot, both guards falling to the floor of the guard towers.

Roger kept the weapon trained on the entry. One of the gate guards, who'd obviously heard one of them fall, rushed out of the guardhouse toward the tower ladder.

"Chris?" Price bellowed.

"I got 'em," he answered.

Roger shifted his body left and caught the guard's head as he moved toward the tower. Just before he'd had a chance to grab the ladder, Roger sent a 7.62 bullet flying into the man's dome, his head nearly splitting apart as he hit the dirt.

The remaining guard had seen his friend fall and ran to see what had happened to him.

"Let's get the bastard before he sounds the alarm!" Roger yelled.

He and Price quickly darted for the gate. As they came around the guard shack, Roger rushed the soldier, snatching him by his uniform and yanking his AK to the ground.

"You're coming with us," Roger said.

He pulled the soldier by his collar to the inside of the building as Captain Price hid the other's body. Roger turned the inside light off.

"We have some questions to ask you," Roger said to the man. "Either you cooperate, or you end up like your friends."

"I'm a dead man if I talk!" The soldier said in broken English.

"Would you rather die sooner or later?"

Roger shoved the man into the desk chair, removing his handgun from its holster and pressing it to his head.

"I can just kill you right now if you'd like." Roger said.

"Please!" The soldier yelled. "I have a family!"

"This is your last chance!" Roger said as he pointed put his finger over the pistol trigger. "Talk, or die!"

"OK!" The man said. OK, I'll talk!"

Captain Price rounded the corner and joined Roger.

"Who is in charge of this installation?" Asked Roger.

"You better answer him, mate," Price said casually as

he leaned his body on the doorway. "This man is unstable when he's angry."

"I'll ask you one last time," Roger continued. "Tell us who is in charge here, or you get a bullet to the head."

"OK, fine!" He shouted. "It's Colonel Bortnik. Colonel Bortnik's the one in charge!"

"See? "asked Roger. "That wasn't so hard, was it?"

The Captain moved in closer to Roger so they could prevent the soldier from running out.

"Now," Roger added. "Where can I find this Colonel Bortnik character?"

"Down there," the soldier said, pointing down the street. "He's inside that big building over there. That is his office."

Well," Roger said as he looked over at the Captain. "Thanks for your cooperation."

Roger pointed his gun right at the soldier's head.

"I thought-you were going-to let me go," he stuttered.

"I lied."

Roger squeezed the trigger on his Sig Sauer handgun, sending a bullet into the head of the soldier, blowing blood back onto the wall and causing him to slump to the side of his chair.

"Let's go," Roger told Price. "We need to get this guy and figure out what is going on in this place."

"Watch our backs, boys," Price said into his earpiece. "We're heading inside."

The two men transferred the body of the soldier to the back of the building. They made their way down the fence line, out of the glare of the post lights that ran down the single stretch of road. For four hundred meters, they moved cautiously toward a patch of trees that filled the edge of the way across from the Base headquarters building.

"What do you think, Captain?" Roger asked as they remained low to the ground.

"Well," Price answered. "We can't bust in there without knowing how many soldiers are present. But we need to hurry before anyone realizes there is nobody guarding the gate. After that, we'll be surrounded."

The men faced a dilemma. If they rushed in with a large number of Russian Soldiers inside, they'd risk a base-wide alert. If the dead bodies were spotted, they'd risk a base-wide alert. They'd both been in impossible predicaments before. They didn't figure this time to be any different. But the longer they remained there, the bigger the chance of them being found out.

But then, there appeared a stroke of good fortune. A high-ranking Russian officer stepped out from the building door and lit a cigarette.

"Captain, do you know Russian Army rank structure?"

"Well enough," Price replied as he glanced through the binoculars. "Three stars between four red lines? Looks like a Colonel to me. And it says Bortnik on the name tag."

"Let's go snatch this asshole before anyone else shows up," said Roger.

The men crept along the side of the parked vehicles to the front of the building to give them more cover. As they reached the front walk, not twenty meters from the

Colonel, Roger rushed in and grabbed him, causing the man to lose his cigarette.

"What the fuck?" the Colonel asked in Russian. "Who are you?"

Captain Price, being the only of the two who knew Russian, got into the Colonel's face.

"Give us your car keys!" Price said in Russian. "Or we kill you right here!"

The Colonel reached into his uniform pocket and dangled his keys in front of them. Price snatched them from his finger.

"My men will kill you before you ever get out of here!" He said.

"I swear to God," said Price. "If you make a sound, we will kill you. Now move!"

Roger gripped the Colonel's arms behind his back, drawing his sidearm from its holster and shoving him forward while Price hit the button on his keyless entry.

"There we are," he said, pointing to a black Mercedes parked in the front of the building entrance.

Price unlocked the trunk, and Roger hurled him in there and slammed it shut.

"Come on, "said Roger. "We need to hurry before they notice he's missing!"

But as they backed the car out in haste, two Russian soldiers opened the door and spotted the men in the front seat of the Colonel's vehicle.

"Go!" Captain Price yelled. "Get us out of here!"

Roger raced for the outside of the base to pick up the other two.

"Hurry, get in!" Roger shouted.

New teammates Bailey and Dixon dove into the backseat as Roger pushed the accelerator.

The Russian soldiers had set off the alarm, and the base lit up like a Christmas tree as the loud piercing alarm sounded against the surrounding mountains.

A Russian military jeep had taken off after them and was closing in fast.

'Shoot those bastards!" Roger shouted.

Price rolled his window all the way down and began firing his rifle at the oncoming Jeep.

"Shoot the tires!"

The.Captain shot at the front tire, watching the jeep flip over as it rolled down a steep hill. Suddenly, the entire base was bustling. Men were no doubt headed their way.

"We need to lose them!" Price shouted as Roger steered off the road and into a large ditch, driving that Mercedes as fast as he possibly could.

"I don't know if she can handle this!" Roger said.

"We don't have much choice!" Price replied. "We need to lose this car!"

Just then, Roger spotted an old Jeep sitting in front of a deserted auto shop.

"I have an idea," he said.

Roger slammed on the brakes, skidding to the side.

"Can you hotwire it?" he asked the Captain.

"I've done it from time to time."

"Good," he continued. "Let's go!"

Price entered the cab of the Jeep. Sparks began to fly at him as he fooled around with the ignition wiring. *Minutes had gone by* as the team waited.

"Hurry up!" Roger said.

"Almost got it!" He answered.

Suddenly the engine fired up, and Roger grabbed the Colonel from the trunk, tossing him into the back of the Jeep.

"Let's get the hell out of this place!" He added as they sprang into the vehicle.

Roger tore through the parking lot, leaving the Mercedes behind them at the side of the road just in time to see a Russian Helicopter buzzing overhead where the Mercedes sat.

"Oh my God," said Roger. "We dodged a bullet on that one!"

Bailey and Dixon held Colonel Bortnik between them, not allowing him to budge an inch.

"Where are you taking me?" the Colonel asked.

"That's the least of your concern right now, Colonel," Roger told him.

They rode for a few more kilometers, and Roger pulled off to the side of the road.

Captain Price hopped out of the Jeep and grabbed the Colonel, lifting him over his shoulder and carrying him to the wood line. Price dropped him against a tree and began tying his arms behind it with a heavy rope.

"Now, Colonel Bortnik," Roger said as he crouched on

the ground in front of him, pistol in his hand. "You are going to answer our questions. Or, we will just leave your body here for the animals to feed on. It's your choice!"

"What do you want to know?"

"Shit," Roger replied. "I didn't think you spoke English."

"I do," Bortnik answered. "I am an educated man."

"So," Roger said. "As an educated man, you know you are in no position to piss me off!"

The Colonel didn't speak a word.

"So," Roger continued. "What is the Russian President's plan here? To nuke the US coast?"

Bortnik smiled up at Roger, then spit on his boots.

"You Americans are so simple-minded," he said. "You have to think bigger. You are here looking for something, while what you should be after is already on its way!"

"What the hell are you talking about?"

"It fits in a normal-sized container, something you can put into a duffel bag."

"Where?" Roger asked. "Where is it going?"

"Where do you think?" Bortnik asked maliciously.

Roger cocked the slide of his gun back and pressed it to the Colonel's left eye.

"Where, damn it? Where is it heading?"

"I guess you'll have to watch CNN to find out!" Bortnik shouted. "You will see soon enough!"

Roger's eyes suddenly saw red as he thrust the gun harder into the Colonel's eye.

"Now, kill me," the Colonel continued. "I'm already dead anyway!"

Roger pushed that gun into Bortnik's face as hard as he could, pressing the trigger as bright red blood splat against the tree behind him.

Roger and the Captain's eyes met, full of worry and angst.

"Shit," Roger said. "We were played. It was a fucking diversion!"

"It seems so," Price replied. "Come on, boys. Let's get out of here."

They left the Colonel's body tied to the tree and rushed for the Jeep.

"I need to contact HQ," Roger added "We have to hurry. I have a terrible feeling about this!"

CHAPTER 28

ROGER, CAPTAIN PRICE, and the rest of the team waited in the lobby at CIA Headquarters as Richard Weber sat in on one of his many weekly meetings with the agency's Director. Roger had gotten prior authorization from both the British and American Government to bring the SAS members along.

The agency had done that from time to time, loaned out agents and Special Operators to their allies in the UK, and vice versa. But that was something that the general public was never privy to.

Sitting in an office building wasn't the way the men had wanted to spend their time. But Weber had asked them to wait for him.

The Russian President, who'd been vilifying the United States regularly, had gone entirely silent. There hadn't been a peep from him in over a week. The United States Government, and especially the American President, had gotten used to Petrov swearing at them weekly. But suddenly, it ceased. Those who knew the Russian President had a reason for concern.

"I don't care!" Director Cabot shouted to Weber as they left his office. "We haven't heard a damn thing from the man in a while! Do we assume that he just changed his mind, just like that?"

"I honestly don't know what to assume, director," Weber replied. "I really don't know!"

"Yeah, well, neither do I. That's why we have operatives in country!"

The team glanced up at the both of them, not really sure of what they were talking about, specifically. But the men knew it had something to do with President Petrov.

"Captain," the Director called out as he glanced over at Price. "I'm glad you guys are on board. What a mess it has been!"

Captain Price shook the Director's hand as he moved toward him.

"Of course, sir," Price said. "Glad to be here. Our interests are quite aligned, Director. We are happy to provide assistance."

"I'm sorry it had to be under such circumstances," the Director added. "It's a disgrace that we still have heads of state behaving like mad children. Children with the power to launch nuclear weapons. A nuclear war cannot be won, so it must never be fought."

"Yes, sir," the Captain replied. "I agree with you, wholeheartedly."

Suddenly, Director Cabot's cell phone began to ring. He reached into his pocket, bringing the phone to his ear.

"Have you heard, sir?" asked the voice on the other side.

"Heard what?"

"Obviously, you haven't heard yet."

"Damn it, Maddie," he said into the phone. "What are you talking about? I don't have time for this. Just spit it out!"

"Sir," he continued. "An explosion has just gone off in the middle of downtown Washington. We think it was nuclear. The number of dead is unknown. But it's bad, sir."

"Holy hell," he uttered.

Director Cabot released his grip on the phone, and it fell hard to the floor.

"Sir?" the man said into the phone. "Sir? Hello? Are you there?"

The Director didn't need to relay this information to the team. They'd already overheard it through the phone by how loud the caller was speaking. By the time Cabot hung up and got into gear, they were already halfway to the parking lot, running at breakneck speed.

They jumped into the four-door Dodge Charger rental car that Roger had picked up in nearby Virginia and sped out of the agency parking lot, breaking every traffic law on the books as he raced out and down the highway closer to Washington DC.

"You better believe this has something to do with Petrov and that other fucking asshole!" He said. "There is no way it doesn't!"

The blast itself was small by nuclear standards. The fallout had been predicted to blow northeast in a steady gust of wind toward Maryland. Still, those within the blast radius stood little chance of survival.

"I agree," Captain Price replied. "But let's get there first. We can worry about that after we help these people!"

"There may not be many people left to help!"

Roger kept his foot to the floor, tearing down the road as they came up to the Interstate exit outside of the capitol. He made an abrupt right turn as they rolled up to a HAZMAT checkpoint at the intersection just past Arlington Cemetery. They could see the black ash and debris falling from the sky, not far away as they rolled halfway down the exit ramp.

"Damn," Roger said. "That's not good."

Roger put the car into park, and all four hopped from the vehicle.

"Roger O'Neil, CIA," he said, flashing his badge to the female African American Army Colonel in charge of the HAZMAT team. "We need to get in here."

Only feet from them, the triage tent was continually being loaded with the dead and severely wounded. Emergency personnel with yellow HAZMAT suits pulled down to their ankles were running in and out of the tent, doing whatever they could. There wasn't much to be done. Many of the exposed were being laid on stretchers. Most seemed to be merely waiting for their turn to die.

"Do you have authorization?" Colonel Myers asked as

Roger, and the team watched in dread as loads of bodies were being carried in. "I can't let you in otherwise."

"Yeah," Roger replied. "The United States fucking Government! That's my authorization!"

The Colonel slipped her way past the team and out through the door of the large tent and began checking over one of the HAZMAT teams outside as they prepared to go through decontamination.

"If you do not have an authorization," she added, "I cannot allow you to enter."

"Fuck it!" Roger said as he fumbled through a stack of HAZMAT suits lying on a tabletop. He snatched four suits and gave one to each of the other team members. "I don't have time for this bureaucratic bullshit!"

"Sir!" she shouted from across the tent as Roger and the men made their way outside. "It is too dangerous. I cannot allow you to pass through!"

"Oh, yeah?" Roger asked as he got into her face." You want to stop me? Then shoot me! Or allow us to pass so we can do our damn jobs. This is way above your pay grade! You want to call the Director? Then call him!"

The Colonel backed away as they pulled the suits up over their heads.

Meanwhile, the downtown DC area was desolate. Dead bodies littered the streets and sidewalks, with not a single breathing person in view. Cars that had been making morning commutes were toppled over. The occupants were frozen in place as if something had flushed all of the air from their bodies.

Buildings and businesses were utterly destroyed, with only a shell of their former selves remaining. The district had been strategically obliterated. The place was eerie and dark. Smoke rose up where structures once stood.

"How could this happen right under our noses?" Roger thought as they remained speechless, looking in horror at the total devastation.

Roger and the team walked tentatively down the roadway, looking and searching for any signs of life in the ash-filled remnants. Ground zero started to become more apparent the further into the destruction they went. The capitol building was completely demolished, except for a single stretch of wall that still stood loosely, as if it would come crashing down at any slight of wind. Every building and structure around them had been burned to a crisp in the intense heat of the explosion.

All of a sudden, a woman came screaming out from a corner of charred rubble, dashing right for the team, her burned arms held in front of her. She was yelling something that they didn't easily understand. The woman had seemed to have lost her sense of reality. She sprinted toward them as if she wasn't going to stop. As she got closer, running as if something was chasing her, she fell face-first immediately in front of Roger.

Roger bent down and turned her over with his gloved hand to check for breathing. But, as he gazed into her bloodshot eyes, seeing white foam spew from her purple lips, he knew she was gone. There was nothing they could do to help her.

"Poor lady never had a chance," Roger said through his mask. "None of these people did."

The team kept marching on, with Bailey and Dixon taking up the rear of the formation.

"They didn't see it coming, sir," Bailey said. "Just going about their everyday lives, not knowing their own fate. Makes me furious!"

"It makes me angry too, Sergeant," Price said. "The only question now is, what are we going to do about it, Roger?"

"The people down here," Roger said. "Congress, the senate, business owners, tourists, monuments, Over two hundred years' worth of history! All gone in a flash! Fuck!"

Suddenly, Roger hit his knees and began pounding the pavement erratically. He screamed at the top of his lungs, his voice slightly muffled through his HAZMAT suit helmet.

"Fuck!" he cried out.

Roger had appeared to be losing the battle with his anger. In a flash, he felt as though he was beginning to lose control, beating the surface of the road as hard as he could.

Captain Price snatched Roger up from the ground by the back of the suit.

"Get a grip, mate!" The Captain said, shoving Roger by his shoulder. "It's a tragedy, unquestionably. But we still have a job to do here! We don't have the luxury of wondering why it happened. Our mission is to eradicate those responsible!"

The Captain touched the front of his helmet to Roger's, looking straight into his eyes.

"We will have vengeance, Roger," he continued. "You better fucking believe that, mate. We will get every single one of the assholes. They will pay in the worst possible way you can imagine. Now, you are in charge here, mate. Just take a deep breath and get yourself together!"

"You're right," Roger replied as he rested his hands on Price's shoulders. "I don't know what the hell came over me."

"It's ok, lad," Price replied. "We're all human. But right now, people need us, whether they know it or not. Let's get on with it, yeah?"

There is something I need to do first," Roger told them.

They followed Roger to the decontamination area, stepping through the station one by one as they were sprayed down from head to toe. They left their suits on the table beside the tent as they made their way back to the Charger. As the rest of the team got into the car, Roger waited, reclining back onto the hood. He had a personal call to make.

"Honey?" he said into the phone. "It's me."

"Roger!" Kate yelled. "My God, we've been so freaking worried about you. I haven't had a good night's sleep in weeks!"

"How are the kids?" he asked, trying to change the subject.

"They are fine. The kids just want to see their dad again."

"I know," he said. "I'm really sorry, babe. I just couldn't risk calling you from where I was. But, listen, I have something to tell you."

"What? Did you hear about that explosion in DC? It's all over the news. It's shocking!"

"Well," he answered. "That's kind of what I need to explain."

"What do you mean?"

"That's where I am," he added.

"What?" Kate asked.

"Don't worry, I am not hurt. But I have some things to finish up down here. I can't really explain it all right now. But just trust that I am fine, ok? Tell Patrick we'll go horseback riding when I get home. It won't be much longer now. I will be home soon. I love you and the kids."

"We love you too, babe," she replied.

"Ok, hun, listen, I have to go. But I'll call you later, ok?"

"Ok," Kate said as she blew a kiss through the phone. "Please be careful!"

"I will, babe," he answered.

Roger hung the phone up and slid it back into the pocket of his tan, khaki trousers. He bounced from the hood and jumped back into the car, turning the key as the V8 Hemi engine began to roar furiously.

"So, Roger," the Captain said. "What's next?"

Roger thought to himself for a brief moment while

staring through the front windshield, his hands gripping the steering wheel tightly as if he was trying to flex his muscles. Who placed the bomb? Was there a secondary target?

"We find out who set it," he said intensely. "And any other targets that might be out there. Then we burn their house to the fucking ground. And anyone who had anything to do with it! They will regret the day they decided to kill innocent people!"

"Now that is the man that I have come to know and respect!" Replied Price. "So, what are we waiting for?"

CHAPTER 29

MIDTOWN, MANHATTAN
NEW YORK CITY

DOWNTOWN MANHATTAN WAS bustling with hordes of businessmen and women going about their noon business, visiting shops, and hurrying down the sidewalk to grab a bite to eat on their lunch breaks.

Double-decker tourist buses were conducting their daily routes, showcasing the city to their many eager patrons, mostly those from out of town.

The roads were filled with flashy cars and taxi cabs picking up the random passenger in a rush to get back to their perspective offices. The walkways were brimming with pedestrians ambling along in both directions. Each had their own place to go.

Subway trains traveled in opposite directions as the sharp sound of rails vibrating underground resonated throughout the streets. It had been a regular, busy New York day for a city of millions. But that day was far from typical.

Over two hundred miles away on Virginia highway 123, Roger was running them back to Langley when he received an urgent call on his cell phone. He put the phone on speaker, setting it upright on the center console.

"O'Neil?" Weber said, sounding like he was out of breath. "O'Neil, we just received an update."

"What is it?" Roger asked, with all eager to hear what Weber had to say.

"We have just uncovered CCTV footage of a yellow moving Van that was traveling in the direction of downtown Washington early this morning, the same general area of the blast. We believe it is the vehicle that was carrying the bomb. We are still trying to determine who rented the truck. But it will almost surely be under a false name."

It seemed that President Petrov had decided against launching a large ICBM but employing a smaller version that could easily fit into a box and be moved around without drawing much attention to it. It was small enough to fit in the trunk of a car but large enough to do significant damage to a city. Not to mention radiation fallout.

"We already know who is responsible," Roger replied. "That's a no-brainer. But we need to find the person who carried it. All of them must be dealt with!"

"There's something else," Weber stated.

"What?"

"We've been exchanging information with the National Security Agency. NSA satellites have located an identical truck speeding up I-95 toward New York City. It is not confirmed yet. But we suspect it to contain a secondary bomb. Currently, it is traveling up the interstate, closing in on Philadelphia. We need to try to intercept before it reaches its location."

"Okay," said Roger.

"But we need to confirm this before engaging. We can't risk killing an innocent person. You aren't even supposed to be operating on US soil. But since this operation began in Russia and landed you back here, we can make an exception. We don't have the time to brief officers from other agencies. Nobody knows this issue like you and your team. But be very careful, O'Neil. We don't want CIA involvement as a headline in the Sunday newspaper. We must remain discreet."

The agency had no definitive proof that the truck was heading for New York. But a city of so many people seemed to be the most likely target.

"So, what do you need from us?" Asked Roger.

"We have a helicopter fueled up and ready to go. There is a Delta team standing by who will provide support. Get back here as soon as you can and get on board. You need to hurry!"

"Roger that!" Replied Roger. "We're on the way!"

Roger pushed that Dodge Charger as fast as it would possibly go, zipping around highway traffic, speeding for CIA Headquarters. Meanwhile, an unmarked CIA helicopter buzzed on the helipad as a team of Delta Force Operators in civilian clothing waited for the team to arrive.

Suddenly, the car came barreling around the corner,

skidding into a hasty parking job as the team snatched their gear and ammo and hurried for the chopper.

"Sergeant First Class Bradford!" the Caucasian, barrel-chested Delta Operator in charge said over the noise of rotors whirling, his four-man team standing beside him.

"Sergeant!" Roger said as he climbed into the open door, the team close behind. "We can do formalities later. We need to get this bird in the air!"

"Roger that!"

Sergeant First Class John Bradford was a ten-year Delta veteran. Being a former Army Ranger, he'd always dreamt of being at the tip of the spear of American operators. Closing on twenty years of distinguished service, Bradford wanted to put off retirement for as long as possible. He enjoyed the job too much.

Each team settled in on opposite rows, balaclavas covering their faces. They assembled, facing one another as the helicopter lifted off from the CIA helipad heading northeast toward the I-95 Highway.

"Glad you guys are on board!" Roger said into his earpiece. "I'm Roger O'Neil, CIA. These guys next to me are all SAS."

"Captain Price!" the Captain shouted. "This is Sergeant's Bailey and Dixon."

"SAS?" Bradford asked. "I've worked with you guys before! A couple of times in Iraq and Afghanistan. And once during a raid on an ISIS compound in Syria. This is my team, Sergeant's Johnson, Manning, Martinez, and Walsh!"

"Nice to see you!" Price shouted. "Too bad it always has to be under these circumstances. But, I'm happy you lads are here!"

The chopper flew fast, following the Highway over Baltimore. Every man was busy doing a gear and weapons check, ensuring everything was in order. Roger removed the Sig Sauer P229 handgun from its holster, cocking it back and inspecting the chamber. Squeezing the trigger and hearing the slide ram forward, he inserted the fifteen round magazine and tapped the bottom hard to make sure it was locked.

As the bird raced in the direction of New York City, Roger suddenly received a radio call.

"Charlie 1-3," Weber said. "This is Charlie 1."

"Go for Charlie 1-3," Roger replied.

"Roger, Charlie 1-3. We have some updated intel. The driver has just exited I-95 onto 495 toward the Lincoln Tunnel. It looks like he's going right for Midtown Manhattan!"

"Shit!" Roger said. "All those people!"

"Exactly, Charlie 1-3. We need you guys to step on it!"

The pilot flew that helicopter as fast as it would go, following the Interstate toward New York. *Fifteen minutes later,* they zipped past the Statue of Liberty to lower Manhattan. Roger yanked the helicopter doors open and unfastened the harness around his body.

It was the middle of a sunny afternoon. The city that never sleeps undoubtedly was alive and hustling on that day. The large projector screens at Time Square were showing footage of the events in DC. People were mortified.

Everyone was glued to the screens as if another 9/11 had taken place. But this was significantly worse. There was no detailed account yet of the number of casualties in the District of Columbia. But it was estimated to be well over ten-thousand, including congress men and women, and diplomats. It was sure to come in a matter of days, or even weeks or more. But a bomb set off in the middle of NYC would cause many more fatalities. The fall out alone from both would ravage people with radiation poison and disease.

One of the most densely populated cities in the world, a detonation anywhere within the New York City limits, would be catastrophic. It was the ideal target for any rogue nation or organization that wanted to deal mass casualties.

"Charlie 1-3," Roger heard over his earpiece. "We've tracked the target to Times Square. He's just parked in front of the ABC News building. We have no ID on the driver yet! We've hacked into local CCTV footage. But his face is concealed behind a black bandana. He has not left the vehicle yet, over."

"Roger that, Charlie 1. We'll be on location in two minutes!"

Roger paused momentarily. He had something burning in his mind.

"Charlie 1," he said again. "What about the President, Vice President, and the rest of them?"

"As far as we know, the Vice President and the rest of

the staff made it into the bunker shortly after the blast. But there were congresspeople inside the capitol building. They didn't make it."

"Damn," continued Roger. "So many innocent people down there."

"Oh, shit!" Weber said suddenly.

"What, Charlie 1?" Roger asked. "What is it?"

"I just realized that President Cash is in the hospital not far from there! You have to stop this man! I'll see about getting the President moved promptly!"

"Damn it," Roger answered. "Roger that, Charlie 1."

Roger hit the side of the seat.

"Fuck!"

"That's not good," Captain Price added.

The helicopter began to dip low just above the skyscrapers of Midtown Manhattan.

"I can't drop you guys up ahead," the pilot said over the radio. "There are too many people down there. We're going to have to drop you off in Bryant Park. It's the only place we can safely hover."

"Roger that," replied Roger. "We'll need to hump it from there."

The chopper started to lower, hovering over the park lawn as Roger tossed the ropes to the bottom. Civilians quickly rallied around and watched curiously, snapping photos as the men slid down both sides to the ground below. They hadn't wanted to panic anyone. But they needed to get to the location quickly. No other means of transport would've sufficed.

"Good luck, boys," the pilot said as he climbed higher into the sky.

"OK, listen," Roger said as they knelt on the ground. "Captain Price, you are with me. The rest of your team holds across the street. Sergeant Bradford, I need two of your team on overwatch. Send your sniper and a spotter to any adjacent building and take up a position facing the square from one of the windows. "Roger," Bradford said.

"Guys," he continued. "Be extremely careful. We've already had one bomb go off today. With any luck and some help from above, we can prevent a second. But we do not want him to see us coming. If he does, this mission will be over!"

"Got it," Price said.

"Try to blend in as much as possible," Roger added. "Don't pull your weapons until you know you need to. We don't need to cause a city-wide uproar just yet. Okay, let's move."

The men began jogging down the street and toward Times Square. While most of them followed Roger down the walk and around the crowd of pedestrians, Sergeant's Manning and Martinez broke away and went in another direction.

A quarter mile away, as they rushed around the buildings, they spotted the yellow moving Van up ahead.

"I've got the target vehicle in view," Roger said into his earpiece as they turned the corner and hurried across the busy intersection.

"Roger that," Charlie 1-3. "Proceed with caution."

"Okay, guys," Roger said. "Let's spread out a little. We don't want to seem obvious."

The Captain followed Roger as the other's went in another direction, trying to blend in with the masses. He and Price took a seat at one of the many tables that filled the center of the walkway just ahead of the Armed Forces Recruiting Center.

"I have eyes on the target," Roger said.

Roger removed his handgun from the concealed holster in his pants and hid it in a folded Newspaper that had been lying on the bistro table.

They stood by, observing as the man appeared to be watching people walk by the Van. Perhaps he'd been waiting for the square to fill with evening shoppers.

"In position," he heard Sergeant Manning say into his radio. "We're in the Hard Rock Cafe across from you, over."

"Roger that," Roger answered.

As Roger glanced back over in the target's direction, he noticed a Hispanic-looking NYPD Officer approaching the Van.

"Shit," he said. "He has company."

"I see 'em," Price replied. "We need to intercept. If he gets agitated, he could detonate the bomb."

"Follow me," Roger said.

Roger held the newspaper under his arm. The pair got up from the table and started to move in the Officer's direction, trying to get to him before he reached the Van.

"What are you guys doing?" Manning asked into the radio.

"Just go with it," Roger answered. "NYPD about to crash the party."

Roger increased his walk to a near run, aiming for the Officer before he could cross the intersection.

"Excuse us, Officer," he said. "Can you come with us, please? We have a pregnant woman over here about to give birth. She's in a bad way."

"What?" the Officer asked. "Where?"

"Come. We'll show you."

The Officer followed the men across the street to the corner in front of the Bubba Gump Shrimp Company.

"Listen, Officer… Sanchez," Roger said as he glanced down at his name tag. "I'm with the CIA."

Roger opened his wallet to show his badge to the policeman.

"We're in the middle of an operation that we can't explain to you. Would you kindly stay away from that section of the road until we give the all-clear?"

Officer Sanchez looked at both of them with a distraught glance. He was speechless.

"And please make sure no other officers get close to that corner."

The Officer just nodded his head and backed away.

"Much obliged," Roger said as he and the Captain made their way back to the other side of the street. "Thanks for cooperating."

Roger had assumed that the target wasn't a suicide

bomber. But he'd been sitting there an awfully long time. It was as if he'd been waiting for something.

"We need to move on him," Roger told Price. "We can't risk another encounter like that."

"I agree," the Captain replied.

The both of them moved tentatively toward the rear of the Van so the driver wouldn't spot them. Roger put his hand inside the newspaper, gripping the pistol grip on his handgun.

"Manning, watch our backs," Roger mumbled.

"I got you covered," Manning replied.

"OK, Captain," Roger added. "I got the driver's side. You take the other. Be extremely cautious. He may have a trigger device in his hand."

Price reached for his pistol and made his way along the side of the Van to the passenger side door as Roger mimicked his action on the other side. As he neared the door, Roger peeked into the window. The target sat, stagnant, his face partially masked.

"Don't fucking move!" Roger said as he pointed his gun at the man's head.

He didn't acknowledge their presence or even look in Roger's direction.

"Roger," Price said, looking down at the target's hands. "We have a dilemma over here!"

Roger glanced down at the man's right hand and noticed his thumb held tightly on a button.

The man stared into Roger's eyes and uttered a chilling phrase.

"You all will die!" He thundered, drawing attention from the groups of people outside.

Roger and Price glimpsed at one another. He bowed his head downward to tell Price something without having to speak.

Abruptly, Captain Price leaped for the trigger device, squeezing it as hard as he could and jerking it from his hand. *At the same time,* Roger had gripped the man around the throat, locking him in place so he couldn't move as Sergeant Bradford and the rest of the team members dashed for their location.

"Death is too good for you, asshole," said Roger. "Instead, you're going to spend the rest of your life isolated, staring at a prison wall!"

Roger dropped him to the sidewalk, putting a knee into his back and placing plastic cuffs around his wrists and ankles so he couldn't move. People from all around began to watch curiously as they tried to figure out what was happening.

"Charlie 1," Roger said into the mic. "The Captain has the detonator. Get a bomb unit over here ASAP to disarm this damn thing! And get them to evacuate the city! We don't need these people close in case something goes wrong!"

"Roger that," said Weber.

"I also need a transport to get this guy back to HQ for interrogation."

"Got it, Charlie 1-3. Stand by."

"Don't worry, partner!" he shouted to Price. "A bomb unit is on the way!"

"I hope they hurry. I can't bloody hold this thing forever!"

"Just don't fucking let go!"

"No, shit!" Price replied. "Evacuate New York City? Millions? That'll be problematic!"

"I know!"

Roger pinned the target's body to the ground as the other men stood above them. Suddenly, a loud PA speaker began to part the crowd as NYPD cruisers started to fill the streets surrounding the truck.

"You Americans are so stupid," the man said from underneath Roger's leg. "You are so fucking predictable."

"What?" Roger asked, grabbing his chin and yanking his head back. "What are you talking about, you bastard?"

"Your leader," he said. "You can't protect him! Our plan has already been set in motion. You won't stop us! The man they sent before missed. But we will not!"

"How do you know where the President is?" Asked Roger.

"We know everything," the man answered.

Roger released his head to the blacktop with a snap, bloodying his nose as he looked up at Sergeant Bradford.

"Oh shit," he said.

At that instant, Roger had understood just how vulnerable they and their President were.

"Watch him until they load his ass up," He told Bradford. "Don't let the asshole budge an inch. And have one of your men relieve Captain Price until the bomb unit arrives to disarm this damn thing. We have to go now!"

"Roger that, CIA," the Sergeant answered.

CHAPTER 30

NEW YORK

THE BOMB COULDN'T have been left in a more detrimental location. New York City streets were notorious for being hectic. It wasn't the ideal place to be able to keep things secret. Then again, it's precisely why the location had been chosen as a target.

But the team needed to keep this information on a need to know basis. If the general public got wind of what was in that moving truck, there would be a city-wide panic on their hands.

But at the same time, some had already started to figure it out. After the bomb that had gone off in Washington, the entire nation was glued to CNN and Fox News. Yet for all of the commentary coming from American reporters and politicians, Russia remained silent. There wasn't even so much as a claim arising from the mouth of the Russian President. Then again, there didn't need to be. People, and especially Roger's team, were profoundly aware of Petrov's

stance on America. Perhaps he'd been attempting to pro-
voke a war with the US all along.

US citizens everywhere were in a state of turbulence.
People on the New York City streets had begun to get
out of their cars. They were shouting at NYPD Officers
who were sending traffic away from the perimeter of city
blocks. Most were demanding to know why they were
being diverted. It was complete chaos in downtown Manhattan. Millions of people all hit the street at once, causing
enormous traffic jams on both sides of the borough. Cars
were at a standstill.

The trigger man had just been handcuffed and tossed
into an unmarked agency vehicle for transport back to
Langley. The man was a terrorist. He wasn't headed to an
ordinary jail. Where he was going, nobody would ever hear
from him again. But the agency needed to interrogate him
first, for as long as it possibly took.

Roger and Price began to sprint down the Manhattan
sidewalk, hoping they could make it to the President's
location in time. But President Cash was blocks away
from them. Counting the jam-packed traffic and the covered walkways, running in a direct line was proving to be
impossible.

"Bailey, Dixon," Roger said into the earpiece. "You
guys stay and assist the Delta Team. Price and I will
handle this!"

"Roger that!"

He and the Captain tore through a retreating crowd
down West 46th Street, heading in the direction of New

York University Hospital. But no matter how fast of runners they were, Roger knew it would never be quick enough.

"Damn it! We need to get a car!" he shouted, reducing his sprint to an abrupt halt.

"What do you suggest?" Price asked.

Roger looked around the area a bit.

"There!" he said, pointing to a police cruiser sitting nearby, blue lights flashing at the side of the street. "Come on!"

Roger knew the sirens would be the one thing they might need to get through New York City traffic. Cars were at a delay just outside of the cordoned-off area.

"Sorry, officer!" Roger said to the Police Sergeant guarding a corner of the intersection. "We need your car!"

The men didn't wait for the officer's reply. Instead, they jumped into the police car, flipping the siren switch, and scrambled down the street as fast as they could go.

But they didn't make it half a block before running into a traffic jam.

"Damn it!" Roger said.

Cars were packed on both sides of the road as New York City Police Officers tried to direct them away from the location of the bomb.

"Hold on, Captain!" Roger yelled. "We're taking the scenic route!"

Roger jerked the steering wheel to the right, bouncing the curb and racing down the sidewalk, blaring the horn as loads of people dived into city shops that dotted the downtown walkway.

"Charlie 1," Roger said into his mic. "The President is in trouble! We are heading to him right now! We have a team standing by at the location of the target vehicle. Are they on the way?"

"Roger that, Charlie 1-3," replied Weber. "The bomb squad is only a few blocks from the target location!"

"Good. We'll end this! Just focus on getting rid of that damn bomb!"

"We will, Charlie 1. God speed and good luck!"

Roger steered the vehicle one way, then the other to avoid hitting pedestrians in his path.

"Get out of the bloody way!" Price shouted out of the window as they drove right over cafe tables and chairs, tossing them, broken to the side of the street. "Move!"

People screamed as Roger drove that police car through everything in his path, full speed ahead to 2nd Avenue and barely missing pedestrians diving out of his way and cursing him down. Further down, the traffic lightened up, and he took an abrupt right and veered off the walkway back into the street.

"The hospital is only a few blocks from here!" he said to Price as he slammed the gas pedal.

Roger sped onward down the New York City streets like a man on a mission, swerving through the left and right lanes to avoid the traffic. He wasn't going to be slowed down, no matter what.

"Be advised, Charlie 1-3," Weber said over the radio. "They are preparing to move President Cash as we speak!"

"No!" Roger shouted. "Tell them to stop, Charlie 1!"

But the Secret Service had already begun wheeling President Cash on his bed to a waiting van parked in front of the hospital entrance.

As the medical center came into view a block away, Roger caught a glimpse of the Van, engine idling by the exit ramp.

"This isn't right!" he said to Price. "There are too many buildings around. He could be in any one of them!"

Roger skipped the curb at forty-five miles per hour and skid sideways to a stop in front of the hospital's main door. He and Price darted from the vehicle, moving straight for the double doors where the President and his Secret Service Agents were about to exit.

But they didn't make it. The President was pushed through the doors just before they could get there, his body revealed to anyone who'd wanted to do him harm.

As if it happened in slow motion, Roger glanced back at Price, then plunged headfirst into the President's path just in time to hear a muffled popping sound coming from hundreds of meters away.

Roger sprawled out on the concrete; a quarter-sized bullet wound to shoulder. Fortunate for him, the van was blocking the shooter's vision.

"Get him in there and go!" Roger yelled in agony to the four Secret Service Agents as they quickly loaded Cash into the armored van. "Go! Get him the hell out of here, now!"

It was too late to move the President back inside. The

only thing they could do was safeguard Cash and protect him at all costs.

The agents darted for the front of the vehicle under sniper fire and quickly shoved the president inside. Wheels spun as they made their way out to the street toward an unknown location.

Roger lay flat on his back, staring up at the building towering above him.

"Fuck!"

"Come on, mate!" Price said. "We need to get you inside before he finishes the job!"

Captain Price ran to Roger's side, quickly picking him up and carrying him into the hospital lobby as a bullet from the sniper's Rifle shattered the door glass. People started screaming while Price spread him flat across the bench.

"Damn, that hurts!" Roger cried out.

Price raised Roger's button-up shirt. He spent a minute looking over his body, trying to assess the damage.

"I think you'll be ok," he said. "No major arteries or vital areas hit. Damn, you were lucky."

"I don't feel lucky," Roger replied. "I feel shot."

Price seized Roger's hand, squeezing it tightly.

"You just saved the President's bloody life, mate. You realize that?"

"Yeah," Roger answered with a painful grin as he gazed up at the ceiling. "Yeah, I guess I did. Although I'm somewhat regretting it right now."

"You must have nine lives, mate!" the Captain replied.

They laughed at one another in a moment of amusement, Roger's chest throbbing in agony with every chuckle.

"Ugh," Roger said as he started coughing.

"Oh my God," one of the nurses said as she came around the corner. "What happened to him?"

"He was shot," Price replied.

"Jesus, Mister. You need to be seen right now!"

"No, I don't," Roger said. "It's only a shoulder wound. Just bring us some gauze, alcohol, and a bandage."

"Are you sure?" she asked. "It looks pretty bad."

"Please, just do it, miss," Price told her. "And hurry. We have somewhere to be!"

The nurse rushed over to the nurse's station, snatching medical supplies from beneath the counter. She ran back over and gave them to the Captain.

"Thanks, miss," he said.

"Are you sure you don't want a doctor?" She asked.

"I'm fine, miss," he answered. "Nothing we can't handle."

The Captain started cleaning the wound and dressing it right in the middle of the lobby, people watching them in utter disbelief.

"There you go, mate," Price said as he finished taping the bandage to Roger's chest. "You're as good as new. Sort of. How does it feel?"

Roger moved his arm in a circular motion.

"Well, it hurts like a motherfucker," he said. "But I can still use it. That's all I need right now."

Captain Price jerked Roger upright on the bench.

"You sure you are good to use that arm with that hole in your shoulder?" Asked the Captain.

"As good as I'm going to be," Roger answered. "Let's go. We need to hurry! We aren't out of the woods yet!"

Roger tugged his shirt back down as they hurried for the car. He quickly popped the trunk and checked inside.

"That's what I'm talking about!" He said as he pulled out an M4 Rifle and a 12 gauge tactical shotgun. He tossed the shotgun to Price.

"You drive!" he told the Captain, pitching him the keys.

The two of them hopped into the police cruiser and shot around the circular drive into the street, heading for the Secret Service Van blocks away from them. Roger switched the siren on, and they began zigzagging through the city traffic.

"Charlie 1," Roger said into his mic. "We have no visual. Which way did they go?"

"First of all, what's your status, Charlie 1-3?"

"I am fine, Charlie 1," Roger said. "Which way did they go? We need to find that van, now!"

"They are currently traveling south on 1st Avenue, Charlie 1-3. About ten blocks from you!"

"Roger that!"

Captain Price whipped the vehicle around and jumped back onto the sidewalk, blasting the horn and sending pedestrians diving for cover.

"Police emergency!" Roger said as he snatched the PA system mic. "Please get out of the way!"

Up ahead, he caught a glimpse of the black Secret Service Van as it passed through the intersection.

"There it is!" Roger said to Price. "Step on it!"

Suddenly, a black Kawasaki Ninja Motorbike came gliding around the corner of East 11th Street, a couple of blocks ahead.

"Shit!" Roger shouted. "I think that's the bastard up ahead! Catch up to that bike!

The bike driver reached into the inside of his black leather motorcycle coat, pulled out a Bison submachine gun, and began firing armor-piercing rounds at the Van tires.

"Hurry!" Roger yelled. "Before he succeeds!"

Secret Service Agents discharged their 9MM handguns from the cab of the van. But with the versatility of the bike, he was proving to be a hard target to shoot at. All of a sudden, one of the rear tires popped with a loud gun like noise, sending the van sliding all over the four-lane street.

"Shit!" Roger yelled. "They're going to crash!"

The van fell over onto its side, sliding sideways across a canal bridge, slamming into the guard rail and breaking it in two, half the vehicle protruding over the edge as the rear door busted open. The van was teetering halfway over the side, looking as if it would tumble over at any second.

President Cash, still strapped to the hospital bed, had suddenly been flung over face-first against the inside of the vehicle. Roger hit the brakes.

The motorcycle came to a skidding halt one hundred meters from the van, leaving black tire marks and smoke rising up behind him. Suddenly, he aimed the Bison sub-machine gun straight for Roger's head. In a movement he'd practiced many times before, Roger raised the M4 with a sudden fluid motion, and pressed the trigger. The bullet struck him in his shooting arm, right above the hand and sending the submachine gun falling to the street.

Roger and the Captain got out of the car and surrounded the man, blood spilling from his wrist. Roger shoved him from the bike, pressing his right boot onto the top of the man's bloody arm.

"Ahhhh!" he screamed.

"Go help them get the President out of there!" Roger told Price. "This one is mine!"

"Right, mate!"

Captain Price rushed for the van to assist the Secret Service in retrieving the banged-up President from the rear. He hopped into the back, pulling the President's hospital bed out as the agents countered the weight in the cab.

"You guys can get out now!"

As they departed the cab, the truck lost its balance and plunged forty feet to the water below with a crash.

Only feet away, Roger leaned over and removed the red motorcycle helmet from the man's head, his Rifle still trained on him.

"Well, well," Roger said as his face flushed with anger. "Nikolai. It is so lovely to finally meet you face to face.

"You won't do it," Nikolai replied as he stared up at Roger. "You westerners are too soft. Russia is the only true power!"

"Well, then," Roger said, flicking the safety off of his M4 Rifle and pressing the tip of the barrel on Nikolai's forehead. "Allow me to prove you dead wrong! And, don't worry, Nikolai. You will see your precious President in hell! Dasvidaniya, asshole!"

Roger squeezed the rifle trigger at point-blank range, the 5.56 bullet ripping half of Nikolai's head apart, brains flying everywhere as the blood coated the street around him. Roger spit on the man's dead body.

"Good riddance, you fucking prick."

Roger spun his body around and locked eyes with Captain Price as they nodded to one another as sort of a silent gesture.

"Target down," Roger said over the radio. "I repeat, the target is neutralized."

Roger ran to Price and the agents to help them remove the bloodied President from the Secret Service transport Van. This time, they'd opt for an ambulance for the evacuation. One of the Secret Service Agent's retrieved his hand-held radio to call for EMS.

"You saved my life again, son," President Cash said to Roger, blood trickling down the side of his soaked head. "Both of you. I have no words to display my gratitude."

"Mister President," Roger replied. "It was our duty and our pleasure. We are just glad that you are okay."

"I'm fine, but," Cash answered. "The Capitol. All of those people, innocent people, dead in a second. I've tried to avoid war my entire presidency. But, perhaps, I should've been on the other end."

Roger snatched the President's hand.

"Don't do that to yourself, sir," he said. "It wasn't your

fault, or America's, for that matter. It was always that bastard Petrov. He's the evil doer behind all of this."

"What would you suggest, then?"

"Me, Mister President?" Roger asked. "Well, I would recommend you concentrate on getting better, sir. We will handle the rest."

As the ambulance pulled up, agents and emergency medical technicians began to load President Cash into the back. Roger and the Captain watched them close the doors and didn't take their eyes off until the ambulance rounded the corner street and drove out of sight.

"You know what we need to do now, right mate?" Price asked.

"Yep," Roger answered, balling his fist tightly. "I know exactly what we need to do!"

CHAPTER 31

DAMASCUS, SYRIA

IT WAS THE middle of a warm desert night in the Syrian capital city. The battle of Damascus, where rebel forces had captured part of the city during the Syrian Civil War, was all but disappeared and forgotten.

Syrian armed forces had driven them out of the area with preemptive strikes and fierce bombing. Abdullah's Army had received prior intel on the operation and pushed the rebels out after three weeks of intense fighting.

Now, the Syrian President was snoozing soundly in his bed, an attack on him and his closest allies the most distant thing from his mind. Later that morning, Abdullah had a rally scheduled, a speaking engagement in front of thousands of pro-Abdullah supporters at his Army's museum close to downtown Damascus.

Kilometers away from his presidential residence compound, Captain Price had perched himself on top of a high hill overlooking the back of the museum. Wearing traditional Arab garb and a Keffiyeh around his head, he'd been there for hours. And he'd wait there for hours more if that's what it took.

He glanced at his watch as the hand struck 6 AM. It would be an eventful day, for sure. But not in the way most would expect. Price waited patiently for the Syrian President to show as scheduled. The Captain observed through his high-powered binoculars as people had already begun to crowd around hundreds of meters from him.

An hour had passed by as Captain Price envisioned what would happen next. He was there to assassinate a target. And that was precisely what he was going to do As the sun began to rise high into the sky, warming up half of his face, his eyes remained fixated on one part of the road ahead.

Suddenly, a three-vehicle convoy passed around the hill and into his sights. The armored Presidential Limo was sandwiched right in the center, being protected by heavy machine guns on both ends. But, however powerful those machine guns were, they wouldn't serve to help the Syrian President on that day.

Abdullah's motorcade turned onto the street that led up to the museum. As the convoy parked in formation at the back of the building, bodyguards stepped from the Army trucks and opened the back door of the Limo. Out stepped President Ali Abdullah, all decked out in his favorite black Armani suit with Navy Blue tie.

The richest man in Syria, he'd wanted to portray a humble existence to his people. But those who'd understood and knew what the man was capable of knew better. After all, he'd gassed his own citizens to stop a protest. He was a dictator. He'd approved, and even glorified attacks on those who wished to challenge his policies and his presidency.

In fact, half of the Syrian population wanted him gone. During the Syrian Civil war, many had hoped that the United States military would kill him so they could build democracy. But Americans didn't want an all-out war with Syria. But, this time, he'd overstepped his bounds by selling his nuclear stocks to the Russians. For that, he would pay dearly.

Abdullah moved from the Presidential motorcade to a waiting wooden podium that stood in front of the museum, facing mounds of hyped-up Syrian citizens. He snatched the microphone and brought it closer to his mouth.

"Thank you for coming," he said in Arabic to his crowd of supporters jammed packed at the front of the museum lawn and the walkway that led up to it.

They began to cheer loudly at the mere presence of their leader.

"It is a glorious day to be a Syrian," he continued. "We have emerged victorious, largely due to the cooperation and assistance from our allies in Russia! The West will no longer taunt us! We will not tolerate Western influence in our country, period!"

The crowd cheered and elated even louder, almost drowning out the President's voice. Abdullah began to clear his throat.

"The propaganda and the constant bickering from the US President will no longer stand!"

Hundreds of meters away, Captain Price had been watching and listening to the loud commentary coming from the Syrian President. He was less than impressed.

"I've had about enough of this bloody shit," he said to himself. "The guy must love to hear himself talk."

The Captain reached into his shirt pocket, recovering a detonating device from inside. He brought the mechanism to the front of him and rested his thumb firmly on the button. Not willing to wait any longer, he pressed down. A bomb that had been situated inside of the large podium went off, sending pieces of the Syrian President's body flying all over, vaporizing him from existence.

"Now you no longer have to worry about us Westerners anymore, asshole," Captain Price uttered as he slipped silently down the back of the hill and disappeared into the Syrian streets. In a state of pandemonium, Syrian citizens and security guards raced toward what was left of the Presidents body, blood coating the floor where he had stood just seconds before.

Thousands of kilometers from the Syrian Capitol, Roger had been lying in the prone in a bell tower overlooking the Palace Square in Saint Petersburg, Russia. All day he'd perched in that spot, monitoring one hundred eighty degrees around the large building in the center of that square. His suppressed .338 Lapua Sniper Rifle sat to the front of him, bipod resting flat on the floor.

He'd gotten information that the Russian President

was due to arrive that day to rally young cadets at one of Russia's many military academies. He would surely be boasting about Russia's successful attack on the United States Capitol. However, he had largely underestimated the response. Believing that America would declare nuclear war with Russia, Petrov let his guard down; a fatal mistake.

President Petrov may have had supporters within his own government. But the people silently cursed him. The CIA had determined that if he was to be eliminated, the Russian people would quickly revolt. Even the majority of the Russian military scorned Petrov. But, he ruled out of fear. There was only one thing left to do.

Roger inserted the magazine into his weapon and took a peek down the road to his left. There, far away and barely visible, the convoy was traveling fast down the street and over the hill. He followed the movement of the motorcade all the way to the outer edge of the square. Russian Presidential Security Officers bolted from one of the armored Range Rovers as they came to a standstill, standing in a circular configuration around the vehicles and carrying their AK-47's in front of them.

They were doing what they'd always done, trying to protect the Russian President from any one of a million people who denounced him and everything he stood for. Petrov had always been able to somehow repel many attempts on his life over the years.

On that day, though, the tide would change. Roger planted himself behind the glass of that powerful rifle, his legs straight behind him and consistently running through his tactical breathing. He was prepared to end what he had gone there to do. It was finally time.

As the President exited the armored car, his bodyguards surrounding him, the top of his head was barely visible. People had begun to move in closer to catch a tiny glimpse of the Russian leader. Petrov walked with his security personnel toward the main door of the military academy. As one of his guards gripped the doorknob to open it, the President turned immediately to wave back to the gathering crowd.

In a split-second, as Petrov acknowledged his people, his head had become completely visible from Roger's position seven-hundred meters away.

"Bad move, jackass," Roger mumbled, feeling the ease of the newly oiled bolt as he slid it forward.

He loaded a round into the chamber, feeling the coldness of the metal as he firmly rested the tip of his finger on the trigger. He took a deep breath and let it out. Roger felt an adrenaline rush shoot throughout his entire body as he prepared to exterminate a parasitic insect who'd destroy the world just to prove a point.

He brought the butt of the rifle tight into the pocket of his right shoulder, his left hand gripping beneath the barrel.

"Have fun in hell," Roger said under his breath. "You'll be in familiar company."

With the crosshairs surrounding the Russian President, Roger squeezed the trigger and watched as Petrov's head had nearly been taken clean off from the overwhelming power of that bullet. Blood started to spurt from his neck as his body collapsed to the ground, Russian citizens screaming in horror.

As the President's security detachment began to yell obscenities while attempting to locate Roger's sniper nest, he had descended the stairs of the empty cathedral. He'd left his rifle bag in the garbage can and vanished into a Russian crowd, cap over his head on a busy Saint Petersburg Street. Like a ghost, Roger had reappeared and then disappeared, leaving his vengeful mark on the future and fate of the Russian leadership.

Three days later, as Roger lounged on his living room chair, his wife and children by his side, he flipped the television on. There it was, all over the evening news.

> Coming to you, live from Al-Jazeera, this is Nayla Muhammad. President Boris Petrov has been assassinated by an unknown individual or individuals during a planned speech at the military academy in Saint Petersburg. The identity of the assassin is still not clear as the Russian authorities work tirelessly on the investigation. But, what is clear is Alexander Bortsov, one of President Petrov's fiercest critics, will step into his shoes. Bortsov has vowed to take a more liberal approach to his government as he seeks to undo the damage and devastation caused by the late Russian President.
>
> Concerning the West, Bortsov promises to work

with America to strengthen its unsteady relations over the years. Syrian President Ali Abdullah has also been killed, coincidentally on the same day. It isn't clear yet if the two incidents are connected. It is believed by many within the Syrian government and international community that he was murdered by one of the rebel forces in the country. The future is unclear for the nation of Syria. The late president's next in command, Ahzar Kashmir, has taken his seat. It is not known what direction he will take the country in. But, All in all, I would say that tomorrow may be looking bright, and much more modern for Russia and its people. Coming to you from Qatar, I'm Nayla Muhammad. Back to you, Adeel.

"What was that about, honey?" Kate asked him. "You know anything about that?"

"I'm not sure, babe," Roger said, smiling as he wrapped his arms around them tightly. "But I think the world just got a tad bit better."

Roger picked up his buzzing cell phone from the glass coffee table in front of him and answered it.

"You see the news, mate?" Captain Price asked before Roger could utter a word.

"Yep," replied Roger. "Just saw it."

"I think we just started something, Roger."

"I think so," Roger answered. "I believe you may just be right."

"All right, mate," said Price. "Just wanted to check-in. I'll leave you with your family. God bless, brother. Until we speak again."

"Same to you, my friend. Same to you."

Roger and the Captain had become close friends throughout the whole ordeal and everything they'd been through together. They'd remain that way. If one needed the other, they each would be there in an instant.

Roger tossed the phone onto the sofa. He turned the TV off and walked toward the wooden front door of their ranch-style log home. He snatched his cowboy hat from the wall-mounted rack and set it over his head.

"Come on, son," he said to Patrick. "Get your boots on. Jack isn't going to ride himself."

"Yes, sir!" The boy shouted happily, glad to be with his father once again.

Patrick was all smiles as he ran through the front door to follow his dad to the barn. It was the beginning of a new period for the O'Neil family. Whatever the future brought with it, Roger would be ready. But for now, he had some catching up to do.

As Kate stood in the doorway, watching the two men in her life mounting their horses in the paddock, Roger grinned back at her. She knew he had secrets buried deep inside of him. But at that moment, he was hers, and she was his. Until he was needed again, home is where he would remain.

THE END

WHAT DID YOU THINK OF STRIKE POINT?

Dear reader:

First of all, thank you for purchasing STRIKE POINT. I know you could have chosen any number of books to read, but you picked this one. For that I am extremely grateful!

I hope that it added value and quality to your everyday life. If so, it would be really nice if you could share this book with your friends and family by posting to **Facebook** and **Twitter**.

I'd like to hear from you and hope that you could take some time to post a **review** on **Amazon**. Your feedback and support will help this author to greatly improve his writing craft for future projects.

I want you, **the reader**, to know that your review is very important and so, if you'd like to **leave a review** and have a minute to spare, it would really be appreciated. I wish you all the best, and thanks again for purchasing STRIKE POINT!

— John

ABOUT THE AUTHOR

John is a retired US. Army combat Veteran, author, horse and animal lover, and adventurer. Joining the Army shortly after the September 11, 2001 terrorist attacks in the US, he served multiple tours overseas between 2003 and 2013. Subsequently, he was medically retired for an injury after being medevaced and sent to Landstuhl Army Medical Center in Germany in 2010.

Although John has always enjoyed writing, it wasn't until recovering from surgery that he began to take it more seriously. Writing has since become a passion for him, and he loves to share his stories with the world of book lovers.

John now lives in North Carolina with his wife Elizabeth, whom he met while stationed at Joint Base Lewis-McChord in Washington State in 2011. He is also a lover of cats. John and his wife share their home with two beautiful Sphynx cats.

In addition, he studies the German language, and enjoys traveling, especially to Europe, and meeting new people. Feel free to drop him a line anytime! Vielen Dank!

MORE BOOKS BY JOHN ETTERLEE

THE COLD STORM

Follow John

Twitter: www.twitter.com/JEtterleeWrites
Facebook: www.facebook.com/jbetterlee
Instagram: www.instagram.comjohnetterlee.author
www.johnetterleebooks.com

Printed in Great Britain
by Amazon

10344201R00207